GOBBELINO LONDON & A MELEE OF MAGES

GOBBELINO LONDON, PI: BOOK 4

KIM M. WATT

Buy the book. Gift the book. Read the book. Borrow the book. Talk about the book. Share the book. Just don't steal the book.

Book thieves will be thrown into the Inbetween.

But still, if the cat winks, always wink back.

For further information contact www.kmwatt.com

Cover design: Monika McFarland, www.ampersandbookcovers.com

Editor: Lynda Dietz, www.easyreaderediting.com

ISBN 978-1-8383265-4-8

First Edition April 2021

10 9 8 7 6 5 4 3 2 1

To friends who are family,
And family who are friends.
Yours, mine, and everyone's.
You are extraordinary.
Thank you.

1

THE LOGISTICS OF CAT CHESS

We were playing chess at our beaten-up old desk when a magician called to ask us about a dead man.

Which isn't entirely outside our area of expertise, but still. Those are two things I'd rather not deal with again. Once bitten, twice as likely to get infected, or whatever.

Anyway, to be clear, Callum was playing chess. I was mostly pointing out that the rules were arbitrary and illogical, and that he shouldn't complain so much. It was, after all, a cat's natural instinct to knock stuff on the floor, and if he had so many objections to it then he should get himself a human chess partner.

"*Don't,*" he said, pointing at me. "You said you knew how to play."

"I *do,*" I insisted. "It doesn't mean I agree with it. Human rules are ridiculous. I mean, the bishops I get – religious warriors are always tearing off in weird directions on a mission from their god of choice. But you can't tell me knights ride into battle at right angles. That's just impractical. And how would they ever finish a quest if they can't go in a straight line?"

Callum glared at me. "Those are the rules. It's a *game*, not an actual bloody battle."

"Are the knights drunk? Is that why they can't ride in a straight line? Or are the *horses* drunk? That could be it." I patted one with a paw, knocking it over, and he made a frustrated noise.

"Can you play or not?"

"And then you've got castles running about the place. When has a castle ever actually got involved? Was it the human who came up with the rules who was drunk? Someone was definitely drunk." I knocked over a pawn and watched with my ears pricked as it rolled to the edge of the desk.

"Right. I don't know why I thought this was a good idea," Callum said, grabbing the tatty cardboard box the game had come in. It was missing one queen, and we were using his lighter instead, which made me think he'd got the set out of the bin rather than a charity shop, which was our usual shopping destination. The career path of the private investigator is not as lucrative as one might imagine. Nor as glamorous. And it seems to involve a lot more running than I generally approve of, usually from someone or something that wants to do terrible things to us.

"I don't know why you thought it was a good idea, either," I said.

"I should've just asked Mrs Smith to play," he told me. "Not that she's any clearer on the rules, but at least she wouldn't have whinged this much."

"I'm not *whingeing*. And I totally know the rules. I just don't agree with them." I tapped another knight experimentally. "Cat chess makes much more sense."

Callum paused with his hand raised to sweep the board clean. "Cat chess? That's a thing?"

"Sure. It just involves fewer drunk knights and more actual fighting." I considered it. "Also naps."

"Custard, too, I suppose."

"Oh, now that's a good idea. Do we have any?"

Callum *hmph*ed and abandoned the box. "I need a cuppa anyway. Or possibly some sort of cat tranquilliser."

"You're just grumpy from nicotine withdrawal," I told him as he got up and padded into the little alcove that passed as our kitchenette. "Have a biscuit."

He said something unrepeatable about my opinions and clattered around with the kettle, still muttering to himself. I was fairly sure it was less the health benefits that had convinced him to try quitting smoking than it was our rather dire lack of cases, and therefore income. We'd been dodging the landlady for the last month, and if it wasn't for our extravagantly coiffed across-the-hall neighbour Mrs Smith accidentally making too much food and buying too many groceries on a regular basis we'd have been going pretty hungry. Of course, if Callum would stop taking cases that paid in knitted river weed scarves and rosehip foot tinctures we might be doing a bit better. Opening our books to Folk cases – magical cases – had not exactly filled our coffers the way I'd hoped.

But, thanks to Mrs Smith, there was custard. Callum put a bowl in front of me and sat down with his cup of tea, his fingers twitching toward the desk drawer where his last packet of cigarettes was stashed. He stopped himself, ran a hand back over his scruffy hair, and sighed.

"We need some work, Gobs."

"You're not telling me anything I don't know," I said, sampling the custard. We usually got what we could at the corner shop down the road, which meant weird off-off-brand products that were a month past their sell-by date. Mrs Smith went to the proper supermarket, and the custard was excellent, although she'd probably disapprove if she knew it was me eating it rather than Callum. "We need to get a bit more proactive, I think."

Callum tapped his fingers restlessly on the mug. "More proactive. What do you recommend, then? Radio ads? A bit of an infomercial? A flyer drop regarding magical investigators for hire?"

"Your nicotine withdrawal is definitely showing." I licked my chops. "I just mean we could get a little more inventive. Really *find* some cases. And not magical bloody ones that pay in moonlight in a bottle."

Callum looked at the bottle resting on a pile of tatty paperbacks. It had once held cheap vodka, by the look of it, and was currently shedding a weak pool of silver light on the covers. It was more impressive at night, but we hadn't been able to work out how to turn the damn thing off, so it spent most of its time in a drawer. "It's a really nice light, though."

"Which doesn't pay the rent."

"No, but how can we just *find* cases? It's not like there's a PI bulletin board anywhere."

"Sure. But what if, say, a local pawnshop lost some

stock, and we just *happened* to know how to get it back, and—"

"*No.*" He opened a packet of biscuits that were so far off brand I couldn't even tell what they were meant to be. They were just called "Biz-Kit". "We are absolutely not robbing a pawnshop."

"Well, *we* wouldn't do the robbing. That's just silly. We'd—"

"No." He examined a Biz-Kit dubiously.

"Oh, come on! Your family was like the last great criminal enterprise of the north. I'm just talking about borrowing some stuff from a pawnshop and giving it back again."

"And I got out of all that, remember?"

"I'm not suggesting we expand into G&C London, Criminal Endeavours. Just a little dabble before we end up starving and living in the car."

"We're not starving," Callum said, and we both watched a moth crawl out of the Biz-Kits and venture off across the room. He sighed, pushed the packet away, and pulled the desk drawer open.

"No!" I snapped. "Come on – you've almost done a week!"

"I can't have no biscuits *and* no cigarettes," he said, in the sort of tone that indicated he was going to descend into the depths of despair without them. That, or break something.

"Then stop being so bloody *moral* and let's go and find some money for biscuits!"

He pulled the cigarette pack out of the drawer, accompanied by a small green snake who was clinging grimly to one corner with his teeth. Callum sighed and set both the snake and the packet on the desk. "I'm not robbing a pawn shop to pay for biscuits."

"You're being ridiculous," I complained. "I'm not saying *we* rob it. We just make an arrangement—"

"No." He pried a corner of the packet open while the snake hissed at him, and extricated a cigarette.

"Don't do it."

"Just leave it, Gobs," he said, the words a sigh. He flicked the lighter, the flame lighting his face and turning the shadows under his eyes into bruises. These days it seemed as though every time I woke up in the night he'd be sitting at the desk reading another cheap paperback with a torn cover, or staring out the window with a mug in one hand. I mean, given our cases – and often our clientele – a little insomnia was to be expected. Personally, I had regular nightmares about Komodo dragons chasing me through endless sewers while oversized land crabs nipped my toes and creatures from the void dribbled on my neck, but I don't think Callum slept enough for nightmares. I think some of his memories filled that gap for him, and they were from older times than our cases.

Now he inhaled on the cigarette and started to lean back in his chair, and I launched myself over the abandoned chessboard. He yelped and tried to shove the chair away, but I barely touched down on the desk in front of him before jumping again. I hit his chest, swiped the cigarette out of his mouth and onto the scarred lino floor, then flung myself back again. Callum lunged forward, but I was ahead of him, skittering across the old desk and snatching up the packet of cigarettes before I shot straight off the other side and onto the floor. Green Snake watched me go with a bemused tilt to his head.

"*Gobs!*" Callum yelled, and grabbed the Biz-Kits, waving them at me threateningly. "Give them back!"

"You told me not to let you have them," I said around the pack, rather indistinctly.

"I've rethought that. Give them here." He came around the desk and beckoned to me with his free hand, not lowering the Biz-Kits.

I eyed them warily and edged toward the window, keeping the desk between us. "Nope."

"I'll give you more custard."

Tempting. "No," I repeated, jumping onto the windowsill.

"Tuna. I'll get some tuna."

"With what money?" I managed.

He waved a little helplessly. "I'll get some."

I examined the window. It was open just enough that I thought I'd be able to force the packet through the gap. "How?"

"Don't do that," Callum said. "Don't just throw them out."

I stared at him. "*You* should've thrown them out. Why'd you even keep them?"

"What's that? I can't understand you."

I almost dropped the packet to repeat myself, then narrowed my eyes at him. "*Ha.*"

"Come *on,* Gobs. Give them to me and we'll talk about the pawnshop thing."

"Talk now," I said, and snuffled. The stink of the damn things was getting up my nose.

"Jesus, just *put them down,*" he snapped, and shook the Biz-Kits. "Don't make me do this."

"You won't," I said, and he hurled the pack at me. I squawked and leaped off the windowsill, bolting for the kitchenette as the biscuits bounced off the glass behind me. "You *turnip!*"

"*Give them to me!*" he shouted, and lunged forward, trying to block the door and trap me in the tiny kitchen area (I harboured suspicions that what the landlady described on our legally questionable lease as a "full service kitchen" had once been an airing cupboard. It was that sort of size). I shot between his legs, teeth still clamped firmly onto the cigarette packet, and headed for the window again. Callum spun and threw himself after me. His hand slipped off my hindquarters and I growled, leaping onto the desk then to the windowsill, struggling to force the packet through the gap. It caught on one corner, and Callum scrambled to his feet. He slammed the window down, almost catching my paw.

"*Hey!*" I yelled, and he hesitated, a horrified look on his face. I snatched the packet up again and jumped for the desk. Callum almost caught me as I leaped, but I slipped away. I landed badly and slid across the chessboard, scattering pieces everywhere, then shot straight off the other side with a muffled squawk. Callum threw himself over the desk, yelping as he landed on the chess pieces, and plunged after me, catching himself on his hands before he could faceplant onto the floor.

"Gobs!" he shouted. "Stop it!"

I dropped the packet so I could shout back. "*You* stop it! I'm saving you from yourself, you … you *battered squash.*"

"You what?" he asked, peered at me through the mess of hair falling in his eyes. It needed a cut. It always needed a cut, even after Mrs Smith had just attacked it with her kitchen scissors.

"Pancake," I said, and we stared at each other for a moment, then he dived off the desk, reaching for the cigarettes. I tried to grab them at the same time and bit his finger instead – which was an accident, in my defence.

"*Hey!*" he yelped. "Agreement, remember? No biting!"

"Sorry," I said, letting go, then lunged at his hand and wrapped all four paws around it. "Drop them. *Drop them!*"

"Gobs, let go," he said, and tried to pry me off with his free hand.

"Never!" I yelled, suddenly enraged by the twitching of his arm. I tightened my grip, my tail lashing furiously, and yowled, "You'll never get them!" Then I buried my teeth in his thumb, agreement or no agreement.

"*Ow! I will take you to the bloody rescue, you MUTT!*" Callum shouted, trying to shake me off. I just gripped harder, growling.

And things could've got really out of hand, but at that point the phone rang.

Saved by the ringtone and all that.

We stared at each other, me still wrapped around his arm and him with one hand dangerously close to grabbing me by the scruff of the neck. Admittedly, that one wasn't explicitly banned, but it shouldn't need to be. No one can imagine it to be anything but painful and undignified for an adult cat of my standing to be lugged about like a recalcitrant kitten.

I freed my teeth from his thumb and said, "Are you going to get that?"

"Are you letting go?" he countered.

"Are you going to get the phone or the cigarettes?"

He shot a sideways look at the packet, lying half-crushed next to us while the phone continued to blare joyfully. "Both."

"Then no." I dug my claws more firmly into the sleeve of his hoody.

He sighed and sat up, grabbing the cigarettes with his free hand then scrabbling around in the wreckage on the desk.

"Hurry up!" I said. "It'll ring out. And it might actually be a case."

"It'd help not to have a cat attached to me." He found the mobile under a toppled pile of books and thumbed the screen, tucking it between his shoulder and cheek as he shook a cigarette out of the packet one-handed. "G&C London, Private Investigators."

I couldn't hear the voice on the other end, but I watched the angle of Callum's shoulders stiffen, his hand pausing with the cigarette halfway to his mouth.

"Callum North, yes," he said, using the family name he'd abandoned around the same time he'd shaken off his hometown of Dimly. That had been before we'd met, and until recently I'd never wondered why he'd been happy enough to use my name. I mean, London's a good name. I didn't blame him for borrowing it.

Callum wasn't looking at me, his gaze on the desk without seeing it.

"Who is it?" I asked, and he shook his head slightly, taking the phone from his shoulder. I let go, rolling onto the desk, and he started to rub a finger over the thumbnail of the same hand, smearing the blood where I'd bitten him.

"What's this about?" he asked, the words stiff.

I lifted myself onto my hind legs, pawing at his arm. "Put it on speaker."

He glanced at me finally, and shook his head again. He'd swapped to chewing on his thumbnail now. "Mr Lewis, what's the job?"

Mr Lewis? That was familiar, and not in the way that brought warm fuzzy feelings. "*Speaker,*" I hissed, and when he ignored me again I tried to climb to his shoulder, but he just shook me off and stepped away from the desk.

"When?" he asked, then nodded. "Fine. See you then." He put the phone down, blinked at it, then stuck the cigarette in the corner of his mouth and fished the lighter out from among the chess pieces on the floor. I watched him, my eyes narrowed, and Green Snake emerged from the mess of books and slithered up to me. We exchanged glances, then went back to looking at Callum. He lit the cigarette without looking at either of us.

"And?" I said finally.

"It was Lewis," he said, starting to collect the debris from the floor.

"I got that. Who's Lewis?"

He rubbed the corner of his mouth. "Ifan's dad."

"The *magician?*"

"The magician."

"What did he want?" The last time we'd seen Lewis, we'd been hunting for the source of a zombie outbreak in Leeds, and he'd been less than helpful, to put it mildly.

"He has a job for us."

"What is it?"

"He didn't want to go into it over the phone. He wants us to go to the house."

"Oh, that sounds good," I said. "Let's see, the last time we saw him he accused you of being a junkie who was just hoping for a handout. Now he suddenly thinks we can help him?"

He shrugged, knocking ash into an old tin on the desk. "I suppose there aren't too many PI firms in Leeds specialising in Folk cases."

"No, I imagine the rest of them charge in actual money."

He almost smiled at that. "He said it was to do with Ifan."

"Ifan's dead." I saw Callum's mouth twitch slightly as I said it, and I suppose I should have used some human phrase like *passed away* or *pushing up dandelions* or something, but it all came to the same thing. Ifan had been buried in the cemetery where the zombie outbreak had started, and at about the same time, too.

"He didn't say he wasn't. Maybe he just wants to find out what happened."

"I thought it was an overdose."

Callum shrugged, dropping into his chair and rubbing

his face with one hand. "I don't know, Gobs. But it's a job, right?"

"It's a *magician's* job, and the magician in question didn't like you too much. And the last time we went poking around looking for dead people we ended up dealing with zombie hordes. Do we have to repeat that?"

Callum stubbed his cigarette out and looked at me, those shadows looking darker than ever under his eyes. "Ifan was a friend. I at least owe it to him to find out what his dad wants."

I sighed. "I thought we were done with your dodgy past after Dimly. How much of it do you have?"

"Well, less than you. I've only got one life's worth."

"So you should listen to wiser heads."

"When you stop getting yourself killed in every life I'll think about it," he said, and picked up the Biz-Kits, releasing another moth. "We need the cash, anyway. And what's the worst that can happen?"

"Well, now you've said that, anything. He could throw fireballs at us. Dump us in pits of snakes and spiders." I looked at Green Snake. "No offence."

Green Snake flicked his tongue at me, which could've meant anything.

"We'll just go talk to him," Callum said. "Nothing too bad can happen if we just talk to him."

Which sounded like the sort of thing everyone says just before enchanted tadpoles start coming out of their ears, if you ask me.

2

I SHOULD HAVE WORRIED MORE ABOUT SQUIRRELS

ENCHANTED TADPOLES AND DEAD FRIENDS ASIDE, NOTHING more was happening that day, and a cat needs their sleep. Usually a good sixteen hours will suffice, but it was a lot less than that when the pounding started on the door. I jerked upright in my bed on top of the filing cabinet, the morning still damp and dark against the windows.

"London!" someone bawled outside. "London, get yourself up!"

Callum sat straight up with a yelp and rolled off his bed, which did service as an armchair during the day, and, along with the desk, made up the majority of our furniture. "Coming!" he yelled, stumbling to the door before our early morning visitor could smash it off the latch. Not that it would take a huge effort to do so – the structural integrity was pretty compromised. We'd had to repair it more than once after overeager clients had decided *locked* just meant *hit it harder.*

Callum pulled the door open to reveal our landlady, her hand raised to bang on the door again. Two of her sons lurked behind her in the shadows of the patchily lit hall. They had the sort of faces that were designed for lurking, in my mind.

"Morning," Callum said, giving her one of his Callum smiles, the one with dimples at the corners that seemed to encourage a certain proportion of the population to just trust him.

Not our landlady, however. She just scowled at him. "You're behind again."

"I know." He ran a hand over his hair, making it stand up in strange directions. "I'll have it by the end of the week."

"Is that this month's rent, or last?"

He tried the smile again. "I'll get it."

"You'd better. Plenty of people looking for decent housing in this area. Don't think I won't kick you out." She turned and marched down the hall, her sons lurking after her, doubtless to bang on someone else's door. No one in this place was exactly excelling at life.

I looked around at the flaking paint on the walls and the draughty window with the mouldy stain underneath that wouldn't go away, no matter how much bleach Callum had tried on it. "Does she believe herself when she talks about decent housing?"

Callum snorted, pulling his hoody on. "Like we have much choice."

"You're not telling me anything I don't know." I watched him amble into the kitchenette and flick the kettle on. "So I suppose this means we're meeting the creepy magician?"

He put a teabag in a mug and rubbed his hair again, making it even more tangled. "It's all we've got."

"You know it won't really help Ifan? And you hadn't seen him for years, anyway. Certainly not since I've known you."

"I know." Callum hadn't even gone to the funeral, just spied on it from the cemetery gates. That didn't exactly sound like bestie material to me, but Ifan had been there before I'd met Callum. He'd got Callum out of his hometown of Dimly and away from his family – even helped him kick some of the nastier Folk drugs, although the human ones had hung on a bit longer. The only reason we'd stumbled onto the whole zombie outbreak was because Callum had wanted to visit Ifan's grave, so that had been a fun day.

At least Ifan hadn't been a zombie. Or we thought he hadn't – we'd put the zombies down, but we'd never spotted Ifan. Which was probably a good thing, as I wasn't sure Callum would've actually been able to deal with him as needed, and as highly suited to many things as cats are, zombie dispatch is not one of them.

"And I should just point out that the last time we helped a long-lost friend of yours we almost got killed by your long-lost sister. And there was a Cerberus dog."

"Ez didn't actually try to kill us—"

"Okay, so your long-lost friend's recently lost sister did, or whatever. My *point* being, you have too many long-lost whatevers popping up about the place, and it's now company policy that we either avoid them or at least get them to pay up front in case anyone gets eaten by lizards or zombies."

Callum carried his tea to the desk and sat down. “I don’t remember agreeing to that.”

“My name’s first, right? G&C London, not C&G.”

He sighed. “Look, we’ll just find out what Lewis wants. He’s probably just trying to figure out what happened to lead to Ifan … you know.”

“I don’t trust him,” I said. “What if he blames you for Ifan’s death?”

“How? Like you said, I hadn’t been around for years.”

“Who knows what a magician thinks. Maybe he read some chicken entrails and they told him.”

Callum made a face and picked his cigarettes up off the desk. “Is that a magician thing? Entrails?”

“I don’t know. Magicians. Enchanters. Sorcerers. They’re all creepy. Give me indigestion.” I shuddered.

“Custard gives you indigestion. Doesn’t stop you though, does it?”

I sighed. “He’d better pay well. I’ve seen his house. He’s not getting away with a couple of cloaking charms and half a sandwich or something.”

Callum snorted. “I’m sure we’ll work something out.”

“That’s not actually a business model, you know?”

CALLUM PULLED the car up to the big metal gates of the magician’s house just before eight, and we sat there staring at the high walls and waiting for the clock to tick over. The battered old Rover didn’t exactly blend in on the broad, tree-lined street, full of chunky BMWs and flashy Audis slipping past on school runs and commutes.

Houses hid behind high walls and secure gates, and everyone on the street seemed to shop at the same fancy, overpriced stores. Joggers with wireless headphones and bright, unstained shoes peered at us suspiciously, and more than one dog walker snapped a photo of the car in a not-particularly-subtle manner.

Finally Callum checked the time on his phone and got out of the car to ring the intercom button, the collar of his long, stained coat turned up against the damp day. Winter had settled into the north, and not in a pretty, frost-glossed way. Everything was grey and dead and bored looking, waiting for spring to come back and liven things up again.

There was no answer. Callum frowned and tried the buzzer again, then came back and opened the car door, looking in at me. I drew back, just in case he thought I should get out and join him.

"He's not there."

"Probably for the best," I said, and meant it, although the pay would've been handy.

Callum checked his phone again. "Maybe he nipped out for something."

"Or you got the wrong day."

"I didn't get the wrong day."

"You didn't even write the day *down.*"

"It was Tuesday. Today."

"You need a diary," I said, curling my tail over my toes.

Callum swung back into the driver's seat, tucking his tatty coat over his long legs. "We don't have enough cases for me to need a diary."

"So what now?"

"We wait, I suppose," he said, and pulled his cigarettes out while I wheezed pointedly.

"JUST GO AND HAVE A LOOK."

"No one *just goes and has a look* at a magician's private property. There're probably giant guard spiders in there. With fangs. And wings. Maybe tentacles."

Callum sighed. "We can't just sit out here all day. Someone's going to report us for lowering the tone of the neighbourhood."

I peered out the window at a very skinny woman in leggings and an oversized jacket, who was scowling at us and talking on her phone. "Let's just go, then. He's obviously decided he doesn't need our services, and I for one—"

"Don't like magicians, I know. Just poke your nose under the gate and see if anyone's about. He wouldn't have contacted us if he had any choice, I imagine. So maybe something's gone wrong."

"Which would be a good reason for us to stay out of it."

"He might need help. Anything could've happened."

"If I said good, one less magician, would that be considered unprofessional?"

"Yes. Go on." He leaned over me and opened the door, and I stared out at the rain distastefully. The skinny woman had moved on, and there was a squirrel watching me from halfway down the trunk of the nearest tree. I bared my teeth at it, and it chittered at me indignantly.

"If I'm eaten by giant acid-spitting spiders, I'm going to be even more obnoxious in my next life. And I'm coming back to find you."

"Well, that's something to look forward to." Callum shut the door as I jumped out into the drizzle, pausing to sniff the mixed scents of leaking oil from the car and dog pee from the squirrel's tree.

I looked up at the squirrel, who was still glaring at me. "Hey," I said.

"Sod off," it replied. "Bloody cats."

"Oh, lovely. Have you seen the magician go out? Or is he inside still?"

"What do I care?"

I sighed. "Just hoped for a little cross-species cooperation."

"Got any nuts?"

"Not on me, oddly."

"Then take your cross-species codswallop and stuff it." The squirrel scooted back up the trunk, and I grumbled at his retreating tail, but not too loudly. Where you had one squirrel, you had a pack, and if they took the notion of actually stuffing me, they might.

I trotted to the gate and peered underneath. Nothing looked that out of the ordinary. I could smell shift locks burned into the fence, charms that stopped cats appearing within the property the way they appeared anywhere else they fancied. Humans – or at least humans who don't *see* – think cats are simply *around*, without ascribing any sort of importance to it. We're part of the scenery, as unnoticed as abandoned crisp packets and squabbling pigeons. Even those weird sorts who have to talk to every bloody cat they see never really think much about us, other than as objects of devoted attention. Which is, of course, as it should be.

That's how we end up cruising the halls of Downing Street and suchlike. Mostly just out of curiosity, to be honest. It's not like we're sabotaging things. Humans are plenty good at doing that for themselves. But we like to know what you're up to, and we go where we want. Partly we do that by *shifting*, by stepping into the Inbetween, the space that runs between the worlds, and out again somewhere new. Or other cats do. A certain disagreement in a previous life meant I couldn't do it unless I wanted to step out again missing some vital body parts.

Magicians, however, know cats are rather more than just small, adorable gods (although we are also that). Magicians know about the cats of the Watch. They know who keeps an eye on the balance of magic and Folk in the world. If they're any good – like old Lewis – they escape the notice of the Watch itself. But if they're careless or cocky, and the Watch suspect they might threaten the balance by calling human attention to Folk, or using magic to raise themselves over other kinds, they'll get visits. The Watch doesn't go in for much in the way of warnings, either. They tend to favour the sudden attack over any sort of messing around. I knew that first-hand from my dealings with them.

All of this means that magicians, along with most Folk, secure their houses with shift locks, little charms and runes carved into the bones of their property. Of course, a shift lock doesn't stop a cat walking in. It just stops us stepping through the Inbetween and appearing in the living room, but it's something. It kind of takes away the element of surprise, and for anyone who knows the way the world really works, they're as vital as running water. For those who can't make their own, shift locks are cheap enough to buy from the right market stalls. Although it pays to be sure it's the *right* stall. More than one homeowner has activated a charm only to find that instead of locking cats out, they've actually summoned a small demon or – worse – a nymph in, and have to pay twice as much to get them removed. No one needs a nymph sitting in the kitchen sink, clogging the drain with their hair and asking why there aren't any lilies.

I squinted down the drive at the house, but I couldn't tell anything from here. It just stared back at me, blank-faced and empty, a big old car sagging on the circle of gravel that met the steps at the front door, some ragged ivy crawling up one wing of the building and looking more dead than alive. The rest of the garden was much as I remembered it from last year – neglected and overgrown, full of topiary gone to misshapen seed and flowerbeds that were more weeds than flowers. The only difference was that everything looked more dead and mouldering in the winter rain. Lewis hadn't made it up with the gardeners, then.

I trotted back to the car and Callum opened the driver's side door, looking down at me. "Well?"

"Can't tell," I said. "Maybe he's sleeping off a big night. It's unreasonably early."

Callum sighed, tapping his fingers on the wheel. "Can you go in and have a look at the house?"

"Absolutely not. Did I mention the possibility of fire-breathing spiders?"

"Fine. We'll both go in."

"And how do you suggest doing that? Are you going to squeeze under the gate too? I mean, you'd just about make it, but that might get us more than accusations of lowering the tone."

"You're going to open the gate," he said.

"Aw, hairballs. Why do I have to be the one to go in first?"

"It's in your job description."

"I don't have a job description."

"Of course you do. You put the cat in cat burglar." He looked inordinately pleased with himself, and I glared at him.

"Cat burglar? *Really?*"

"Really. Now move it." He pulled the door shut again, and I made a few suggestions about his parentage, then slunk back to the gate. This is the problem with being small yet perfectly formed. Someone always has jobs for you that no one else can do.

Popping straight into a magician's garden seemed like a good way to lose my fourth life, so I examined the gate itself. It was all slick, white-painted metal (with a few streaks of rust – I bet *that* got the neighbourhood watch in a huff), but the walls were invitingly chunky brick and most certainly not cat-proof. And if nothing else, a bit of height would give me a better view of any attack-arachnids.

I bunched back onto my haunches and launched myself at the wall, skittering up to the smooth, damp top before gravity took too close a look at what was going on. I paused there, ears back against the rain, and surveyed the garden, feeling pretty pleased with my reconnoitring skills. Then a squirrel crashed onto the wall next to me, screeching squirrel insults. They're pretty inventive and often nut-based, but I wasn't in the mood.

"Oh, sod off," I said. "I'm nowhere *near* your tree."

"This is *our* wall," he shrieked back.

"It's actually a magician's wall," I pointed out, and the squirrel suggested an unusual use for conkers, then screamed so loudly his ears trembled. I stared at him, and he made a few threatening little darts forward, chattering his teeth.

"I'm not after your bloody nuts, if that's what you're worried about," I said.

The squirrel chittered, and answering calls came from further up the tree.

"Oh, come *on,*" I muttered, and glared at three more squirrels as they jumped down from the tree, tails rigid with indignation.

"Thief!" the first squirrel screeched at me. "Nut thief! Nest thief! *Murderer!*!

"That's libel," I said. "Or slander, or whatever. I'm just — *Hey!*" Because a squirrel had just landed behind me and nipped my tail. "Back off, you nut-addled rodent!"

"Get off!" the first squirrel shouted. "Our wall! *Get off!*"

"Off!" the other squirrels chorused. "Off! Off! *Get off!*"

More squirrels piled down the tree, crowding the branches closest to me and shaking them with their weight.

"Our wall!"

The ones on the wall pressed around me, all sharp teeth and bright furious eyes and sharp-looking claws, and not a shred of reason among them. There never is with squirrels. Either they're all cutesy picture-book paintings you can almost have a conversation with, or they get panicky about their nuts and turn into a horde of hysterical, nippy monsters. Give me a nice reasonable rat any day.

"Callum," I called, but he just peered at me through the windscreen and gave me a *what do you expect me to do* shrug. Some partner he was.

"Get *off!*" one of the squirrels screamed, just about shattering my eardrum.

"Okay!" I yelled. "Okay, okay, I'm going!" I started to slide my paws down the street side of the wall and about three of the damn monsters rushed me, pushing me back. "*Hey!*" I tried to scoot away but the one behind me nipped my tail again, and as I spun to confront him, the others pounced. They hit me in a solid scrum of soft grey fur, and I lost my footing as I was swept up by grabby little paws and long hard teeth and hurled off the wrong side of the wall. I squawked as I tumbled into space, twisting to turn the fall into a jump that was a long way short of graceful, and plunged straight into the magician's garden with my body splayed as I tried to slow myself.

I hit the ground harder than I'd have liked, recovered, and shot straight behind a bushy clump of weeds, panting and waiting for the spiders to emerge. None did, and as my breathing started to calm down I had to admit that I may have given the idea of giant cat-eating arachnids a little too much headspace and frenzied attack squirrels not enough. Not that I'm afraid of spiders or anything, but cat-eating ones were excessive, and just the sort of thing magicians would get up to.

I blinked around, still breathing too hard, and spotted a little pillar to one side of the gates, about a car's length down the drive. It looked very innocuous, which meant it seemed suspicious given the circumstances. Cats don't hold much with the concept of private property or the trespassing on thereof, but magicians were fiercely protective of their houses. The whole place had a greasy sheen of magic to it, and I was half-expecting to be charged by a pack of Cerberus dogs any moment, if the spiders were off the table.

Although, this being a fancy suburb of Leeds and not a pocket town like Dimly, where magic still lived, I supposed Cerberus dogs would be hard to hide. Folk are everywhere – the diminutive, fashion-forward barista at the local coffeeshop who always wears an oversized hoody could well be a faery, while half the plant nurseries in the country are run by dryads, and fauns make excellent sourdough and look pretty much indistinguishable from your average hipster anyway. But humans rarely see them for what they are. Kids do, but as they grow up they get told what to see so often that they start seeing it. Or not seeing it, to be more accurate. Which is why magical Folk can exist quite happily alongside humans, as long as they play by the rules. Cerberus dogs were not playing by the rules. Even the most unobservant delivery driver might notice the dog that just bit him had three heads to do the biting.

No, Cerberus dogs and faeries with their tatty wings

on show are best kept for pocket towns, where humans never go unless they already live half in the magical world, like Callum. So I was probably safe from them, but there was no telling what else a magician might have. Something unpleasant. Geese, maybe. I don't trust geese.

I eyed the sweep of gravel drive that led to the house. It looked even more potholed and weed-ridden than it had when we'd been here in the spring. The grass was long to either side, and could well have hidden a phalanx of advancing geese, if they were crawling on their bellies. Or giant spiders. I craned my neck, but I couldn't see anything approaching. The place felt deserted.

"Sod it," I said aloud. "Let him come in and deal with the wildlife, then."

3

NECROPHILIA IS NECROPHILIA

I TROTTED TO THE PILLAR AND INVESTIGATED IT, FINDING A round flat button hiding under an overhang to keep the rain off. It took a couple of jumps to hit the thing, but a moment later the gate was shuddering open on squealing hinges. Callum drove in, stopped to let me into the car, then nursed the Rover up the potholed drive until he could pull up next to the rusting hulk of the posh old car by the front door. He hesitated, then turned the Rover around so the nose was pointing back down the drive before he switched the engine off. One doesn't get far in this job by not being prepared to run when necessary. Retreat is the better part of victory.

We both stared at the house for a while, waiting for something to happen. Nothing did, and finally Callum ran his hands back through his hair and said, "Well. I suppose we'd better take a look, then."

"You first," I said. "I had to deal with rabid squirrels, and you were no help whatsoever."

"I thought rodents were your thing."

"Not *squirrels*. Squirrels are the worst."

"Good to know." He opened the door and peered around. "Does it seem okay?"

"It's a magician's house. *Okay* doesn't come into it. But I've not spotted any poison arrows or catapults, although it could be that cats are just too small to set them off. They might be saving themselves for humans."

"Encouraging," he said, and climbed out of the car. He checked the garden, then waved me out and slammed the door behind us. It sounded loud in the rain-drenched silence, but our car actually looked pretty good next to the magician's wreck of a Bentley, which was a first. Callum led the way to the front door and stared at it. There was no bell, just a heavy old knocker shaped like the taloned claw of some massive beast. Callum poked it, but it didn't do anything, just sat there looking bland and tarnished. He looked at me, and I shrugged.

"I can't tell. There's so much magic in this place that the door could be completely sentient and I'd have no idea until it bit your arm off."

"Right. I hadn't even considered that the door could be the problem," Callum said, and gingerly grasped the knocker. He gave it a couple of good raps, the noise echoing in the hall beyond, then let go and wiped his hand on his coat. "It's *warm,*" he said, and I wrinkled my nose. The sound of the knocker was still rolling around inside, lasting far longer than it should have, and my tail was pouffing out so much it was taking on a life of its own.

We waited.

The house watched us with empty eyes, and eventually Callum knocked again, then tried the door handle. It turned easily under his touch, and we both heard the latch click open.

"Not liking that." The skin on my back was crawling, the heavy scent of spent magic snaking over the threshold and setting my paws itching.

"It's not a great sign," Callum agreed, and pushed the door wide.

"Which is the sort of thing sensible people say before closing the door again and walking away," I said. "Just pointing that out."

But I stepped up next to him, and we stood staring into the cold, stale depths of the hall. It was one of those grand lofty things, not particularly wide or long, but with a ceiling that swooped up past the first-floor landing to the roof, and a staircase rolling up one side. The last time we'd been here, the hall had been tastefully decorated with dark, angry portraits and a taxidermists' convention–worth of dead, stuffed animals crowding the walls and floor. They had formed a grotesque, endless hunt of snarling foxes and fleeing rabbits, boars and dogs and deer, and even birds hanging from wires like a nightmarish mobile. Odds were there were some cats in there too, but I hadn't looked too closely last time, and I had no intention of doing so now, either. The only thing that could be said for the magician was that he was an equal opportunity lover of the dead, because there had been a tea party of human skeletons in fancy hats set up in one corner of the hall, too. Gods. *Magicians.* Weird as humans and five times as dangerous.

All this I remembered from before, but as the dull light

of the day washed over the room it lit something very different in the dusty shadows.

The floor was covered with bodies. Long dead, taxidermied ones, but still. Bodies. They piled over each other, lips drawn back from sharp yellow teeth in eternal fury, legs stuck out stiffly except where they'd been snapped by the fall from the walls, or in whatever altercation had brought them down. The skeletons had collapsed into a confused, bony pile, and a skull had rolled across the tiled floor to sit near the door, staring sideways up at me. A couple of banisters on the stairs were broken, and the birds suspended from the ceiling were tangled into a feathery, broken knot. Glass from the shattered chandelier sparkled everywhere like a heavy frost.

"Ah," I said. "This seems even worse than the open door."

"You think?"

The tiles shone bone-white under the tangle of ancient, threadbare hides and scattered bits of skeleton, and brightly coloured scarves and the multicoloured feathers from fancy hats were littered about the place like oversized confetti. There was a closed door to either side of us, and at the back of the hall a third stood ajar onto what I remembered as the magician's study, the shadows too deep beyond it to make out anything more than a slice of dark green carpet. It was utterly silent in here, and I could hear rain on the gravel outside, a whisper of musing voices. But it wasn't the cold, gently mourning silence of a mausoleum, where the dead rest. This was expectant. Waiting for the magician to return, perhaps. Or for someone to fill the gap he'd left behind.

"Come on," Callum said. "We'd better check the house. Maybe he's still in here somewhere and needs help."

I sighed. "I knew you were going to say that. We need to put a danger surcharge in our contracts."

"We don't have contracts," Callum said.

"We need to sort that out and all."

THE TILES WERE slick beneath my paws, and the whole place reeked of spent power and ground-in enchantments. It felt empty and not – the half-inhabited shell of a house built for a family but dwindled to nothing more than memories and twisting knots of resentful magic. It smelt of stale tobacco and old whisky and sorrow, and I sneezed.

"That good, huh?" Callum asked. We'd stepped over the threshold and were both standing just inside the door, neither of us willing to go much further until we were sure nothing was going to try to eat us.

"This whole place is just *drenched* in bloody magic," I said. "If Lewis is gone, every two-bit enchanter in the county'll want a piece of this place."

"What, they can take the magic?" he asked, nudging a fallen bird with the toe of his boot. It rolled over and glared up at us with a glassy eye.

"If there's no rightful owner. As long as Lewis is alive, the house and its power is still tied to him, but if he's not, then his heir has to claim it before anyone else can. Or would have to, if Ifan was still around."

"And since he's not?" Callum asked, stepping over a

frozen hare and opening the door to the left. It gave onto a high-ceilinged room dominated by a massive fireplace and empty of anything except two spindly chairs and an unpleasant forest of disembodied antlers on the walls.

"Then anyone who knows how to collect power can siphon it off. Or, preferably, take the whole house. Magicians' homes soak up magic spills and store all the excess power, like a sponge, or a battery. And this is an old house. There must've been a *lot* of spills over the years. You can feel it." And I could. My tail wouldn't calm down, and even the air had that unpleasant, enchanted sheen.

"Lewis' family's been in the area a long time," Callum said, leaving the door ajar and crossing the hall to try the one to the other side. The room beyond it was overstuffed and floral, and smelled as though someone had been eating microwave meals a bit too often. "I don't know how many generations, but more than a few."

"Awesome. *Lots* of power for the taking, then." I shivered, examining the tangle of bone and bodies in the hall.

"That seems bad. And it'd need another magician to take it over?"

"Not necessarily. Just anyone with decent magical ability, really. A sorcerer. An enchanter, even." I still hadn't moved from the door. The stillness of the house wasn't sitting right, and I kept thinking that it wasn't *actually* still. Like something was creeping up on us, just out of sight.

"We'd better hope he just popped out to the shops, then," Callum said, and looked back at me. "Are you going to help me look, or are you just going to sit there?"

"Well, I'm standing, for a start," I said, and a whisper of

movement caught my whiskers, trembling them in the cold air. "What was that?"

"What was what?"

The hair on my back was creeping up even higher, and my ears twitched back. "We need to get out of here."

Callum looked around the hall. "It looks empty."

"It's a magician's house. It might be magician-less, but it's definitely not *empty.*"

"The garden was."

"Yeah, but—" That movement again, a breath across my whiskers, and I took a step back, then shot sideways, almost falling over the skull, which snapped hungrily at my paws as the front door lurched into motion. It slammed shut, barely missing my tail, and a susurrus of tiny movement washed around us.

Callum ran to the door and jiggled the handle, but it didn't budge. He went for the window instead, trying to push up the old sash pane, but it was as firmly shut as the door. "Bollocks," he said, and looked at me.

I glanced back at him, feeling distinctly like I was doing an impression of a rather more elegant porcupine fish. "You could say that," I said, and nodded at the jumble of dead things.

Which were acting rather less dead than they ought to have been. I mean, they were very, very clearly not alive, especially the ones who were missing body parts, but they were also climbing to their cold, dead feet and turning to us with an awful lot of *intent*.

"Callum," I said, backing my tail up to the door.

"I see them," he said, going back to jiggling the handle enthusiastically.

"Which is great and all, but can you just get us out?" I kept my eyes on the taxidermy army. Not all of them were in full possession of all their limbs, but they were untangling themselves from each other and forming tattered ranks of glaring glass eyes and hooked claws and uneven, yellowed teeth, all aimed in our general direction.

Callum let go of the door handle and tried the window to the other side of the door instead. "About that," he said.

"It's not letting us out."

"Apparently not."

I hissed at a ferret as it scampered clumsily toward me, its limbs working in strange, disjointed motion. Although, it was doing pretty well considering that it was so long dead its hide was distinctly moth-eaten and most of its teeth were gone. None of the others looked much better, making it doubly unreasonable that they seemed so intent on making us breakfast.

"Can I register my displeasure regarding this job again?" I asked, while my tail turned into a pretty good approximation of a black feather duster.

"Why not? It'll really help the situation," Callum said, stepping in front of me and booting the ferret away as carefully as he could. Something snapped unpleasantly, and it rolled over a few times then got up and started back toward us again, one of its legs bending the wrong way.

"*Gah.* This is what we get for messing around with bloody magicians," I said. "We should have stuck with the pawnshop idea."

"I'm starting to see its merits," Callum said, and leaned down to offer me his arm. I scrambled up to his shoulder, and we watched the dead things organising themselves. A skeleton had got itself tangled up with a badger, so the creature had a human skull hooked over one paw, and a rib cage over its head. The arms were still attached, and were scrabbling about in front of it, every now and then grabbing one of the other creatures and patting them violently. The birds were heaving and thrashing in the tangle of their wires, and a deer staggered forward on three legs with the bottom half of a skeleton astride it, urging it on. A startled-looking owl was wedged into the skeleton's pelvic bone. Four rabbits and a moth-eaten fox, lurching on stiff limbs, made their way through the tangle of creeping bones and resurrected carcasses and stared at us out of flat glass eyes.

"Hi," I said, and they turned their heads in jerky unison to look at me.

"Friends of the family," Callum said.

"Definitely not burglars," I added.

Their heads ratcheted around to look at each other, then one of the rabbits raised a paw. Everyone looked at it, us included. There was silence, and I realised I couldn't hear the things breathing. I mean, *of course* I couldn't, because they were dead, but that didn't make it any better.

The rabbit brought its paw down. The dead things surged clunkily forward.

"*Run!*" I shrieked into Callum's ear, and he yelped a protest but threw himself toward the door to the overstuffed living room.

We careered through, my claws latched into his jacket to keep my balance as he spun and slammed the door in our wake.

"Lock it, lock it!" I yelled.

"There's no key!" He jumped away from the door, grabbing a giant armchair and trying to drag it across the thick carpet. It didn't move, and the door groaned as our voiceless pursuers piled up on the other side. Scratching rang through the wood, and I jumped clear of Callum, running for a door at the back of the room.

"Leave it! Come on!"

He sprinted after me as the foyer door gave and shattered creatures stalked through with ragged, too-fast clockwork motion, staring blankly and hungrily at us, teeth and beaks clicking. I spun to put my tail to the next door and spied a goose with a human skull on its back, clinging to the bird's neck with its teeth.

"Hurry," I wailed.

Callum hit the door and wrenched the handle down. Nothing happened. He twisted it wildly while the dead things stuttered closer. I could smell sawdust and chemicals and the bitter reek of magic, and I had a moment to consider that, when it came to deaths, this one was not shaping up to be my favourite. As far as one could have such a thing as a favourite death.

"Dammit," Callum said, and kicked a duck that was marching resolutely towards me. I reared back with one front paw raised.

"Plan! We need a *plan!*"

"Run," he said, and scooped me off the ground as a hare jumped clumsily into the spot where I'd been sitting. I squawked, all four legs splayed in fright as Callum dodged a deer and hurdled a lumbering boar. He yelped as the thing caught his jeans on one tusk, tearing them, and almost dropped me as he stumbled on.

"Watch it!" I yelled.

He didn't reply, just booted the boar hard enough to dent its head – its skull must have been either missing or long-rotten – and took off around the sitting room, sending a chunky side table crashing to the floor in his wake, and tripping over a cushion as he scrambled across a fat chair. I threw myself out of his grip, bounced onto a pink floral sofa and skittered up its back, looking around at our pursuers. They were swinging after us, not desperately fast, but more than quick enough, and filled with a terrible single-mindedness.

"We need another way out!" I called.

"I'll just get one for you, shall I?" Callum demanded, banging his shins on another side table and swinging over a faded green chaise longue cluttered with orange cushions. It was like someone had emptied the contents of three living rooms into one in here. A dead bat flung itself at his head and he batted it away, swearing. "Come on, Gobs!"

I bolted after him. The path back to the foyer was clear, and I shot through the door between Callum's legs. He stumbled over me with a curse, jerked the door closed, and ran to the front door, giving it a quick, hopeless tug. It was still firmly jammed shut, so we swerved for the door straight across the hall, the one that led to the empty sitting room. Shadowy movement skittered beyond it, and I stopped so suddenly I just about skinned my snout on the tiles. Callum dodged around me, bounced off the door frame, and yelped as a set of antlers stabbed out of the doorway at him. They were mounted on a wood plaque, and were somehow walking on one side while trying to impale us on the other.

I hissed at them, retreating toward the stairs, then spun as something nipped my tail. The bloody ferret grinned up at me with yellow glass eyes, and behind it the rest of the dead menagerie crowded out of the sitting room, blocking the way to the stairs.

Callum sprinted the length of the hall to where the study door was still resting ajar and threw it open. He ducked aside as he did so, but nothing came chattering out at us. All was dark and still in the room beyond. "Here!"

I hesitated. "It's like it wants us to go in there. That's got to be the worst idea ever."

Callum pointed behind me, and I scuttled forward as the antlers stabbed down where I'd been standing. "Better idea?"

"Hairballs," I whispered, and jumped a toothy, one-eyed rabbit then bolted after Callum. It couldn't be worse than out here.

I shot across the threshold and Callum slammed the door, turning a reassuringly large, old-fashioned key in the lock. There were two bolts on the frame as well, one toward the top and one lower down, so he shot those across and grinned at me. "Nice."

"Sure," I said. "Now we're locked into the magician's inner sanctions. This is what a trap looks like, you know?"

"Sanctum," he said, pressing a hand to the door as if to encourage it to stay shut.

"That sounds like a digestive aid."

"Something you should explore."

I bared my teeth at him, but he wasn't looking. He was staring at the bottom of the door, where small paws were appearing, scratching longingly at the dark green carpet. The wood groaned as weight piled up behind it, but nothing cracked. The old door looked as if it had been built to withstand more than a stampede of stuffed animals.

Callum stepped back and ran both hands over his hair, his body sagging. "Jesus," he said. "I'd expect that from necromancers, not Ifan's dad."

"They're all as bad as each other," I said, trying to get my fur to calm down.

"I'm fairly sure Ifan's dad doesn't want to raise an army of the dead in order to wipe out Folk and enslave humanity."

"He is fond of dead things, though," I said. "Necrophilia is necrophilia, no matter who's doing it."

Callum looked at me, then said, "I know you know that's not the right usage of that word."

"That's not the right usage of dead things, either," I said, nodding at the door, and he made a non-committal noise, then turned to examine the quiet dark confines of the room. The dark, *doorless* confines.

He rubbed his chin and looked at the heavy-paned windows dubiously. "I suppose we need to find another way out."

"You think?"

The door shook pointedly.

4

SOMETHING ANGRY IN THE WALLS

CALLUM STEPPED FAR ENOUGH AWAY FROM THE DOOR THAT nothing was going to grab his heels and pulled his cigarettes out of his coat. Green Snake lifted his head over the edge of the pocket and stuck his tongue out at me.

"Some help you were," I said to him and added to Callum, "I wouldn't light that."

"Stress management," he said, plucking one from the packet.

"Flammable fumes," I replied, and nodded at the room. Callum tucked the cigarette into the corner of his mouth and looked around.

The last time we'd been here this room – the magician's study, or magic chamber, or man-cave, or whatever – had been a creepy showroom of weirdly titled books and shelves of cloudy jars that seemed to move just on the edge of vision. The whole thing had been dominated by an oversized chair and a massive old desk, which had been on the messy side and generously decorated with rings from whisky glasses.

Now … well, the desk was still there. The big chair had toppled to its side behind it, and had taken out the heavy purple curtains on the way to the floor, leaving the windows with their multitude of tiny old-fashioned panes bare. Books were scattered everywhere, torn pages creeping across the floor, and the green carpet was a sodden wasteland of broken jars. Dead, slimy things were congealing among the wreckage, or – worse – were still twitching helplessly. Everything stank of spilt pickling fluid and spent magic and the sharp, astringent stench of panic.

"Huh," Callum said, and picked up one of the smaller chairs that had faced the desk, setting it upright. Its mate was only identifiable as a chair because of the seat lying amid a tangle of splinters.

"Will those windows open?" I asked. "I'm not loving the ambiance." I flinched from something that looked like the love child of a plucked budgie and a grasshopper as it waved feebly at me.

Callum picked his way around the desk and jiggled the window latch. It might as well have been nailed shut, and those small panes were thick to the point of distortion. They weren't going to come out with anything short of a sledgehammer. "Not looking good."

"Awesome," I said, and jumped onto the desk. A pricey-looking laptop was sitting in a puddle of tea with half a cheese sandwich smashed into the keyboard, and various arcane and likely priceless instruments had been stabbed into the wall behind the desk. "D'you reckon there's a spare key or something in here?"

"I have a feeling it won't be the sort of key non-magicians can use," Callum said, stooping to pick a book up from the floor. His frown deepened as he brushed glass off it and tried to tuck its torn pages back into place.

"Then we best come up with a way to break out, hadn't we?" There was a steady, nerve-jangling chorus of scratching going on beyond the door, and I had the sense that they'd keep going for as long as it took to reach us, even if they had to wear the wood down splinter by splinter. I shuddered. I hate dead stuff.

"If we're assuming Lewis isn't coming back, yes," he said, and put the book on the edge of the desk, stooping to grab another.

"It's not looking that likely, is it?" I asked, looking around the shattered room. "Unless he just sort of trashed his own house and went upstairs for a little lie-down. I mean, no telling with magicians, but it seems unlikely."

"And the fact that he had a job for us kind of suggests something else was going on." He stacked a few more books on the desk then lit his cigarette, apparently deciding nothing was going to explode and that the fumes from the broken jars weren't stifling enough on their own. Green Snake hissed at him, then escaped his pocket and went investigating across the floor, avoiding the worst of the debris.

I coughed pointedly, and when he ignored me said, "Who'd attack a magician in their own home? Especially one who's been around as long as you say."

"Another magician?"

"You heard of anyone else around here with that much power?"

"Not in Leeds, no," he admitted. "Maybe not even in the north."

"I don't like it," I announced. "I say we get out of here and get shot of the whole thing. Ifan's not coming back, no matter if you risk your life poking around in magical business."

Callum made a thoughtful noise and went back to methodically collecting books and drying the worst of the muck off them on the fallen curtains, which clashed horribly with the carpet but were probably worth more than our annual rent. Just like the tacky, multi-coloured lamps lying in pieces on the floor. No accounting for taste.

I wondered who – or what – would be silly enough to attack a magician in their own home. It was like going after a dragon in its caverns, and just as likely to end in an untimely incineration. They'd have to be desperate. And *good*, to get through all this and drag the magician off.

Unless, of course, no one else had been involved, and the magician had just conjured a particularly difficult entity from the void and it had taken exception to the fact. That was a more common way to go than magicians liked to let on. But it's not like you can see what you're getting when you go fishing in the void. It's a *void.* You might get a cute little monster with fluffy tentacles and an overbite, or it might be a screaming, boneless nightmare with teeth in its eyeballs. No way of knowing till the thing's in the room with you. Which was why magicians never had familiars. No self-respecting critter of any species is going to put up with that level of employment insecurity.

Callum shook off one of the jar creatures with a yelp

as it tried to scamper up his arm with far too many legs and rolling, stalked eyes, then leaned on the desk and stared at the door, stubbing out his cigarette in a broken glass and lighting another immediately.

"Why don't you just open it?" I asked him. "Get one of those freaky rabbits to eat your lungs. At least you won't be killing mine as well."

He blew smoke at me. "Do I criticise your custard habit?"

"Yes! All the time. And it's not going to give me *cancer*."

"Just clogged arteries and spectacular indigestion."

I growled at him, and started to ask when he was going to begin looking for a way out rather than rescuing dead books, when there was a soft but very clear *thump* from the bookshelves on the far wall. We both froze, staring at each other.

"Did you hear that?" Callum asked.

"The ghost in the walls? Yes."

It came again, a double thump this time, like someone dropping dead chickens on a floor. Lifeless and vaguely distasteful.

"We need to go," I said, and jumped to the floor, trying to avoid stepping on anything that looked like it might bite. "Have you checked all the windows?"

"They're all the same. Gobs, it might be Lewis. Maybe he's trapped in here somewhere." Callum headed to the bookcase where the thump had come from, and stared at it as if waiting for it to tell him something.

"We must be able to break one," I said, putting my paws on the wall and peering up at the windows.

"We can't just leave him in here if—" Callum yelped

and jumped back as a flurry of thuds came from the other side of the shelving.

I jumped onto a windowsill and investigated the latch. "Here, Thumbs – come try this one."

Callum leaned forward and knocked tentatively on the back of the shelving. The response was immediate, two quick thumps. "There's someone in there."

"I *know* that. But there's no telling what sort of someone – or some*thing* – a magician keeps in his walls when he's got a dead menagerie right out on display in his hall." I pawed the window latch, but there was no way I was opening it. Door handles I could usually manage. Heavy old metal window latches, not so much.

Callum tried knocking again, and the thing in the walls replied with such a pounding that one of the few jars left on the shelves crashed to the floor, releasing a waft of eye-watering fumes and a fish with six luminous blue eyes and a floppy fringe of yellow, very sucker-ish limbs. It wallowed sadly in the last of the formula, blinking up at us. Callum picked it up gingerly by the tail and put it in the lid, where at least its stomach was still wet.

"Lovely," I said. "Now what?"

"Come and help me," he said, feeling his way along the shelves.

"I'm not exciting ghosts. I never signed up for ghosts."

"I don't think either of us signed up for this," Callum said, almost to himself, and I wasn't sure if he meant our lives in general, or just the exciting ghosts part. It was accurate, either way. "I think there's a room behind this. There's got to be a way to open it."

I eyed the shelving from my vantage point on the windowsill. Whatever had happened in here had ripped almost everything off every surface, leaving just the odd jar or a couple of books hanging half off the edge. Except for … "There," I said. "Top shelf. Three books standing up still."

Callum stepped back and peered at them. "Lewis is *short.* How would he reach those?"

"You're just unnaturally tall. Maybe he jumped. Or did some magic thing that meant he didn't have to actually touch them. But there's no way they're just sitting there like that."

Callum looked around the room. "Good point. But what if it's not actually a way to open it, but a way to deal with people who *try* to open it?"

We both stared at the books. One was titled, *Lesser Seashells of the Nocturnal Realms,* and I wasn't sure if that was terrifying or innocuous. It could've gone either way. Whoever was on the other side of the shelf set up such a pounding that I was half sure they were going to bust their way through on their own, but presumably they'd already tried that. It sounded like they were angry enough to have already tried, anyway. And also rather less ghost-like than I might've thought earlier.

"We should leave it," I said. "We've already got the undead zoo patrol outside."

"Maybe it's a way out," Callum said.

"Knocky McKnockers in there apparently doesn't think so."

There was another round of furious knocking, as if to underline the point, and Green Snake, who'd been watching from the safety of a broken vase, scooted over to the wall and scaled the back of the chair to reach me on the windowsill. I bared my teeth at him.

Callum looked at the door, where someone's paw had broken off and ended up inside alone. It was twitching hopefully while the steady scratching kept up on the other side. "It can't really get much worse."

"Oh, it definitely can," I said, but he just reached up and grabbed the books on the top shelf, pulling them toward him. They pivoted smoothly on a bottom corner, and I heard the clunk of heavy locks releasing somewhere in the wall. Hot, raw air belched out from behind the shelving, like we'd discovered a passageway straight to the centre of the earth, and the ozone scent of spent magic went from background whiff to so overwhelming that I sneezed. Green Snake dived behind me.

"Told you," I said, and the shelves swung open.

I'D PRETTY MUCH DECIDED there wasn't going to be a ghost inside the walls, but I hadn't ruled anything else out. It might be the magician himself, trapped and enraged. Or, given his affinity for dead things, a whole new army of stuffed pygmy elephants and armoured ostriches. Maybe some trespassers he'd locked up a few decades previously. Whatever it was, it was never going to be good.

What I was not expecting was a furious woman in scuffed, calf-high Dr Martens, her dark hair decorated with multicoloured feathers and her knuckles bloodied. It was so dark behind her she might've been leaning against a void, and the light of the room lit nothing beyond the threshold.

"You bloody took your time," she snapped. "I was knocking long enough."

"*Ms Jones?*" Callum asked. He'd scooped up a piece of broken jar and was aiming it vaguely at her. Her scowl deepened, and he dropped it hurriedly. "Sorry. Wasn't expecting … well."

"Anything that wasn't going to eat us," I supplied.

She muttered something I didn't quite catch as she stepped into the room. It might've been something along the lines of that being able to be arranged. Which might've been more entertaining if we hadn't known she was a sorcerer. That cast any threats in a very different light.

"What're you doing here?" Callum asked. "Where's Lewis?"

Ms Jones ran her hands back over her hair, which looked like it had started the day trussed up but wasn't sticking to the plan so well. She shook some feathers off and muttered again. "I don't know where he's gone," she said aloud. "What're *you* two doing here?"

"He said he had a job for us. He was meant to meet us here at eight."

"What sort of job?"

"We don't know," I said. "*Someone* managed not to ask that question before saying we'd be here."

Ms Jones marched over to the desk, boots crunching on the broken jars, and started going through the drawers. "He's up to something."

"What sort of something?" Callum asked.

She scowled at him, fishing a bottle of whisky out of its hiding place and slamming it onto the desk. "If I knew that, I wouldn't have come here for a friendly chat this morning."

"Looks like it was really friendly," I said, as she pulled the cork from the bottle and took a swig, then held it out to Callum. He shook his head, and she offered it to me instead. I wrinkled my snout and she shrugged, then took another swig. Her face was drawn and tired when she put the bottle down, and she winced as she sat on the edge of the desk.

"What do you know about his son?" she asked.

"Ifan? He's dead," Callum said. He said it steadily, but he was worrying at his thumbnail with his fingers again.

"He the only heir?"

"Far as I know."

"And he's definitely dead."

"I saw the funeral."

"Although there was a small spate of undeadness in the area shortly thereafter," I pointed out.

Ms Jones looked at the bottle, then put the cork back in it. "I recall."

We'd never have been able to stop the undead if it hadn't been for Ms Jones. It didn't mean I trusted her – no one in their right mind trusts a sorcerer. They're so old they've forgotten what it is to be human. But she'd found a zombie antidote when we needed it, and she'd saved Callum. The problem was, I thought she'd had her own reasons for helping, and I wasn't entirely sure she'd forgiven us for losing her book of power earlier the same year. Sorcerers aren't sloppy enough to spill magic like magicians. They hold onto their power. But they accumulate too much of it to be able to pass as human if they keep it physically, so they create dangerous books to sink the excess into, books that take on a sentience of their own. Naturally, she hadn't been best pleased when I'd thrown hers into the Inbetween to stop it tearing the world apart. She'd lost a lot of her power, but I could still smell the magic in her, muscular and restless and vaguely hairy.

"Why're you interested in Ifan?" Callum asked.

Ms Jones looked at him. "I'm not, exactly. Or I wasn't. But I was looking into all the stray magic that's been floating about since the whole undead thing, and the magician seems tangled up in it somehow."

"You *weren't* interested in him?" Callum asked cautiously.

The sorcerer plucked another feather from her hair with a sigh. "Damn things get everywhere. Look, magicians are very into the whole lineage thing for passing on magic. And if this particular one wants to make sure things – like this bloody house – stay in the family, he might be trying to find his son."

"*What?*" Callum looked for a moment like he was going to snatch the whisky off her, but he just scrabbled for his cigarettes instead. "I told you, he's *dead*."

"Did you see him die?"

"Well, no," he admitted, lighting a cigarette and inhaling hard. "But Lewis thought he was dead too – we saw him after."

"He wasn't exactly grieving," I said.

"Rage can be grief, too."

Ms Jones made a quick, impatient gesture. "It's not

unheard of to choose an appearance of death, is it? And death can be deceptive, anyway. It isn't necessarily the end. There are ways to help souls find their way back if they're not truly gone."

"Wait, are we talking necromancers?" I asked. "Or zombies? Either way, I'm not keen."

"Noted," she said, and picked Green Snake up off the floor. He'd abandoned me and gone to investigate her boots, and now he wrapped himself around her wrist, gazing up at her with flat green eyes. "And I don't know yet. I've still not discovered exactly how your zombie outbreak started, or even if the magician was involved at all, and I just came here to ask some questions." She scratched the back of her neck with her free hand and handed the snake to Callum. "It did not go quite as expected."

"No baby goats," I said. "How did *you* get trapped?" Missing book of power or not, a magician should've been no match for a sorcerer.

Ms Jones blinked at me, and Callum tucked Green Snake into his pocket, sighing. "He means no kidding. He won't give it up."

She snorted. "Right. Well. Bloody magician's houses. It all got a little … heated."

Her wave encompassed the devastated room and the taxidermy army, still pawing at the door, and I revised my opinion of Lewis. Tackling a sorcerer – let alone shutting them in anywhere – indicated a rather formidable level of skill. And probably a death wish.

She tucked the whisky bottle under her arm. "We need to go. And I want you to keep an eye on Lewis."

"*What?*" I demanded. "You just said he managed to trap you! He'll turn us into hand warmers. Or me, anyway. Callum he'll probably add to his taxidermy petting zoo."

Callum wrinkled his nose in distaste.

"I don't want you to confront him," the sorcerer said. "Just watch him, try to figure out what he's up to. And for the gods' sakes don't meet him, no matter what job he says he has for you. That feels all wrong."

"Told you," I said to Callum.

"He's definitely up to something," Ms Jones said. "There's been a lot of strange stuff going on – the dead rising were just part of it. There's power in places there shouldn't be these days, and lots of signs pointing back to him."

"You really think he's trying to bring Ifan back?" Callum asked. "You think that's what started it?"

"Maybe. I don't know yet. But someone was raising the dead, even if it was by accident last time, and if they keep meddling it's going to end up opening some doors that should stay closed." She shrugged. "Maybe he's behind it, maybe someone else is. Maybe he's just trying to protect his house and his power. But I really don't like him, so he's my main suspect."

"Well, that seems like as good a reason as any for us to risk our tails," I said. "What're you paying?"

"You still owe me a book," she said. "And an anti-zombie vaccine."

"Expenses?" I suggested.

"We'll do it," Callum said.

"Of course we will," I said. "Why would we not stalk

the scary magician who might be trying to raise his son from the dead? *For free?*"

"I'm not going to let someone turn Ifan into a zombie," Callum said. "We're doing this."

"This is going to be one of our worse ideas, I can tell."

"Do we ever have less than worse ideas?"

"I suppose we must, in order for them to be worse," I said. "I'm starting to have doubts, though."

He sighed. "Me too, actually."

"Are you two quite done?" the sorcerer asked. "Because we should move. You know, before the scary magician type comes back."

"Excellent," I said. "How are you with taxidermy?"

5

A GOOD LINE IN HEADLESS CHICKENS

WE DIDN'T HAVE TO FIND OUT WHAT SKILLS IN TAXIDERMY-charming Ms Jones might possess, as she just took a final glance around the room then put one hand on the window behind the desk. There was a shudder that felt like the house was going to come down around us, then the little windowpanes and their cross-hatched frames melted around her hand and spilled down the wall outside, forming a puddle in the flowerbed that immediately congealed into glass and wood modern art.

"Nice," I said. "That's handy."

She nodded, wiping her forehead with her arm, and uncorked the whisky bottle again. She took a couple of noisy gulps, and blew alcohol-flavoured air over her lower lip. "Move it, then, unless you want to wait to catch up with Lewis in person."

We moved it. Callum went first, checking for giant spiders or armed geese, and I followed. Ms Jones was last out, still clutching the whisky. She stumbled as she landed in the flowerbed, dropping into a crouch and catching herself on one hand. Her eyes met mine as she looked up, and for a moment we stared at each other. Sorcerers don't wear their years the way humans do, but I suppose they have to show somewhere. Her eyes were still vivid, some mix of colour that was both dark and light and that I couldn't quite name, but there were lines pulling at the corners of her mouth and I could smell the exhaustion on her, underneath the power. I wondered again how the magician had been able to trap her. He was powerful, but surely not *that* powerful. Then she got up, brushing her hands off on her jeans, and led the way around to the front of the house, her head up and her stride long.

She stopped by the car and looked at it the way she might have looked at a particularly interesting creature she'd just pulled out of the void.

"Does this run?" she asked, sounding more curious than dismissive.

"Most of the time," Callum said, sliding in and reaching across to open the passenger side. She got in, sprawling her legs out and leaning her head back against the rest. She closed her eyes while Callum poked and prodded the car into urgent life, and we rumbled down the drive. No one spoke as we pulled up by the gate button and Callum cranked the window down to push it. I think we all expected, at the very least, that the gate wouldn't open. More likely the ground would crumble beneath us and we'd plunge down into some pit of hot tar below the house, or hellhounds with teeth that could tear the roof right off the old Rover would be let loose in the garden. And that was if the magician wasn't waiting on the other side of the gate for us, which would likely end up being even worse.

But the earth held underneath us and the garden stayed empty, and there was no one outside as the gate jerkily eased itself open. As soon as the gap was wide enough, Callum pulled straight through and onto the street with barely a pause to check for traffic. Everything was as it had been, all damp and grey and gloriously unmagical. Callum let his breath out slowly, and I flopped down on the back seat.

"Can we skip any more magical house calls?" I asked. "That was more than enough for this lifetime. Or, you know, for this week at least."

Ms Jones opened the whisky bottle, took a mouthful, then said, "I'm parked at the shops down the road." Callum looked at the bottle, then at her, and she scowled at him. "Please tell me you don't think I'm human enough to metabolise this like you would? How insulting."

"What're you doing, then?" I asked. "Is it like magical mouthwash or something?"

She shrugged. "Oh, it's still alcohol. It's been that sort of morning. It takes a lot more for it to affect me, though. Comes in useful sometimes."

I had visions of Ms Jones in drinking contests with Viking warriors, slamming down horns of ale and claiming their plunder. Or matching Leeds locals drink for drink on a Saturday night, which would be just as intimidating, although possibly less bloodthirsty. Possibly. Depended on the night.

"So we just watch the magician?" Callum asked. "That's it? He had a job for us – couldn't we use that to get close to him and see if we can find out more about what he's up to?"

She rubbed her forehead, discovering something matted in her hair and frowning at it. "I mean, you could, but it seems rather too much of a coincidence, him wanting to hire you specifically."

"We're kind of specialists," I said, even though I agreed with her. "He's not going to find the sort of services we offer from your average PI agency."

She twisted in her seat to look back at me. "No, I imagine not. Who would need professionalism and experience when they can have you two?"

"*Unfair,*" I said. "We're very professional. In our own way."

"You forget Ms Jones has been a client," Callum said. "She's probably got her own opinion."

"Oh, I have many," Ms Jones said, sinking back in her seat, but not before I saw the corners of her mouth twitching. That seemed a good sign. I couldn't see her turning us into dung beetles if she found us amusing.

"I did come to the same conclusion," I said. "You know, that it was a trap."

She looked back at me again. "Why would it be a trap?"

"You said it was."

"I said it was too much of a coincidence." She looked at Callum. "Why would it be a trap?"

"There's no reason for it to be," Callum said, pulling into a parking area in front of a small, tidy row of shops. You could tell we were in a fancy part of town – there wasn't a pound shop in sight. There was the sort of cafe where the coffee's hand-squeezed by blue-tongued skinks in home-woven bonnets; an organic food shop where you'd definitely need your own containers, never mind bags; and the others were so expensive I couldn't even tell what they were. One appeared to be a barber's, but it might also have been a showroom for leather aprons and old sewing machines, from what I could see.

A motorbike crouched in front of the cafe, looking at one level like the sort of ageing, nondescript bike no one would even look twice at, and at another uncomfortably *alive*, hungry and waiting, all black leather hide and hunching chrome bones. Callum parked next to it, and I picked my way onto the edge of his seat, avoiding Green Snake. He was rubbing his head on the sorcerer's hand.

"Callum and Ifan were besties, back in the day," I said. "Maybe Lewis figures he can use that."

Ms Jones let the snake wind around her fingers, frowning slightly. "How did you know him?"

"He used to come to Dimly when I was a kid," Callum said. "We were friends, is all."

"You were both into imp dust and unicorn horn," I pointed out. "Is that really a healthy basis for friendship?"

"He helped me get off it, too, remember?" Callum said, then sighed. "But, yes, we both used back then."

"Horn, huh?" Ms Jones said, lifting the snake to eye level. They stared at each other. "Bad stuff."

Callum didn't answer. He didn't need to. Unicorn horn has two functions – well, three, if you count the original use, when it still belongs to the jumped-up horses and they get all stabby-stabby with it at the slightest provocation. The other two uses were when it was ground to dust. If taken, it could give humans – and others – the sort of high that opened gates between dimensions and turned your mind inside out, if you weren't careful. Or it could be worked into weapons that could kill anything, including every one of a cat's nine lives in a single blow. Bad stuff alright, no matter who had hold of it.

Ms Jones lowered the snake and let him coil into a little green puddle on her lap. "Did you see much of Ifan after you left Dimly?"

"No. He helped me get clear of my family, then we sort of … lost touch."

She sighed. "Look, it might be that Lewis just thought you knew more of what happened to Ifan than you said at the time. Or it might be something more." She looked at him speculatively. "What do you think?"

"There isn't anything more," Callum said flatly, taking his cigarettes out. I didn't say anything. When I'd first met Callum, all I'd known was that he could see enough of the true world to rescue me not just from some truly unpleasant humans, but from the sneaking tentacles of a monster reaching out of the Inbetween. He never seemed surprised by what he saw, but he still appeared as firmly clueless about the magical world as any human. These days I wasn't so sure what I really knew of him, because these days I knew he'd grown up in the magical pocket town of Dimly, that his family traded in unicorn horn, among other things, and that Callum was aware of far more than he let on. *Was* far more, I thought sometimes. But I wasn't sure what that meant, exactly. I didn't see all of Callum. I couldn't. Maybe because he couldn't see it himself, some part of him always lost behind old memories he'd locked up and abandoned. Sometimes I smelled it, though, a whiff of something wild and drenched in unknown things.

Ms Jones made a non-committal noise and startled me by scritching the back of my neck with long fingers. I flinched slightly, then relaxed. Her fingers were cool but gentle.

"What about you?" she asked.

"Me? Well, obviously I am exceptionally talented," I said, and Callum snorted. "What? I don't believe in false modesty."

"Some modesty'd be nice," he said. He hadn't lit his cigarette yet, and he rolled it between his fingers thoughtfully.

"The Watch don't like you much," Ms Jones said, her fingers still moving gently in my fur. I half-closed my eyes, arching pleasurably against her hand.

"The feeling's mutual. They keep killing me."

"Why?" Her voice was soft, whispering of warm beds and thick blankets.

"I don't know," I managed. My legs were going weak, and I sank down onto my haunches.

"Think."

My eyes closed, and for a moment all was sleepy violet bliss, then the dark deepened and my belly fell away as teeth closed on my neck, claws dug into my sides, and the *whisper-snap-snarl* of unknowable beasts closed in while cats held me, trapped me, offered my scent to ancient things while they whipped away into living worlds—

I jerked away from Ms Jones, lashing out with one paw, my teeth bared in a snarl. She pulled back, but not before I laid thin lines of blood across her hand.

"What was *that?*" Callum asked, putting a hand on my back. I jumped away, stumbling into the footwell, and spat at him. My heart was going too fast, and my mouth tasted like I'd just thrown up a hairball that had been brewing for too long. "Gobs!"

"What did you do?" I hissed at the sorcerer. "What did you *do* to me?"

"Nothing," she said, inspecting her hand. "Just seeing if you might remember something."

"Death is not something I want to remember," I spat. "Not one of them. Not ever. And definitely not *that* one." Not the one where the Watch had given me to the beasts of the Inbetween.

She regarded me for a moment, then nodded. "Of course. But it may be that there's a reason the Watch keep killing you. And maybe it's something to do with why the magician wanted you."

Green Snake had been peering at me from the sorcerer's lap, and now he abandoned her and slithered down next to me. I hissed at him and jumped through to the back seat, trying to settle my fur down. "This is *nothing* to do with me. The magician wanted Callum. And I can't help it if the Watch take exception to such a free-thinking individual as myself."

"He was rude to the wrong cat," Callum said. "That's my guess on all the deaths."

Ms Jones snorted. "I can see that. Look, maybe you're right, and it's nothing to do with either of you. I'm sorry, Gobbelino."

"Alright," I said, although my joints felt shaky and loose. "Sorry about your hand."

She examined it again, smiling slightly. "I suppose I deserved it." She put her hand on the door, then said, "I think the zombies were a symptom of whatever's happening around here. A little unexpected bonus from some deeper magic going on."

"Zombies are a really rubbish bonus," I said.

"I don't think there were meant to be zombies," she said. "They were no use to anyone. Completely uncontrollable. But someone's stirring things up, and whether the magician started it or not, he's in it now. And the Watch never even addressed the zombies. They're looking in the wrong directions, deliberately or not."

"Yeah, we've been getting that impression too," Callum said.

Ms Jones grunted. "The Watch may once have been the keepers of peace between humans and Folk, but I don't know what they are now. Can't trust any of them."

"Except Claudia," I said. The calico Watch lieutenant had not only helped us out more than once, she had, so far, not tried to kill me. Which meant she was by far my favourite Watch cat.

"Except Claudia," Ms Jones agreed. "But I can't find her."

"She's missing?"

"Can't say. I just know that I haven't been able to contact her through our usual channels."

I was momentarily put out that Ms Jones and Claudia had usual channels. It seemed distinctly unfair. "We need to try to find her. She might know more about what's going on."

Callum tapped his fingers on the wheel. "So, things

still haven't settled after the zombies, and Lewis is hunting for Ifan, who's meant to be dead. But can we really be talking necromancers? I thought they were meant to be extinct. Proper ones, anyway."

Ms Jones shrugged. "Supposedly. *If* you listen to the Watch. Anyhow, we might not be talking necromancers exactly, but certainly someone messing with death magic."

"That wannabe-necromancer lot in Headingley were doing a good line in headless chickens," I said. "Although they reckoned that was nothing to do with raising dead people and more to do with reanimating dead pets for well-paying clients."

"Yes, I think this may be a little advanced for chicken-raisers," the sorcerer said. "Look, just keep an eye on the magician, but don't get near him. And if you've got any way of getting in touch with Claudia, try that." She opened the door, swinging out into the rain. "And for the gods' sakes, stay out of trouble. I've enough to be dealing with."

She slammed the door on us and swung astride the motorbike, dropping the whisky bottle into a saddlebag. The bike started up without her doing anything, a low rumble like the growl of a beast stalking through deep forest. I shivered and jumped into the front seat, tucking my tail over my toes, and we watched Ms Jones slide out onto the road and cruise away, the rain parting around her in strange ways, as if reluctant to touch the bike.

Callum finally lit his cigarette.

I looked at him. "Really?"

"Let's just say magicians, necromancers, and sorcerers make me crave a little nicotine." He cracked the window and sent a swirl of smoke up into the dull day, exhaling like a sigh.

"Well, I suppose pretty much all of those will dial our life expectancy right down anyway."

"Exactly." He rubbed his forehead. "Gobs, what if he really isn't dead?"

"Ifan?" I said. "We saw his grave. You watched him get buried."

Callum tapped ash through the window, his mouth twisted. "I saw *something* get buried. And we found his grave dug up, remember?"

"Yeah, along with half the other graves in Harrow Hill. Zombie outbreak, remember?"

"We never saw his body. Not at the market, not anywhere." He took a quick drag on the cigarette.

"The magician said he overdosed."

"Ifan wouldn't."

"Well, I'm sure he wouldn't *mean* to. Most people never *mean* to. But—"

"No. Ifan was never … I was serious when I was using. I was lucky to survive it. But he was a … a dabbler. Enough to experience it, never enough to get hooked. He dabbled in everything – human drugs and unicorn horn and imp dust and occultism and spiritualism – everything. But he never lost sight of himself. He just *dabbled.*"

"Doesn't always stay that way," I said. "Sometimes what we think we're dabbling in is dabbling with us."

Callum shook his head. "No. I mean, maybe, but maybe Ifan dabbled in something he shouldn't have and now he's just lost or something. You know that can happen with magicians."

"Yeah. But Ifan was dabbling with necromancers, remember? You said yourself, we don't want a zombie Ifan. Or anyone."

"I know that," Callum said. "And Lewis wouldn't want that either, I'm sure. But what if he really isn't dead, Gobs? What if he's alive somewhere, and Lewis is trying to get him back, and we're going to ruin it all by helping Ms Jones?"

I looked at him, at the lines digging into his forehead and the cigarette clutched in his hand like a lifeline. Ifan had helped him get out of Dimly, away from his complicated, criminal family, away from the unicorn dust, but he hadn't been around when a very much not-dabbling Callum had scooped me up as a kitten. And he hadn't been around since, either. But some friendships don't have expiration dates. Some friendships are stronger than time and distance and the wounds of life.

I sighed and looked at my paws. "We can't know if we don't look."

He looked down at me. "You think we take the case?"

"It's not like we have a choice, anyway. Sorcerers don't exactly *ask* you to do things, do they?"

He snorted, and scritched the top of my head, his fingers scented with cigarettes and exhaustion. "True." He seemed about to say something else, then just shook his head and said, "So shall we try and find the magician, or d'you want to see if we can get a message to Claudia?"

"I prefer the idea of finding Claudia to stalking magicians, oddly. Let's see if Pru can get hold of her." I found it best to keep the lowest of low profiles when it came to the Watch, just in case they took it in their heads to turn me into monster munchies again. The lovely, if alarmingly hairless, Pru always seemed to be able to find Claudia when needed, though. Which was useful, if almost as annoying as Ms Jones and her usual channels.

"Why don't I have usual channels?" I asked Callum. "You know, we sorted Dimly out. And the book of power. *And* the undead."

"Maybe she just likes Ms Jones more than us," Callum said, turning the key and grinding the engine into life.

"That's blatant species-ism. And against her own species, no less."

"I think it might be more to do with personality than species."

"I have a wonderful personality."

"Sure you do."

"I *do*. You like my personality."

"I have no choice in the matter," he said. "You won't go away."

I huffed at him, and he pulled the car back out onto the street, and we set off in search of the dead and the lost and the unknown.

6

TEA, MISSING CATS, AND URBAN GORILLAS

Pru's human, who had looked rather like a barefoot Norse goddess – if an almost undead one – last time we saw her, had a cafe in Headingley, which seemed an excellent occupation for a human. There'd be no end of decadent treats on offer for a discerning cat, even if the trade-off was Pru having to wear fancy collars. But any cat that can carry off being bald has no issues with a bit of bling. And they kind of suited the whole Norse-goddess-and-friend aesthetic.

We parked up not far from the cafe and ventured out into the rain. Headingley itself was all coffee-drenched cafes with blackboard menus and expensively battered tables rubbing shoulders with charity shops and second-hand record stores and overcrowded bookshops, and the odd fancy store where a T-shirt costs fifty quid thrown in just to keep things interesting. The pavements were crowded with students clutching coffees they probably couldn't afford, and old women with pinched, disapproving faces towing shopping bags on wheels. Everyone was brandishing umbrellas or hunching into their jackets, and Callum adjusted the collar of his coat, as if that was going to do any good.

Pru's cafe didn't look any different. There were still plants pressing against the windowsills as they searched for the winter daylight, and the rich scent of coffee washed around the closed door. Callum paused outside, looking at something in the window that I couldn't quite see.

"What?" I asked.

He looked down at me, his face set in uneasy lines, then crouched to offer me a lift rather than answer. I jumped to his shoulder and balanced there as he straightened up. It's true that there are certain problems associated with my otherwise ideal stature – some things just aren't in my sightline. But now I saw a collection of posters in the window. Or not posters exactly, but rough, homemade flyers, printed at home or photocopied too many times, or both, all pixelated and badly done. There were some really dubious font choices and colours going on too, giving the whole window the feeling of a primary school bulletin board. Only where that would be an explosion of joyous chaos, this was a tangle of heartache. I could almost smell the grief coming off the signs, as if the hands that had put them up had left smudges of loss behind.

The one thing every flyer had in common was at least one picture of a cat, and the word *Missing* emblazoned across the top. They were crowded across the window, too many for me to count, that heavy grief creaking at the edges of my vision. Front and centre was one done a little better than the rest, the paper glossy and the photo in focus. Pru's narrowed green eyes stared back at me, her smooth bare skin hanging loose on her bones and her head tilted just slightly. And yeah, there was that flashy collar. This particular one was pink, with glittering stones set all over it, and it should have made me snort with amusement but it didn't. Not this time.

"Hairballs," I said, when I found my voice.

"I know," Callum said, and we were both silent for a moment.

I couldn't keep looking at Pru, with the *Missing* in red army-style lettering over her head, and I jumped back to the ground, tail twitching. "This does not seem good."

"I know," Callum said, wiping his mouth with one hand and keeping his voice low. Humans talking to cats on the high street is one of those things that tend to tip beyond eccentric into unacceptable.

"That's a lot of missing cats. A *lot.* And Pru ..." I stopped. I didn't know what I wanted to say. It's not fair? I mean, it wasn't fair for any of them, whatever had happened.

Callum crouched down and rested a hand on my back. "We'll find her. Never mind magicians and necromancers and all that. We'll look for her first."

"Unless it's all part of the same thing. Those shoddy chicken-raisers are just around the corner, after all. Maybe they've advanced their experiments into cats."

Callum sighed and waited for a grey, shrunken man to pass, glaring at us disapprovingly. "It could just be coincidence."

"Sure. Just like the undead popping out of the cemetery with your dead boy buddy." I peered up at the window. "There's no point hanging around out here. Shall we talk to her human?"

"Sure," Callum said, and looked as if he were about to say something pointless, like, *are you okay?* or some other human banality that didn't mean what it actually said. But he just twisted his mouth slightly, as if he were biting the inside of his cheek, took a final look at the poster and pushed the door open.

A bell jangled cheerily next to us, swinging on a long cord that almost whacked Callum in the head as we stepped in. The light was low and mellow, the overhead bulbs shining in filamented constellations above the wooden tables. The hairy waiter we'd met last time wasn't behind the counter, but Pru's human Katja was. She didn't look quite the barefoot Norse goddess that she had last time we'd seen her, but she also wasn't trying to eat anyone's brains so I counted that an improvement. She looked up and gave us the sort of non-committal smile someone uses when their mind's only half on the job.

Callum returned the smile and went straight to the counter rather than sitting down. She drew back as if afraid he'd grab her, and they stared at each other.

"Coffee?" she asked finally. The word had unfamiliar accents draped over the corners.

"Um, please," Callum said, tapping his fingers uneasily on the glossy wood of the counter.

She waited expectantly, then when it became clear he wasn't going to say anything else she asked, "What sort?"

"Oh. Right." He examined the shelves rather helplessly. "Tea would be better, actually."

I looked at my paws, shaking my head slightly and wishing I could be the one asking the questions. But Pru had said her human was *very* human, so even if I talked to her the odds were she'd either think I was just mewling or that she was having a small mental break and needed to cut back on the coffee. Looking at the shadows under her eyes, I thought the second option was pretty viable.

Katja gave Callum a curious look and took a fancy glass teapot off the shelf behind her. "Earl Grey?" she asked. "Bergamot? Green? Chai?"

"Just regular," Callum said. "You know, builder's tea."

"English Breakfast, then," she said, and chose a canister from the shelf above the teapots. She had heavy bracelets on her wrist, and they clanked as she opened the tin to scoop the tea out.

I arched my whiskers at Callum expectantly, and he scratched his chin. "I see you've got a few missing cats around here."

"Yes," she said, the word pinched.

"All recent?"

She spoke to the teapot rather than him, her shoulders high and tight. "It's happened over the past couple of weeks."

"Is … have you lost one?" Callum asked. He was doing his patented gentle voice, the one that people always seem to want to trust and confide in.

She nodded, concentrating on the teapot, then turned around to find a cup and saucer, taking her time about it. "My cat Pru vanished last week," she said finally. "Really *vanished.* I just woke up and she was gone. She's not even meant to be outside during the *day,* let alone …" She stopped and put both hands flat on the worktop behind the counter, not looking up.

"I'm sorry," Callum said. "I really am. They take up a huge space in our lives."

She nodded, and put the tea on the counter in front of him, her face pale and her jaw sharp. "I don't even know where to start looking. I asked the police, but they said oh, it's just a missing cat. What do I expect them to do? Don't they have enough to deal with? And then they told me to leave the station because I was causing a scene." She sniffed, and shoved a sugar bowl at Callum. I suddenly had a vision of her back in Norse goddess mode, and wished I could have been there to watch. "They told me to check with the RSPCA and the other rescues, but no one's seen her. The rescues have even lost cats. How do *rescues* lose cats?" She frowned at Callum, and he gave a rather helpless shrug, then glanced at me. I just stared back, because it wasn't as if I could say anything. But this was sounding worse and worse. Either it was necromancer-related – so who knew what they were up to when they should've a) been extinct, and b) been hiding from cats due to the Watch if they weren't extinct – or it was human-related. And that could get all sorts of creepy. You know, like serial killer creepy.

I stood up on my hind legs and tugged on Callum's jacket. I was getting sick of trying to see what was going on from down here. He looked down, and Katja followed his gaze and spotted me. A smile twitched the corner of her mouth.

"Hello, handsome," she said, and my ears perked up. "You can put him on a stool if you want," she said to

Callum. "If anyone complains about cats in here I'm just going to throw them out, anyway. It's that sort of day."

"Fair enough," Callum said, and pulled out the stool next to him so I could jump up. Katja and I looked at each other, and she scratched me between the ears.

"Fancy some cat milk?" she asked, and I put my ears back.

"He's not so keen," Callum said. "He goes for the full fat stuff."

"It's not good for them," Katja said. "It gives them indigestion. They're lactose intolerant, you know."

I huffed, and Callum nodded. "Trust me, I know all about the indigestion. But he won't drink cat's milk. I've tried."

I put my paws on the counter and snuffled at the biscuit on the edge of his saucer. Katja pushed me back gently. "Regular milk, then. I suppose a little can't hurt."

Callum sighed. "Well, not till later, anyway."

She smiled and went to find a bowl. "We need more info," I hissed at Callum. "*Just vanished* isn't exactly helpful."

He sipped his tea and whispered behind the cup, "I'm trying."

"Ask about the chicken necros. They used to meet here, right?"

"I've got this, Gobs. Shut up."

I huffed, but fell silent as Katja came back and put a cat's bowl in front of me. It was probably Pru's, and suddenly I didn't want it.

Callum put his cup down and said, "We might be able to help."

"How?" Katja asked.

"We're— I'm an investigator." He took one of our cards from his coat pocket, shaking off Green Snake. We were down to the last few, all classy white print on a matte black background. We needed to find another printer in need of an urgent covert move and willing to pay in cards and plaques, otherwise we'd soon be down to scribbling our phone number on the back of napkins.

Katja took the card and read, "*G & C London, Private Investigators.*" She lowered it and said, "Are you G or C?"

"C. Callum."

"Katja," she said, and Callum nodded just as if he didn't know exactly who she was. "You'd take on a missing cat case? Business not that good, or something?"

Callum smiled, which wasn't exactly a denial. "We tend to take on cases other people don't. And dealing with animals is kind of my speciality."

I snorted, thinking that was taking the definition of animals and casting it fairly far and wide, but Katja just looked thoughtful. She checked the cafe, but the only people in were two young women taking photos of their coffee and cake, an old man turning over tarot cards, and two older women bent over the same magazine like it was a treasure map. No one was looking at us.

"You'd really take this case," she said.

"Of course," Callum said. "I don't know what I do if I lost Gobbelino."

"Gobbelino," she said, and scratched me under the chin. "That's a cute name. I like that."

I arched my head into her hand, smelling coffee and sleeplessness and memories of a starker, harder country layered under the skin. I was glad someone appreciated me.

"I mostly call him Gobs," Callum said. I glared at him, and Green Snake peered out of Callum's pocket at me with what could've been a smug expression.

Katja snorted. "Alright," she said. "Please. I don't know what to do next. I've walked around the neighbourhood about fifty times. I've knocked on every door. Pru does go outside sometimes, even though she's not meant to, but she always comes back. She *always* comes back." She stopped, pressing her fingers to her mouth.

Callum reached forward as if to touch her arm, then patted his pockets instead and offered her a cigarette. She started to take one, then drew back and shook her head. He put them down. "We'll find her," he said. "Can you tell us anything else? Has there been anyone unusual around?"

"No," Katja said. "It's just been the normal people we get in. I mean, some of them are a little unusual, but that's normal."

Callum poured milk into his cup. "What about regulars? Any that have suddenly stopped? Or new ones started?"

Katja frowned. "Not that I can think of. We have a few groups that are always in – there's Friday Scrabble, then book club on Tuesday, and another one Thursday, which is really margarita club. Then there's the urban guerrilla farmers, and the lot that raise mushrooms …" She trailed off with a shrug. "No one that I can think of in particular."

"No one really interested in Pru?"

"No. I mean, people are always a bit curious because she's a Sphynx cat. They like putting her on Instagram."

I nosed Callum's arm, twitching my ears in a way I hoped indicated that I didn't feel he was entirely taking the questioning in the right direction. He looked at me, noticed Green Snake, and pushed him back out of sight before turning to Katja.

"A friend of mine told me there used to be a group here that were into the occult," he said. "Have they been about at all?"

I thought that made it sound like the necros been playing with Ouija boards in the corner, but Katja said, "Oh, *them.* I kicked them out ages ago. I was actually in the group for a bit because it seemed like it should've been fun, but they got really weird. They had some very strange ideas."

"Could they have maybe come back when you weren't here?" Callum suggested.

"Maybe," she said. "But why would they want Pru?"

"Did they ever say anything about doing stuff with animals?" Callum asked.

"No," she said. "It wasn't that kind of weird."

"No, no, I don't mean— No." He shook his head, looking horrified. "Not like *that.* Just, you know, some of these occult groups I've come across do sacrifices and things—"

Katja caught her breath, her fingers digging into the counter. *"Sacrifices?* You think Pru has been *sacrificed?* Like, what, some cult thing?"

I glared at Callum pointedly as he shook his head, raising both hands as if to push the suggestion away. "No, no, of course no one would do that. You said she's a Sphynx cat, right?"

"Yes," Katja said, not looking reassured.

"So she's valuable. And if that group were really upset about you kicking them out, maybe they stole her as a bit of revenge."

Katja frowned. "I suppose. But I haven't let them meet here for *ages*. I did think that maybe some dodgy breeder had stolen her or, you know …" She took a deep breath. "Dogfights. The cats being used as bait. Because most of the missing cats aren't purebreds, they're just moggies. And it's just so *sick*—" She stopped and turned away, busying herself with something at the sink.

"Oh, no," Callum said. "I'm sure it's not that. No one would take a Sphynx cat for that. The moggies, sure, but not her."

I growled, and he gave me a slightly panicked look.

"But why take *any?*" she asked. "What *for?*"

"Um." Callum stared at his cup. "Animal trafficking."

I blinked at him, then narrowed my eyes. It was as close to an eye-roll as I could get.

"What?" she asked, turning back to him. "Animal trafficking? In domestic cats?"

"Yes, definitely," Callum said, nodding rather too eagerly. "Animal trafficking. Cat trafficking. Huge demand. I've come across it before. Quite common. I mean, not that common, or I'm sure you'd know about it, but I have seen it. Them. The, uh, traffickers."

I looked at the ceiling. One of these days we're going to have to talk about his people skills. He might be great at all the human emotions rubbish, but he was terrible when it came to concocting any sort of believable story.

Katja helped herself to a biscuit from a jar and

munched it, frowning. “I didn’t know it was such a problem.”

“It can be,” Callum said. “Or, you know, it might be that group. The ones you kicked out.”

“They might be traffickers?”

“Maybe?”

I put my snout to his arm, so he could feel my teeth through the sleeve of his coat. He stared at me, and nodded.

“D’you know, just leave it with us. We’ll follow up all the leads.”

Katja looked at him for a moment, then said, “Sure. Okay.” She sounded less reassured than she had when Callum had first offered to help. I didn’t blame her.

He straightened the front of his hoody a little, which just made the hole at the neckline more obvious. “Is there anyone else you think we might look at?”

“I didn’t even know about cat trafficking. Now I’m wondering if the mushroom people might have taken her for compost or something.” She gave a half-hearted smile as she said it, and Callum smiled back, putting both hands on the counter.

“We’ll find her. I promise.”

She looked at his hands, nodded, then said, “Do you need a deposit?”

“Oh, no, we’re just happy to help,” Callum said, then yelped as I bit him.

"THAT WENT WELL," I said, once we were outside and heading down the road, Callum with his head down against the rain and me perched on his arm and tucked inside his coat. Green Snake was in an inside pocket next to me, and kept nudging my ears. "Cat traffickers?"

"I bet people do traffic Sphynx cats."

"Not us common lot, though," I pointed out. "Her dog-baiting theory was much better."

"I hope it's not that," he said.

"Me too." We were both silent for a moment, then I added, "Although, if it is necromancers, it might be worse."

"I know. I don't know what to hope for."

"No." I peered out at the street. "Are we checking out the necros' house first?"

"We're in the area," he said. "Plus, we need to see if the magician's been around there anyway."

"D'you think we'll be welcome after getting their headless chickens killed last time?"

"I mean, technically they were already dead."

"Fair point, although I think letting them out onto the road really cinched the matter."

"True. You may have to do some more sneaking – they'll recognise me."

I sighed. "Of course I will. And on another point, I can't believe you didn't take a deposit."

He adjusted his coat. He had to have it open to tuck me inside, and I could see rain soaking the neck of his hoody. "Pru's our friend."

"Do you really object to making money that much?"

"Katja was upset."

"I'm sure not paying us really made all the difference."

Callum sighed and pulled the coat shut, trapping me inside.

"*Hey!* It stinks of cigarettes in here!"

"I'm getting soaked."

"Yeah, but I'm suffocating." I clawed my way up his chest and poked my head out of the coat. "Katja's nice, though. Especially now she's not a half-zombie."

"*Hmm.*"

"Nice cafe, too."

"Tea was too fancy."

"Picky, picky," I muttered, and retreated back into his coat as the rain got heavier. Then I pushed my head back out again and said, "What about the gorillas? Should we be worried about gorillas?"

Callum made an exasperated noise and tucked his coat a little closer, just about squishing me. "Not those sort of gorillas."

"There's more than one?" I asked, but he didn't reply, and after a moment I ducked back down again. Let him deal with the gorillas. Although what the world was coming to when you had gorillas wandering around Leeds, I didn't know. The zombies had been bad enough.

7

CELLARS ARE NOT MY HAPPY PLACE

THE DOOR TO THE NECROMANCER'S HOUSE – OR EX-HOUSE, by the look of it – was still painted black, just as it had been when we'd been chasing zombies back in the spring, but the windows were blank and curtainless, and we could see an empty room through the one closest to the steps. There was no furniture, no rugs on the painted wood floors – not even the usual ghostly outlines on the walls where paintings had been. It looked not just wiped clean, but reset somehow. And the smell of the place was the same. Last time the most alarming thing we'd encountered had been the zombified chickens – which, to be fair, had been pretty alarming – but the whole place had reeked of something far deeper and older, seeping out of the ground. Something more than a bit of nasty avian resurrection magic. Now there was nothing.

I jumped off Callum's shoulder and we stood on the doorstep like a couple of gatecrashers who'd crashed the wrong house. At least it didn't look like I was going to have to do any sneaking.

Callum looked at me. "What d'you think?"

I snuffled the door, but it was about as magical as your average tea parlour, where the odd person's been knocking on wood or throwing salt over their shoulder. Low-level, habitual magic, more baked-in tradition than anything active. "They've gone," I said. "They've bloody well gone, and taken Pru with them."

"We don't know that for sure."

"We do. Missing cats, missing necromancers, and magicians trying to get their dead sons back? Did you honestly believe your own cat trafficking story?"

"It could still be a coincidence," he said, without much conviction.

"I've about as much time for them as I do for mermaid tea parties."

He didn't answer, just put his hand on the door as a kid ran past on the street, jogging trousers flapping wetly around his shins. "Shall we check?"

"Sure. It's not like it can be any worse than a taxidermied assault team, right? I mean, this lot only *specialise* in dead things."

Callum snorted, then knocked a couple of times. There was no response, but we hadn't really expected one. Not with those blank walls. He tried the handle and it turned under his hand. "Huh. Again."

"It's because no one with half an ounce of common sense just walks into a house belonging to magicians or necromancers," I said. "You don't have to lock the door when your house can simply eat any intruders."

Callum pushed the door open, releasing a wave of cold, stale air, flat and lifeless. The hall was empty. No runner on the bare floor. No sideboards. Just echoing silence that felt far vaster than the narrow entrance of the little terraced house should have been capable of. Callum stepped in carefully, and I followed, snuffling warily with more than just my nose. Your usual five senses aren't all that handy when it comes picking up magic.

"Anything?" Callum asked.

"Nothing. It's been stripped clean. You couldn't even imagine zombie cockroaches in this place."

"I suppose we should look around. I mean, we're here."

We looked at each other, and after a moment I sighed. "The worst of it was in the cellar. I didn't even go down there, but Pru said she did. She said it was where all the power was coming from."

"Fun," Callum said.

"I know. I really bloody hate cellars."

We went upstairs first, because it was as far from the cellar as it could be, but it was pointless. The whole place was freshly painted, and the hard carpets had so much detergent still clinging to them that I kept sneezing. Even if there had been anything up here to find, I wouldn't have been able to see it past my streaming eyes. There was even new grout in the bathroom, and fresh sealant around the sink, and not so much as a single zombie chicken feather stuck in a corner. The whole place smelled astringent and characterless, and we finally wound up in the little, well-bleached kitchen, looking at an old door still gleaming with shiny white paint.

"Just once I'd like to have to investigate a nice home furnishings store," I said. "Something with lots of cushions and no sharp edges."

"Noted," Callum said. "But have you ever been in one? It takes about two days to find the exit again at the best of times. And by then you've bought five candles and half a dozen jars you didn't even want."

I blinked at him. "I did wonder why we had jars. I asked for a fluffy blanket."

"That's a home furnishings store for you." He opened the door, which creaked obligingly, and flicked a light switch just inside. Pale illumination washed up the stairs to meet us, along with the scent of fresh concrete.

"Well. No stinting on the home renovations, then," I said, venturing onto the top step and peering down. The freshly painted wooden railing gave me a good view of the barely set concrete washing across the entire floor to meet the newly plastered walls.

"Can you tell if anything was here?" Callum asked.

"No. They've drowned the lot. Sealed it off." I looked at my paws, tail flicking. "There's got to be something that'll tell us where they've gone. We have to be able to find Pru."

"We will." Callum led the way back into the hall and sat down on the stairs, taking a cigarette out and lighting it. The ugly, harsh scent of it was almost welcome after the over-cleanliness of the house.

I sat down in the middle of the bare hall, looking around, while Green Snake crept out of Callum's pocket to investigate the stairs. He kept shaking his head like the fresh paint scent was getting up his nose too.

"How much do you know about necromancers, Gobs?" Callum asked, looking around for somewhere to flick the ash. Eventually he found a receipt in his pocket and tapped the cigarette into it awkwardly.

I shrugged. "The usual. As much as you do, probably. These days, they're not even meant to be around. The Watch wiped them out when they tried to take back the world from humans, forced the oldest and strongest of them out of this reality. They were sorcerers then, of a particularly nasty sort. They didn't like the fact humans were pushing Folk to the edges, and felt they personally were owed some sort of worship. You know, for wearing black and messing around with the dead or whatever. Which would've been funny if they weren't sorcerers. It was war in the end. Big war."

"It usually is," Callum said. "I don't think there's ever a small war, certainly not for anyone in it."

"Yeah, well, this one ended with the necromancers destroyed and the Watch *becoming* the Watch. Before that cats just kind of did their thing. We were the observers of everything just because it interested us, but we didn't get involved. Then we realised someone had to make sure humans and Folk stayed separate, or there'd just be more and more clashes, and at some point it'd wipe everyone out. You can't trust gods or sorcerers for that sort of thing, and most other kinds don't cross over so well between Folk and human worlds. So here we are."

"Here we are," Callum said, squinting against the smoke. "So how do we have necromancers now? I mean, *do* we have proper ones?"

"We shouldn't," I said. "But magic does its thing, just like nature. It always grows back where you least expect it. So maybe we were always going to have necros capable of raising more than a few chickens eventually."

"Fun," he said, examining the hall. "And now we have *missing* necros, which is even more fun."

"I never thought I'd actually *want* to find a dead-raiser. Ugh. How long d'you think they've been gone?"

"Not sure. I mean, everything still stinks of paint, but if it hasn't been aired out properly then it could be two weeks, maybe?"

"Two *weeks?*"

"Or less. I don't know. I'm not a painter."

I sighed. "I don't suppose we know any other necromancers we can drop in on for a friendly interrogation?"

"Not personally, no."

I looked at the bare walls, my stomach tight and nauseous. "Why would they take Pru? Why would they take *any* cats? They should be *avoiding* us, not … whatever they're doing."

"We'll figure it out."

I looked up at him. He was worrying at his thumb again, scratching at the skin where it met the nail. It looked a little raw and painful. "Are you thinking about Pru or Ifan?"

"Both."

I scratched my shoulder with a back paw. "It was a pretty crappy thing to do, if he's alive. To let you think he died."

Callum nodded, and the edges of his voice were rough when he answered. "He'd have had his reasons."

"Oh? Like what? Avoiding alimony? Life insurance scam?"

"Yes, those sound like just the sorts of things magicians worry about," he said. "Look, I'm not saying he was the best person. Maybe he needed to vanish for his own reasons. Or maybe it's all just Lewis' grief getting the better of him, and Ifan really is properly dead."

"Do you want him to be alive?"

He shot me a sideways look and took a drag on the cigarette. "Of course."

"Even though he might've lied to you?"

"He always lied to me." He smiled slightly. "He lied to everyone. That was just Ifan. You never knew whether you were getting the whole truth, or part of the truth, or nothing like the truth."

"Wow. So the whole faking his death thing would be totally in character, then."

"Not far off, anyway."

"He sounds like such a fantastic friend. Just really sound, you know?"

"I wasn't an easy person to be friends with." Callum's smile faded, and he went back to worrying at his thumb.

"You make it sound like that's changed." I watched him for a moment longer, but he didn't smile again. Eventually I said, "After all this time, you still think you owe him so much?"

He looked at the cigarette rather than at me. "It's not about owing him, although I do. It's knowing he'd do the same for me."

"Would he?"

"Yes." Callum's voice was flat and certain. And that was it, really. Humans tend to get hung up on Family with a capital F, as if it's the same thing for everyone, as if just by sharing a smaller gene pool with them than you do with others that you're somehow promised a certain solidarity, a certain connection. But Callum already knew his family wasn't *really* family, not in the way it matters. Because it's not necessarily about who married who. It's the people who stick by you that matter, and often that's nothing to *do* with family. Sometimes it's not even anything to do with species. But those are the ones you hold to, the ones who don't turn away when things get hard, or ugly, or just plain boring.

The ones who'll get you back from the dead if you can be got back at all.

I sighed and looked around the hall. "I suppose we could have a look in the backyard. You never know. Maybe they've left a 'necromancers and how to find us' brochure in the garden shed or something."

"That would be handy," Callum said.

WE LET ourselves out the kitchen door and poked around the skinny backyard, walled in on each side by the fences belonging to the adjoining houses in the terrace. At the back, a gate opened onto a walkway between the gardens on this side and the ones belonging to the houses opposite. It was just big enough to take the bins out to the road at the end, and was a bit overgrown with scraggly grass and weeds. The grass in the yard itself was cropped brutally short, and even the bins smelled more of bleach than rubbish. There were no sheds, but there was a plastic storage thing that was big enough for a couple of bikes. Callum unlatched it and checked under the lid, but it was as empty as everywhere else.

It didn't take us more than a couple of minutes to check the whole area, and I looked back at the house, digging my claws into the grass. "I don't understand how they've done it. It *stank*. The magic was so deep in the earth there's no way they should've been able to just … *this.*"

Callum nodded. "Maybe they moved a while ago. You know, not long after we came by last time. Maybe we worried them. Which means they've had months to get everything cleaned up."

"Well, that's helpful." I poked around the edge of the fence one more time, hoping to find *something*. Anything. The complete absence made it feel as if we'd got the wrong house, misplaced the necromancers entirely and therefore any chance of finding Pru, as well as the other cats with their grieving, painful posters. I wondered if I should be looking for Claudia myself. As much as I had no desire to come across any Watch cats, she needed to know about this.

But the whole thing sat uneasily. I knew Callum and I were good at what we did, but the Watch were better. They'd *know* about this. Claudia would know. And the fact that no one had shut this down already – whatever *this* was – made it something else. Something that matched up with the way other things had been ignored recently, zombies and unicorn weapons trade and other things that threatened the balance of the world. Something that was willing to sacrifice cats for an end goal I couldn't see or understand.

"We'll find her," Callum said. "It's the most important

thing right now. Ifan's not getting any deader. Or not-deader." He considered it. "Maybe."

I looked at him. "So was it the fancy tea that got you interested, then? Because I can get behind someone who gives you fancy tea, even if she did sneak me lactose-free milk."

"Nothing to do with Katja," he said. "More to do with Pru being one of the nicer cats I know."

"Hey," I said, following him out of the back gate. "I'm better than *nice. Nice* gets you shortbread biscuits and fancy tea. I get you cases and *introductions* to people with shortbread biscuits and fancy tea."

"I can get my own shortbread biscuits," he said, closing the gate behind us.

"Whatever," I said, and trotted after him as he tucked his hands into his coat pockets and headed for the street.

And I almost missed it. The path was just wide enough for the concrete walkway and a border of ragged grass to either side, but buried in the grass was a drain, the grate almost completely overgrown with dandelions. Who knows why it was there – it wasn't like the path was wide enough for a car, and the rain was running calmly down the centre of the concrete walkway, demonstrating clearly that it had no use for the drain. It was a leftover, a forgotten thing, and the smell came out of it and hit me like a fist. I squawked and jumped back, splashing myself with rainwater.

"Holy piglets," I said. "Hairballs. Hairballs on … on broccoli sprouts."

"What?" Callum asked, turning back.

I crept slowly forward again, trying not to breathe too deeply as I pawed at the overgrown edge of the grate.

"What is it?" Callum asked again.

"It's still here. Or something's still here." I took a careful sniff, bracing myself. It was like finding the edge of a scab and ripping it clear, releasing the blood that lay underneath. The scent flooded around me, old and crawling and *alive*. It was something raw and brutal and remorseless and . . . I didn't want to be there. I did not want to be anywhere near whatever had – or was still – making that scent, and I'd have been over the fence and gone if it wasn't for Pru. I took a step back, shaking my head to clear it, and Callum dropped to his knees next to me. He tore up big handfuls of the tangled weeds, scraping the old layers of earth away until he uncovered the drain.

We both peered at it. It wasn't some decent broad thing, but a round, rusted hole with a thin, broken grate on top of it. It looked like I'd barely get my head inside the thing. I looked from it to Callum and repeated, "Hairballs."

He shook his head. "Yeah, I don't think you're getting in there, Gobs."

"I have to. It's the only lead we've got."

"You won't be much help if you get stuck."

"I won't," I said, although I wasn't actually all that sure.

"I don't know. All that custard."

"I'm a fine figure of a cat," I snapped. "Anyway, you always say I'm scrawny."

"Yeah, but Mrs Smith's been keeping us pretty well. We should probably start taking the skin off the chicken."

"Sod off," I said. "Just open the damn drain, would you?"

Callum shrugged and dug his fingers around the edge of the grate, trying to shift it. It was solidly stuck, the weeds winding around it and tightening it in place. Eventually he pulled his keys out of his pocket and used our apartment one to clear the dirt and plants away while Green Snake looked on.

"Careful," I said. "Don't break that key. We don't want to have to ask the landlady for another one. She'll probably just kick us out."

"I'm aware of that."

"Can we rethink Katja's deposit?"

"No."

"We're going to starve."

"We're not going to starve," he said with a sigh, still digging at the grate. "Not the way Mrs Smith keeps feeding us."

"I have suspicions that she keeps trying to sneak worming pills into my tuna," I said. "The cheek of it!"

"Imagine."

"I do *not* have worms."

"No, you're just always hungry."

"I can't believe you'd accuse me of having *worms.*"

"Less accusation than a statement of fact," he said, finally levering the grate off. It snapped as he pulled it free, scattering rust into the darkness below, and we both peered into the shadows. Under the stench of the magic I couldn't really smell anything else. I didn't know what I was going to be jumping into down there. The last time I'd been in a drain I'd been running from a Cerberus dog and a murder of crows, and I'd been threatened by a one-eyed rat and chased by d'wyrms, whatever they were when they were at home. I wasn't exactly keen to relive any of it.

"You don't have to do this," Callum said. "We'll figure this out. I can't help you in there."

I didn't look away from the drain. "There's something down there. There *has* to be. Nothing smells that strong and ends up being just nothing. Maybe they haven't gone at all. Maybe there's a cellar *under* the cellar, with a different way in."

"So we find the different way in."

"Starting where? We've looked everywhere." My tail was flicking anxiously. I needed to get in the horrible drain now, else I wouldn't do it at all. "And I could be wrong. Maybe it's not another cellar, but they've sealed something up. In which case there's no other way in, and the only way to know what's going on is for me to take a look."

"Oh good," Callum said. "So they sealed the cellar over some necromancer mistake, which sounds pretty much as bad as it can be, and now you're going to go in and poke it. That sounds great." We looked at each other, and Green Snake poked his snout into the drain then retreated rapidly, shaking his head like someone had slapped him.

"What other lead do we have?" I asked.

Callum looked up at the house. "We can check again."

"We both know there's nothing there."

"We'll go back and wait for the magician to turn up."

"We don't know that he's definitely working with the necromancers," I pointed out.

"We don't know that they're definitely behind the cats disappearing, either."

"We know it's the most likely, unless we really do have a cat trafficking ring that *just happens* to have kicked off about when the necromancers moved out."

He looked at me for a moment longer, then sighed and said, "Be careful. Don't hang about. And don't talk to anyone. And come back straight away. "

"Yes, Dad," I said, and wriggled into the gap.

8

THE TOYS ARE REVOLTING

IT WAS A HEADFIRST DROP INTO A SHALLOW STREAM OF water that didn't actually smell too bad, other than the insistent stench of magic. As far as nasty things I might land in, I couldn't pick up anything worse than a whiff of leaf mulch, which was a win in my book given the way the day was going. I landed clumsily, splashing water into my nose and snorting as my hindquarters caught up with me. They were smarting a bit, as the drain had been a squeeze right at the last moment. Callum had nudged me with his boot to force me through, which was completely undignified, and I intended to tell Pru just how much she owed me when I finally found her. Although it was also possible that taking the skin off the chicken might be a good idea if I was to continue my career of crawling into drains. But given that the skin was the tastiest bit and I really hated drains, I'd reserve judgement on that.

The drain headed in the direction of the house and I padded cautiously forward, my nose full of the greasy stink of old magic and the water splashing my face. It was bigger now I was down here. Still not a huge drain, but high enough that I could walk without crouching, my head slung low. My ears pricked forward as I tried to catch any whisper in the darkness. The closer I got to the house, the more the stink of bleach started to drown the reek of magic. Normally I'd welcome that, but right now I wanted anything that might give us a clue as to where the necromancers had gone, and bulk-buy cleaning products were not going to help us with that.

I sifted through the smells, trying to pick individual threads out of the mess of old magic and new cleaners. There wasn't just bleach down here. Every magical thing leaves a trace, and even the most pernickety of magic-workers have to clean up after themselves on occasion. Sometimes as a matter of urgency, and sometimes from necessity because too much magic has seeped into the soil and started conflicting with each other. I mean, it's pretty common knowledge that mixing bleach and vinegar can get bad fast, but that's not a patch on mixing a conjuring spell with a banishing spell. That sort of thing can tear an abyss straight into your backyard.

That's why magicians' houses get so weird. They may not have the focus of sorcerers filling their books of power, but they kind of create a legacy of controlled magic spills. They allow all that stray magic to build up in the walls of their houses, using the power to draw a cocoon around them like a small, toothed creature draws wool around itself as it hibernates. It's addictive, that power. Always there's the desire for one more layer, one more wrap of protection. And if they're not controlled at least a little, abandoned spells can start taking on a life of their own, mixing and matching with other magical fragments. Which brings us back to the risk of unfriendly, overly toothy creatures breaking out of voids and different dimensions when you're around magicians.

I don't know why anyone would mess around with such things, to be honest, but that's humans for you. They're always poking around, craving power and prestige, as if that's ever going to do anything helpful. What they really need is a nice cosy bed, a full stomach and a decent fire. That's all anyone ever really needs in this life. Or any other.

Given the stinking tunnel I was currently padding through, though, I had a feeling that our zombie chicken necromancers had maybe not been as careful as they could have. They hadn't exactly given the impression of being experts at this sort of thing, and it seemed to me that somehow they'd stumbled on a house with power there for the taking. They'd likely been drawing on that magic without ever really understanding it, adding to the spillage and probably having some pretty curious results. I wasn't even sure the chicken-raisers understood what a necromancer *was*, considering the woman we'd met had been going around saying that their whole deal was comforting people by resurrecting their dead pets, or by communing with the already-dead and giving people *closure*. I've never heard of a necromancer giving people closure, unless the closure in question involved wounds inflicted by their own hand.

All of which suggested that, if they'd suddenly abandoned their power supply and were taking on cats, someone new and distinctly more formidable was in charge. Or things had taken on a life of their own. Ugh. Give me a raiser of the dead who knows what they're doing any day over these amateurs. At least you know what you're getting then.

The drain was angling down slightly, looking like it was going to go straight under the cellar. Which was both where I wanted to go and also not at all what I wanted. I tried not to think about what might have dribbled down here over the years, and instead just thought of trying to find any sort of clue as to where the chicken-raisers might have gone. It was utterly dark in here now, the light of the drain long-lost behind me, and I was relying on the twitch of my ears and the whisper of air across my whiskers to tell me of side drains and new openings as I padded steadily on.

Which meant I stepped into the gap before I even realised it was there.

I felt the flare of empty space even as my hurrying paws carried me into it, and I tried to jump back but it was too late. I pitched forward with a squawk into a far wider gap than the one I'd arrived through, with no idea how far it went down or what was waiting at the bottom. I bumped off a side, hissing, and twisted into the fall, hoping my feet were going to be pointing the right way by the time I hit. Then I did the only thing anyone can do when things get entirely out of control. I relaxed and went with it.

It's amazing, even when you don't fall for long, just how much time you have to think while doing the falling. I had already decided that I was probably going to land in something that stank and was distinctly squishy, which I wasn't looking forward to. But it was better to think of that than to consider falling into some gloopy mess of sewer water where I'd have to swim among various unidentifiable things, or, worse, smashing into some hard and stabby surface. Although, to be honest, given a choice between that and sewer scum, I don't know. I mean, I'm a cat. I do bounce.

But I hit both sooner and more gently than I expected. For a moment I thought it actually was some sort of stretchy, solidified sludge that gave softly then flung me back up again, like I'd landed on some horrifyingly *warm* trampoline. I yelped as I was thrown clear, getting my paws under me and stumbling onto a hard rock floor. I found my footing and dropped into a crouch, freezing where I was and blinking around at a low-ceilinged chamber illuminated in dull, unhealthy light.

It should have been dark in here. *Really* dark. I hadn't seen even a glimmer of illumination before I fell, and I should have, against all that velvet black. But all around me now was a soft luminescence. I couldn't entirely tell where it came from, but the odds seemed good that it was some sort of freaky, previously undiscovered, and probably sentient fungus. It felt like the sort of day and place for sentient fungus.

The unhealthy light outlined a chamber twice as tall as I was, with curved concrete walls and the dark arches of pipes leading off in four different directions. Two of them were blocked with heavy wire mesh, and one of the others was jammed halfway to the top with some unpleasant debris. I could smell the rot of it from here.

I'd crashed to the floor pretty much dead centre in the

chamber, and there was a rumpled *thing* there, at least as big as I was, all mud-caked and grimy. It could've been a pile of rags, except for the fact that it was currently pushing itself up to sitting, grumbling. I stared at it in the pale, green-tinged light. The creature stared back. It was possibly the oddest thing I'd ever seen, and I've come across a *lot* of strange things. A lot. It seems to have turned into an occupational hazard for me. Never mind all your average magical critters, like imps and faeries and sludge puppies. I've seen tree dragons and ceiling monsters and flamingos (and you can't tell me they aren't weird). I've even come across the beasts of the void, and while I couldn't actually *see* them, I certainly felt them. There were lots of tentacles, lots of teeth, and lots of claws.

But this was possibly even weirder. It was like looking at a large teddy bear, if a teddy bear could sit up and rub its chest and make little *ooh* sounds of distress. It was very soft, and had probably been very fluffy at some stage, judging by the matted, stinking state of it.

It gave its belly another rub and said, "That was completely uncalled for."

I opened my mouth, shut it again, then said, "Sorry. It wasn't actually how I intended to make my entrance."

The creature looked at me and said, "How did you intend to make your entrance?"

"I didn't," I admitted. "I was planning against making any sort of entrance, really."

The creature grunted, and we regarded each other. My fur was sticking in all directions from my fall, and the magic stink was so thick and cloying it was making me want to sneeze. It was hard to tell colour in here, but the creature looked like it might've been pink once. Its belly was a slightly paler shade of stained, and there seemed to be rainbows tattooed onto it. I wondered if that was some sort of hardcore sewer monster tattoo, like a human getting a death's head. But I figured that was hardly the most important thing right now – I needed to get answers and get out before I ended up with my own hardcore sewer monster tattoo.

"I was looking for the necromancer's cellar," I said. "Can you point me in the right direction?"

"The People Above are gone," the creature said. "They used to send us chickens, and sometimes rats, but they're gone now."

I shuddered. Chickens were one thing, being scatty enough that losing their heads made little difference to their conversational skills, but I liked rats. Bloody necromancers.

"They didn't leave anyone behind?" I asked. "Any cats, perhaps?"

"Nothing. They left us with nothing."

"And they don't have any extra rooms down here or anything?"

"No. Down here is our world."

"Right. Very nice." This was one wasted sewer trip. "How would I go about making an exit, then?"

"We don't go out," the creature said.

We. Hopefully that was the royal we. Maybe having a rainbow tattoo marked you as the posher sort of sewer monster.

"Personally, I'd like to go out," I said. "That's my world. But I fell."

"We all fell," it said, and as it spoke things started crawling out of the corners. *Lots* of things. Some were matted and fluffy like the creature in front of me, all stained to the same dank non-colour. Some were angular and multi-jointed, some plasticky and evidently missing some bits, and at least a couple of them I recognised as the sort of toys parents queue up for outside toy stores before Christmas. Or they *used* to be. I doubted anyone'd be queueing for these ones.

"Right," I said, and peered around the eerily lit drain. "Well, you've obviously made the best of it. Good to meet you and all that. Appreciate the hospitality, but I've got friends waiting." I scooted backward, retreating toward the one open drain. It pointed in the wrong direction, heading deeper rather than back the way I'd come, but anything was better than being in here with the mutant toy department. I wondered if the chicken-raisers had been sinking excess magic into toys, or if it was just some hideous spill that had swept up any discarded toy in the neighbourhood. Not that it mattered either way – the end result was still the sort of weirdness that made my paws itch.

"You can't get out," a one-armed robot-type thing said, grinding forward on broken treads. "Once you're down here, you have to stay."

"I'd rather not."

"It's actually very nice once you get used to it," Rainbow Bear said.

"Sure," another creature chimed in behind me, and I

twisted to face it. It looked a little like a tiny horse with some very, very strange proportions and another of those weird rainbow tattoos on its rump. "And it's much better than being pawed by small children and dragged around the place."

"I try to have as little to do with small children as possible," I said. The horse-thing was between me and the drain, and I figured I could probably get past it, but I'd have to be fast. There were too many others for me to tackle all at once. "I'll just be off." I took a step toward the horse, and Rainbow Bear growled.

"You need to stay," it said, and grinned at me. "The People Above no longer send us gifts."

"Unfortunate," I said. "That must've been handy."

"But now here you are," the bear said, and I *knew* he'd just been some cuddly soft toy at some stage, but his teeth weren't standard issue for any toy I'd ever seen. "A new gift from the Above."

"Right," I said, and bolted.

Weird horse had been joined by a phalanx of little naked figures with cones of multicoloured, matted hair, all daubed in mud and waving tiny spears at me, and I ploughed straight through the middle of them. They tumbled every which way behind me, screeching some impressive curses that I'd have liked to remember for later, but I didn't have time to worry about it right now. I plunged into the drain, the light fading behind me until I was running flat out into the darkness, hoping I wasn't going to smash straight into a wall. But even if I did, it was still better than the alternative. I was not going to end my fourth life being eaten by an eyeless doll or a stuffed bear. That was just too undignified to even consider.

I thundered down the tunnel, hearing the pursuit of plastic feet and soggy paws under the swift scrape of my own. They were fading behind me, their legs definitely not made for running. I mean, they weren't even made for *standing,* most of them. I stretched out, sleek and swift, my paws sure on the hard surface of the tunnel, knowing that they had no hope of catching me now I was away. I was *made* for this, I was pure feline grace, I— My paws hit slime as the water returned and I lost my footing, squawking as I flopped into the sludge and scooted along on my side under the power of my own momentum. I scrambled up and kept running, paying a little more attention this time. I'd scraped my snout.

There was a faint lightening in the dark ahead of me, and I started yelling just on the off chance Callum had gone poking around different drains. Hell, even a random friendly cat person would be fine. Anyone to get me out of here, because my pursuers were still following me, and I could hear the rattle of wheels on stone. They had transport.

"Callum!" I bellowed as I came to a skidding halt under a drain. The sides were sheer, but I leaped up anyway, scrabbling at the sides, trying to claw myself up toward a tantalisingly close rectangle of grey sky. "*Callum!*"

There was a flicker of movement, and a small form slid onto the grate and peered down at me. I blinked up at it.

"You've got to be kidding me," I said, and Green Snake swayed his head from side to side, staring at me unblinkingly. I couldn't tell if that was snake talk for amusement, or encouragement, or just *hey, look at the cat in the hole*. I looked over my shoulder, the splashing and rumble of tiny wheels growing closer. "Help," I hissed at the snake. "Find Callum! Help me!"

Green Snake tipped his head at me, then retreated.

"Hey!" I yelled, but he didn't come back, and I had no idea if he understood anything I'd said. "Great. Just great. This is super helpful. I always wanted a snake as a sidekick."

The splashing was getting closer, and it sounded like there were even more of them than I'd seen at first. There was some nasty chanting rising up with it as well. It sounded awfully like a lot of small voices shouting, *Strip the bones and eat the stuffing! Strip the bones and eat the stuffing!*

I was fairly certain they weren't talking about the sort of stuffing you had at Christmas dinner.

"Callum!" I yelled. "Callum, *hurry up!*" I scrabbled at the walls that led up to the drain again, but they were too steep and smooth. There was nothing to get my paws into. I flung myself up once more anyhow, skittering on the concrete and feeling grit jam up underneath my claws. Cats and gravity can sometimes have a fairly casual relationship, but gravity was not having it this time. I splashed back into the water just in time to land on top of one of the hairy little plastic figures. I hissed and jumped away as it tried to bite me.

"Sod off, you little monster," I snarled at it. "What the hell even *are* you anyway?"

"Strip the bones and eat the stuffing! Strip the bones and eat the stuffing!" The chant rang out around me as the crea-

tures started to march into the faint circle of light from the drain. Rainbow Bear was sitting on top of a toy truck, and behind him smaller creatures scooted along on toy cars, using sticks to push themselves at an alarmingly impressive pace. I was going to have to run again. I couldn't wait any longer, or they'd be on me, and I had no intentions of letting any of them touch my stuffing.

"Green Snake, damn you!" I yelled, and batted a tatty bunny with vampire fangs away. I spun to sprint on into the darkness, then the lid of the drain crashed away and a hand grabbed me by the scruff of the neck and hauled me into the glorious, sodden day. I've never been so happy to have such an undignified exit.

Callum deposited me on the pavement and stared down at the group of bedraggled toys in the drain. They glared back up. A plastic dinosaur clutching a small yet unnervingly sharp kitchen knife in its tiny paws roared impressively.

"Jesus," Callum said.

"I know. Bloody necromancers. Never mind zombie chickens – they've raised an army of murderous toys."

"Evidently," Callum said, and ducked back as some sort of punk fairy with an impossibly tiny waist and a huge head hauled back on a slingshot and sent a marble flying out of the drain. "Right. We done here?"

"Well, I'm not going back in," I said, and looked at Green Snake. He stared back at me with his flat, expressionless eyes. "Took your time about it, didn't you?"

"I'd never have found you without him," Callum said, sliding the cover back over the toys. "He knew which drain you were in somehow."

"How?" I asked suspiciously, and the snake tipped his head at me again.

"Who knows. Maybe it was just luck." Callum picked Green Snake up and popped him in his jacket pocket. "We could do with some luck."

"I'd like *more* luck," I said, following him as he headed back down the street. "So far today we've been attacked by dead animals, misplaced a magician, found a sorcerer, lost Pru *and* Claudia, and I've been chased by a pack of renegade sewer toys and thrown over a wall by the squirrel mob. Plus my paws are dirty. I don't feel that lucky."

"Just sounds like an average day," Callum said.

"Can we agree that we need better cases? My patience is wearing thin."

"We can *agree* that," Callum said. "Don't know that it'll change anything, mind. Lift?"

"My paws will only improve your jacket," I said, and he snorted, then scooped me up. We walked back to the car like that, with Green Snake looking out of Callum's pocket and me balanced on the skinny line of his shoulder. No one even looked at us twice.

Humans.

9

A NECROMANCER HOUSEWARMING

"WELL," I SAID AS WE SETTLED INTO THE CAR, BOTH Callum and I liberally dampened from the drizzle, "I guess we're no further forward. There certainly wasn't anything left under the house unless you count the My Little Ravenous Monsters."

"We found something," Callum said, lifting Green Snake out of his pocket and setting him on the dashboard.

"I'm *sorry?*"

"I checked the bins," Callum said, coaxing the car into coughing life.

"You checked the bins? But *we* checked the bins. There was nothing there."

"Nothing in the ones in the yard. The recycling was out for collection and it hadn't been emptied yet."

I closed my eyes and took a deep breath. "You mean you let me crawl into a sewer full of feral stuffed toys who wanted to eat *my* stuffing, and *then* you checked the recycling bin?"

He shrugged. "I wouldn't have noticed the recycling if

Green Snake hadn't found it. Besides, you were very fixed on the sewer. I thought maybe you wanted to go in. "

I glared at him. "I have never wanted to go into a sewer. If you had ever had to go into a sewer, you would understand that."

He looked at me, then nodded. "Fair enough."

"And next time can you open *all* the bins before I have to crawl into a drain?"

"Sure. Can you wait until I've opened all the bins before you start crawling into drains?"

"Whatever," I said. "What'd you find?"

He pulled a crumpled envelope out of his pocket and opened it, taking the letter out to show it to me. "It's a change of address confirmation from the power company. They're stopping the service here and starting it at a new address." He pointed at it. "That's where they are."

I squinted at the address, and sighed. "Well, hairballs. With bells on. In gravy."

"At least we know where to go."

"I was in a *sewer.* With toys. Biting me."

"Nothing bit you."

"How do you know? I could be bitten under my paw."

"You'd have told me if you'd been bitten," Callum said, and pulled out of the parking space. "I wouldn't have heard the last of it."

I growled, and Green Snake flicked his tongue at me. Whatever *that* meant.

I CLEANED my toes pointedly as we rattled along the road, tangling with the steady flow of traffic in and out of Leeds.

"So we're off to the necromancer housewarming?" I asked finally, when my toes were mostly free of tunnel grit and sewer muck.

"It's not far," Callum said. "We may as well check it out."

"Then, what? Just knock on the door and wander on in?"

He gave me an amused look. "Maybe we can find another drain for you."

"*No.*"

"Alright, then. I can't exactly knock on the door, but we can see where it is, and come up with a plan for figuring out if they're holding Pru somewhere."

"You mean I'm going to have to sneak in. Again."

"You are exceptionally well-suited for sneaking."

I narrowed my eyes at him. "That is both insulting and a compliment, and I know pointed flattery when I hear it."

"And you never turn it down."

"What would be the point in that? It's only the truth." I considered it, then said, "Alright. But have we got any snacks? I need to keep my strength up if I'm going to crash a necromancer house party."

Callum took the tub from the open glovebox and popped it open, setting it on the seat in front of me. "Fancy cafe milk wasn't enough?"

"It takes it out of you, getting chased by rabid underworld playthings." I didn't want to admit I hadn't touched the milk. That I'd been able to feel Pru's presence like a ghost, and it kind of took the edge off my appetite.

He snorted, but left me with the tub. I had to share with Green Snake, which seemed a bit off. I doubted cat biscuits were snake food.

On the other hand, he had proved useful. And he had surprisingly impressive fangs for a small snake, so I kept my protests to myself.

IT DIDN'T TAKE LONG to get to the necromancers' new digs, which weren't exactly a step down, but certainly weren't a step up, either. Rather than a little mid-terrace in the depths of Headingley, they'd found themselves a little detached bungalow on the muddled edges of Roundhay. It looked pretty much the same as its neighbours – squat, tired and a bit grubby and wilted at the edges. Paint was peeling on the walls, but the waist-high green chain-link fence around the overgrown garden was tightly kept. There were some mouldy garden gnomes sitting in the weed patches, one with a missing head, and one of the windows was curtained with what looked very much like a crumpled sheet. There were also a couple of tiles missing from the roof. Necromancer business mustn't be much more profitable than the PI one.

Callum parked one house down and across the road, and we sat there for a while, waiting to see if there was any movement from inside.

"What if they have more chickens?" I asked.

"Can you not deal with some headless chickens?"

"There could be toys. I've decided I'm very anti-toy."

"Understandable. But someone has to have a look, and it can't be me."

I sighed. "What about Green Snake? He's even sneakier than me."

Green Snake slithered abruptly into the gap under the glovebox and vanished.

"*So* sneaky," I said. "You can't rely on snakes."

Callum shook his head. "Green Snake can't tell me what he sees, anyway. Just nip over there and peek in a few windows and see if you can spot anyone."

"It's not like they're not going to find me suspicious, you know, even if they don't recognise me. A cat poking around a necromancer house is fairly questionable."

"It's still a better option than me going in. Even if what's her name – Oli – isn't there, I still met that big guy. That's two who might recognise me."

"Ugh," I said. "You suck."

"I know," he said, and opened his door just enough to let me slip out onto the cracked pavement. I checked the empty road then ran across it to slip under the gate into the garden, the loose edges of the wire digging into my coat like sharp fingers. I didn't pause, just ran for the cover of a half-dead bush and crouched beneath it amid a drift of dead leaves, watching the house. There was no stinking magic here of the sort that had been left behind in Headingley.

I wondered again what – or who – had caused them to leave the power source of the old house behind. You don't tend to just *happen* onto that sort of thing. They're usually fiercely protected, like the magician's house. It takes a lot of power and a lot of time to build up a good bed of magic, and no one walks away from that without a good reason. Starting again … it's like a callus, where the first time you lift an axe your hands are ripped raw, but by the time you've been doing it for a year, you don't even feel it. It's the same thing with magic. At first you're drawing from nothing, but then after you've been working at it long enough you have a certain threshold to start from. It must've been something big that caused them to move on. Or the promise of something even bigger.

All the windows to the front of the bungalow were closed and curtained – or sheeted – so I slipped from hiding and ran through the damp grass around the side of the house, my whiskers bristling to attention. The back garden was as overgrown as the front, and the windows were as firmly closed to the day, but there was a scent back here, a slithering whiff of blood and malice. My hackles rose. If it was another damn drain, I wasn't doing it. Green Snake could have a go, if he was so smart.

But the scent didn't lead me to a drain. It led me to a bunker. Or a shed, maybe, because it had a few high, small windows to the back and one decent one to the front, but the rest of it was all ridiculously thick, cold concrete walls with a curved roof of the same material. No one had bothered to paint it, and it looked like a leftover from the days of bomb shelters and hideouts, the windows a mere afterthought, tacked on later in an attempt to repurpose it.

Which would have been unpleasant enough, with the damp musty scent of old concrete mingling with mould and rot, but carved into the grey walls were charms, trapping ones for keeping creatures in and warding ones for keeping creatures out, and ones for hiding and others for securing magic within the four walls. They glared out at me, raw fresh tears in the old stone, and I stood there and stared, smelling a jumble of scents seeping out from under the sigils. Smooth cat signatures and confused human smells and the hairy excited whiff of a dog and plenty more I didn't recognise, all laced about with power and blood.

"Hairballs," I breathed, and in that moment I heard the quick hungry tread of something heavy and muscular, all swift feet and fury. I bolted, launching myself into a sprint without stopping to look around, racing back the way I'd come. There was a bark that just about knocked me over, and that hairy scent swept over me, carried on the thunder of heavy paws.

I sprinted for the side of the house, paws slipping on the damp grass, throwing everything into it. I could smell the dog's breath, so close I half-expected it to ruffle my fur, and when it barked again the noise just about deafened me. I dived into a tangle of broken plant pots, but the dog was right on top of me and there was no time to hide. I broke from the meagre cover and shot for the nearest fence, then turned my flight into a wild zigzag as heavy jaws chomped behind me, spattering my hindquarters with slobber. A scrappy bush loomed in front of me, and I flung myself into its skinny branches, clawing my way upward to the tune of cracking twigs. The dog crashed into the bush below me, and I yowled as it bent under the impact then sprang upright again. I somehow kept my grip and scrabbled a little higher while the dog's barking hit the sort of volume that should come with a warning label.

I reached the limit of the branches, straddling about five of them and swearing fealty to every god I could think of if they'd just hold a little longer. The dog was still barking and shoving its enormous head into the bush, but the branches were as spiky and bendy as they were skinny, and after getting a couple in the eye and one up the nose the dog dropped back and just kept up a steady, furious volley of barks.

"Well, this is subtle," I muttered to myself. "Very low-key."

The dog snarled at me.

"And you know what you can do? You can—" I broke off as there was a bright shout from the direction of the road. "Oh, no."

"Hello?" Callum called again, and I heard the unmistakable click of him opening the gate. The dog looked around, his huge ears pricking forward as much as they could, being of the floppy Rottweiler variety.

"No, hey," I said to him, and he looked back at me, growling.

"Anyone home?" Callum shouted, sounding as if he was definitely inside the garden now. "Hello!"

"Stay," I said to the dog, as he half-turned toward Callum. He whined.

"Hello, hello!"

"*Stay.*"

The dog bolted.

"Hairballs," I muttered, and twisted in the bush, scrambling wildly back through the unhelpful branches toward the ground.

"Oh – hey, sit! *Sit!* Good dog!" Callum yelped, and I hoped he was running. I didn't wait to see, just shot for the nearest stretch of chain-link fence and flew straight over it into someone else's garden, landing among a set of garden gnomes that were fishing in a tiny, stagnant pond. They weren't real gnomes, obviously, because one would not want to crash-land among them. These were a human approximation, which was dead wrong and far less inebriated. Beyond the fence, I heard a door bang open.

"Brutus! *Heel!*" a woman yelled. "You, stand still!"

Brutus. Of *course* the damn thing was called Brutus.

"Standing still," Callum called, and I peered around the gnomes. My angle wasn't great from here, but I could see Callum with his hands up like old Brutus had a gun trained on him, and a young woman with pink hair clicking her fingers at the dog. He was growling, a rumbling sound that carried easily across the gardens, and I was quite happy to have the fence between us. At least the damn thing couldn't eat Callum in one bite.

I wriggled through the tangle of gnomes and decorative stones and out the other side, arriving on a well-kept lawn with some nice high flowerbed borders on the fence side. I kept close to them and ran for the road.

At the edge of the garden I paused and checked around. The car was still in the same spot, the engine off and the doors closed, and with any luck Callum was making his excuses and would be on his way back any moment. Or, failing that, was about to leg it back with the dog in pursuit.

I peered along the pavement at the house, but Callum wasn't on his way out the gate. He was talking to the woman with the dog, which I could still hear growling with the jagged resolution of a chainsaw. Well, I couldn't do anything, and if he had to make a run for it I wasn't going to be left behind. I ran for the car and scooted underneath it, tucking myself in next to the front wheel so I was hidden from the house, then checked on Callum.

He was gone.

The garden was empty.

I blinked at it, and craned around the tyre, checking the street, but the only person about was a man pushing a stroller with one hand and drinking a coffee with the other. I swore, using a few of the more graphic phrases I'd picked up from the toy army, and settled back into hiding, watching the house. It stared back blankly, giving nothing away. I couldn't even hear the dog, let alone see the thing. I waited, not sure what I expected to happen, but certain this couldn't be right. Callum wouldn't have just waltzed into a necromancer's bungalow and got himself nabbed, right? No one could get nabbed in a *bungalow*. It didn't sound right.

The biscuits were sitting heavy and sick in my belly.

THERE HAD STILL BEEN no sign of life from the house when something hit the road with a thud right behind me. I squawked and lurched sideways, bouncing off the wheel and whipping around to face whatever abomination the day had decided to unleash on me next. Green Snake lay on the tarmac, regarding me with unblinking eyes.

I glared at him. "What?"

Green Snake flicked his tongue, then looked at the house and back at me.

"I can't just go in after him. There's a *dog.*"

Green Snake glanced at the house again, then tilted his head at me. I didn't like that head tilt. I had a sneaking suspicion that there was something rude about that head tilt.

"I don't see you doing anything useful."

Another tilt.

"Well, of course I'm going to do *something.* I'm just gathering my resources."

He tilted his head even further. He was going to be looking at me upside down at this rate.

"Well, you come up with a plan, then."

Green Snake looked at the house for a moment, then slithered out onto the road. He moved across it at a surprisingly quick pace, up onto the pavement on the other side, and straight under the fence without pausing, vanishing into the long grass. Only the shake of the odd dandelion marked his passage, charting a straight line toward the front door.

"Fantastic," I said. "*Fantastic.* Callum's vanished, and now the damn snake's going straight in the front door. I should just let him go in the front door. I mean, he's a snake. What are they going to do to a snake? You're already a snake. Life can't get much worse."

The movement of the dandelions stopped and a small

head lifted itself clear of the stems, looking back at me. It tilted.

Of all the things we could've been left with after Ms Jones' book of power nearly tore our apartment – and us – and the world – apart, we got the snake. It could have been anything. It could have been the fridge full of food. It could have been the quite wonderful heated bed, or the double-size apartment that didn't smell of something rotting in the walls. But no, it was a snake, and apparently a snake that was intent on rescuing Callum, which it wasn't going to be able to do, and so I was going to have to rescue them both. I dipped back into my new curse library, added a couple of old faithfuls, then dropped low on all fours and scooted across the pavement, under the gate and into the grass.

I ran straight to the snake and hissed at him, "What are you *doing*, you scaly muppet? There's a dog in here with teeth the size of your head. You want to get eaten?"

Green Snake just looked at me and looked at the house.

"We can't just march in the front door. You have no idea what you're doing. You're a liability."

The snake turned away and started moving again. I followed him, keeping low in the grass. He wasn't going to the front door. He slipped into the flowerbeds that bordered the house and slithered along the wall, his tongue testing the air, moving fast enough that I had to trot to keep up.

We were almost to the back corner when he found the vent. It had the hot, dry scent of laundries, and there was a fluted rectangular grill over it. Green Snake pushed his nose under one of the corners and flattened himself out to some impossibly thin shape, slipping inside while the grate barely moved behind him. He turned back to peer at me through the grille.

"I can't fit in there."

Green Snake didn't respond, so I pawed the corner of the grate to prove my point. It promptly swung off, hanging by one top corner screw.

"Oh. Lovely," I said, without much enthusiasm.

Green Snake stuck his tongue out again, and I peered beyond him into the depths. At least it didn't smell like it was going to deliver us into a raging boiler.

"Fine." I said. The grille had stopped when a corner hit the ground, and the gap it left wasn't exactly huge. I pushed my face in, my whiskers flattening and my ears pinned back, and scrabbled at the ribbed tubing inside. The beds of my claws still ached from trying to claw my way out of the drain earlier, but I was suddenly aware that my rump was stuck out in the garden where the dog could get a really good nip at it, so I hauled with panicked enthusiasm.

I struggled in without much room to spare. Even once I was past the grille I could barely get my legs under me. I crouched there looking at Green Snake, thinking that grates and drains were becoming far too large a part of my life.

Green Snake looked at me with his flat green eyes, then turned and wriggled away into the depths of the vent, sleek and fast.

"Awesome," I said, and crept after him.

10

A TACTICAL CAPTURE

The vent didn't go far, but it was more than far enough for me, with my belly pressed to the bottom of the ducting and my ears brushing the top. It made one tight turn that I barely managed to worm my way through after Green Snake, muttering dire threats about what I'd do to him if I had to back all the way out again. If the ducting was attached to a dryer or something, I didn't like my chances of being able to either bust it off or turn around. But he didn't look back, and a moment later I found my nose pressed to yet another grate, peering out into a gap between the wall and what looked like the back of a freezer. I could smell stagnant water and the heat of dusty coils, and hear the dull churn of the machine's fan. I couldn't see very much from where I was, but I guessed we must be in a utility room of some sort. The air was still and bland, and there was no noise of voices beyond, no sign of movement, just the freezer warbling away to itself.

Green Snake looked at me and put his nose against the grate hopefully. It didn't move, so I sighed and nosed it myself. The metal edges were sharp on my snout, but there was a little bit of movement. It was going to be tight to get through the gap between the wall and the freezer, though, and I looked at him.

"You sure about this? I don't fancy getting trapped in a necromancer's utility room. They probably have demon-powered heating or something."

He tilted his head slightly, which could've meant he didn't understand, or that he was tired of my questions, or that he was just being a snake.

"I don't know why I'm even talking to you," I said, and pushed again, forcing my nose against the grate as hard as I could. It shuddered a little, and one edge lifted away from the wall. It wasn't even screwed in, just shoved tightly into the gap, and I tried a different corner. It pushed clear of the wall, and Green Snake slipped through, vanishing out of sight under the freezer.

"Hey," I called after him. "Shall I just wait here for you, then?" He didn't answer, not that I'd expected him to. I pushed my paws into the gap between the grate and the wall and flattened my forehead against the grate itself, pushing hard. It shuddered, creaking at the corners, but didn't come free. I grumbled, shifted my grip on the wall, and heaved myself forward as hard as I could, the muscles of my shoulders straining and my back legs scrabbling as well as they could in the tight space. The grate gave a grudging screech and popped free, slamming into the back of the freezer. Resistance gone, I tumbled straight after it with a squawk and slid to the floor, getting a whiff of singed fur as my tail whipped into the workings of the freezer. I scrambled up and scooted around the machine into the space beyond, finding myself in a low-ceilinged room with mismatched cupboards on the walls and a peeling linoleum floor. Green Snake was looking expectantly at the door.

"What do you expect me to do?" I asked, inspecting my tail. "You're the snake. Can't you just scoot under?"

Green Snake put his nose to the gap and pushed forward until he rubbed against the draft excluder wedged on the other side of the door.

"Not so clever now, are you?" I asked him, and he stared at me until I looked away and up at the door itself. "Fine, fine."

There was a regular lever-type handle up there, easy for paws, and the hinges opened inward, so we'd be able to walk straight into the necromancer's house without any problems. Fantastic. Just what I wanted to be doing on a … well, any day, actually. Any day you wanted to name, this was a bad idea. I pressed my snout to the door, listening for movement behind it and hoping to hear Callum. I hadn't heard any shouting since the woman had met him with the dog, and I wished I knew how he'd ended up inside. *If* he'd ended up inside, and not in the freaky bunker out back. Probably on the point of some nasty ceremonial knife, either way.

There was no noise or conversation beyond the utility room that I could hear, so I jumped at the handle and hooked it with both paws. It turned immediately, the latch moving smoothly, and as I dropped to the floor the door popped open and rested quietly on the frame, inviting us to come on into the necromancers' lair. I can't say I was delighted, but I pawed it open a little wider and peered through while Green Snake wriggled between my legs so he could have a look too.

"Don't do that," I whispered. "It's weird."

He glanced up at me then ventured out into the hallway, moving smoothly on the old, mustard-coloured carpet. The pattern reminded me of the carpet in the pubs in our neighbourhood – designed to hide burns, tears, and spills of the more unpleasant sort. I followed Green Snake on soft paws, my ears twitching. The hall ran straight from a door at the back of the house, which was the closest to us, to one at the front, the length of it pocked with identically dull closed doors. Now we were out here I could hear the mumble of voices toward the front of the house, level and conversational, as if a neighbour had popped round for tea. Green Snake wriggled toward them, a bright streak against the ugly carpet. I kept close to the wall, not that it'd exactly help if anyone opened a door. The carpet might hide a bit of vomit, but it wouldn't hide us.

The house smelt of talcum powder and cabbage soup, likely a leftover from the previous occupants. I could smell charms, too, but they were as fresh and raw as the wards carved into the bunker outside, and didn't carry the whiff of anything more sinister than shift locks and cloaking spells. The only good thing I could really say about the place was that the low-level magic meant there were unlikely to be threatening toys roaming the corridors. The ghosts of cabbages past, maybe, but that seemed slightly less dangerous.

We came to a stop next to the door closest to the front door itself, and I caught Callum's low tones drifting out.

Evidently they hadn't sacrificed him to greedy gods or shoved an angry spirit inside him yet.

"Well, thanks for the help," I heard him say, indistinctly. "We just noticed you'd moved recently, so I thought maybe my cat might've got caught up in the moving van or something. You know how they are."

"Sure," a woman said. "Always poking into things they shouldn't, cats."

I couldn't tell if it was the same woman from last time, with her *closure* and reanimated cockroaches, but she didn't sound as though she were about to do any sacrificing. She didn't even sound like she was that bothered by the idea of cats.

"Can't reason with them," Callum said, and I was fairly sure he was using the dimples, given the woman's laugh.

"Definitely not. If we see any stray cats around, we'll let you know, but we moved a week ago, so I'm sure he'd have shown up by now."

"I'm sure you're right," Callum said. "Just thought it was worth checking."

"I hope you find him. Is there anything else . . . ?"

"Oh, no. That was it. I'll be off, then."

I waited for the woman to laugh villainously and declare, "You're going nowhere!" Instead she just said, "Of course. Just watch yourself when you leave, okay? The dog's back out in the yard. His bark's worse than his bite, but still."

I snorted, and Green Snake gave me a sharp look that pretty clearly meant *shut up*. I bared my teeth at him, and he showed me his fangs. We glared at each other, and I hissed, "We didn't even need to come in here, you overgrown garden worm."

He hissed back, giving me a closer look at his fangs than I really wanted.

"*I* knew he wasn't captured."

Green Snake flicked his tongue at me, and I was pretty sure he was being rude this time. I batted his head with one paw, and he snapped at it without biting. I supposed I *had* thought Callum was either being eaten by the dog or stabbed with pointy necromancer things, and it was possible that I might have overreacted a *tiny* bit. I probably should've just left Green Snake to it, but messing about with dead things gets you thinking the worst. Our *business* gets you thinking the worst, since the worst-case scenario was pretty regularly the actual scenario. Anyway, it didn't matter. We'd be back out through the vent in a matter of moments, and hopefully the enormous dog would refrain from barking *and* biting.

I started to tell Green Snake that I forgave him for misleading me this once, but in the future he should leave the investigating to those that were better suited to it. He lifted the front part of his body off the floor until his snout was level with mine, and leaned sideways so that he could see past me down the hall.

"Yes, alright, we're going," I said, since he obviously wasn't listening, and he struck out, fangs bared. I spat and jumped back, running straight into a hard pair of leather gloves. Green Snake hit them at the same time, hissing, and the owner of the gloves yelped and shook him off. I twisted wildly, tearing myself loose and darting for the gap between the big man who'd just tried to grab me and the wall. He threw himself forward and I tried to reverse, but the closed front door was at my back. I could smell the garden in the draught that came beneath it, a teasing whiff of freedom, as the man pinned me to the floor. I was just about crushed under the broad expanse of his chest, snarling and trying to bite through the slippery material of his jacket. He grappled me with gloved hands, getting a tight hold around my belly and squeezing the air from my lungs as I wriggled desperately, but his grip was relentlessly tight. He knelt up, clutching me aloft like a trophy, and my claws swept through the air just in front of his nose. He reared back, swearing.

"Stay still, you little monster," he hissed.

"*Callum!*" I bawled. "Callum, I'm in here, I'm—" I was cut off by the man grabbing my whole head in one gloved hand, clamping my jaw shut. I *mrawr*ed at him as much as I could, lashing out with all four paws in the hope of hitting something vital, but the gloves were those big heavy ones of the sort vets use when they're trying to force a pill down you, and my claws just slid on the tough leather.

"Gotcha," the man said, grinning, then squawked and scrambled to his feet with me swinging ignominiously in his hands. He kicked out, sending Green Snake flying from one ankle. "Damn thing bit me!"

I made a noise that was meant to indicate, *serves you right*.

"Is it poisonous?" he asked, staring down at his leg.

I twitched my ears, which meant, *venomous, you parsnip, and hopefully so*, and the man gave a screech as Green Snake struck his ankle again. He tried to stomp on the little snake, swearing, and Green Snake reared back with a distinctly furious tilt to his head. I scrabbled at the gloves, hoping to get free while he was still worried about the snake.

The man swore, aimed another kick at the snake, and shoved me unceremoniously into a sack.

"*Callum!*" I screeched again as he let me go, but the thick cloth drowned my shout like I'd been smothered in pillows. I scrabbled at the sides, trying claw my way out of the sack before the mouth shut, but the material tightened around me like a net. I ripped at the cloth, swearing and spitting and getting great mouthfuls of hessian and charms, and it didn't give so much as a thread. If anything it tightened further, deadening sound and tangling around my limbs as if it were growing there.

"Old Ones *take* you!" I shrieked, and the words fell around me in pieces. I could taste the magic drenching the sack, and I knew I wasn't getting out. Even if I'd been able to shift I wouldn't have been getting out. I was trapped.

"I will *eat your bones* and feed the leftovers to the damn snake!" I shouted, just for something to say, but the sack held the words so close it felt like I was shouting them to myself. I was swept into the air with careless violence, tumbling inside the sack and bumping off a wall as a door opened nearby.

"Hi," the man said, his voice oddly muffled.

"Hi," Callum said, so close I should've been able to jump to him, and I shouted his name again even though I already knew he couldn't hear me.

"What're you doing?" a woman asked.

"Laundry," the man said, and I was tossed about again as he put the sack behind his back.

"Thanks again," Callum said, and I heard him open the front door. "I appreciate the time." There were tight edges to his voice, but I was willing to bet I was the only one who heard them.

"Of course," the woman said. "Good luck finding your kitty." A moment later the door slammed. "What the hell were you doing?" she demanded, apparently to my captor. "Bringing one of the damn things in here?"

"I didn't *bring* it in," he said. "I caught it. It was eavesdropping."

"Not an it," I bawled.

"Eavesdropping? On us?"

"Yeah. With a snake. It bit me."

"Bollocks," the woman said, and pulled the front door open again, letting a whiff of rain in. "Bollocks, *bollocks,* they were together, I *knew* he seemed off—" The door slammed behind her and she was gone.

The man stayed where he was for a moment, then, judging by the bounce of the sack, he shrugged as he turned back into the house. "Not my problem," he mumbled. "I just get to catch the bloody little monsters. And get bitten by snakes. *Snakes.* I probably need to go to hospital, but no one asks about that, do they? No."

"Monsters," I muttered. "I'm not the one putting cats in sacks." The words travelled as far as my ears and no further, but I flung a few of my favourite curses anyway. Sometimes it's the cursing that's the thing, not the audience.

My captor headed down the hall, swinging me like a

sack of potatoes, and a moment later we stopped again. Another door opened and cold air flooded around us, carrying with it the gentle scents of damp grass and chilly air, then a sudden wash of rather less pleasant doggy smell as a wet nose shoved itself into the side of the sack. I screeched and attacked it as well as I could through the heavy fabric, promising dire consequences for such an invasion of my personal space, but neither my claws nor my tirade had any effect. The nose shoved me a couple more times, then was gone, and I swung across the lawn, bouncing off my captor's legs here and there. I already knew where I was going.

"Godsdammit," I announced to the sack, and a moment later we stopped. My captor fiddled with a lock, and I heard a bolt being pulled. He stepped forward, and through the rough material I saw the light change, becoming thin and pale as it coiled damply around us. I could smell magic with brittle, angry edges, smell rage and frustration and an odd, sneaking despair. The fur bristled all down my back, and before I could even begin to prepare myself for what might be waiting the sack was upended.

I tumbled out, trying to catch the cloth as I went. I had no idea if I was being tipped straight into a summoning circle, or a window into the void, or a bloody stew pot. Anything was possible. But I couldn't seem to hold onto the sack any more than I'd been able to claw through it, and I slid straight out into a metal cage that was set on its end. I gathered myself to leap free, but the door slammed shut above me, then the cage was tipped upright, hefted aloft, and slid onto a hard surface that grated under the metal mesh.

I got to my feet, still pouffed out with rage. My cage was at eye level with a big man who had no neck to speak of. He peered at me, then hit the top of the cage with the flat of one huge hand, the clanging sending my ears even further back, and said, "Where did you come from, then? You and your little snake buddy? Were you with that guy in the scruffy coat?"

I gave him an anatomically impossible answer that was more to do with where he could go than where I came from.

He snorted. "Sure, sure. Heard it all before." He hit the cage again. "Is it poisonous, the snake?"

"Maybe if you eat him," I snapped, and he gave me a puzzled look.

"Why would I eat him?"

I just looked at the ceiling and shook my head. He tried to poke me through the bars of the cage, but I turned on his finger so fast that he jerked back, swearing.

"Fine. See how smart you are after tonight. Saved me a trip out, anyway." He grabbed the sack and headed back out the door, slamming it behind him. The bolt shot across on the outside, and I heard the snick of the padlock closing, then all was still. Still, but not empty.

I finally looked around, examining where I was being held. There were three lonely strips of fluorescent lighting on the rounded ceiling, casting the whole place in a nasty pale glow and turning the bare dirt floor below a tarry black. The window in the opposite wall was scratched and filthy, and there were rough tables beneath it piled with broken garden tools and empty plastic plant pots and stained garden gloves all grown over with cobwebs.

"Nice of you to join us," a familiar voice said, and my head jerked sideways so quickly I just about tore a muscle. Under the mingled stink of charms and old weedkiller, I'd barely caught the scent of cat, but there she was in a matching cage, her pale green eyes narrowed.

"Pru."

"Last time I checked. Please tell me this isn't your idea of a rescue attempt." Her bare skin was rendered almost translucent in the chilly light, and her tail curled and flicked irritably. I tried not to look at it. It was far too naked and rat-like for comfort.

"Well, I found you," I pointed out. "It's a start."

"What's next then, civvy?" a rough voice asked to my other side. "You going to break us all out with your dainty little paws?"

I turned and found a burly ginger tom glaring at me with orange eyes, his heavy shoulders scarred and patchy. "I got in, didn't I? And my paws aren't *dainty.*" Although, next to him, they were of rather more compact and pleasant proportions.

"It's called being captured," he said. "Not *getting in.*"

"That was tactical," I said, and turned pointedly back to Pru, ignoring his snort. "I've got a plan."

"I hope so," she said. "Because they wanted nine cats for some reason, and guess what number you are?"

"Eight?" I asked hopefully.

"Guess again, junior," the tomcat said behind me, and I sat down, scratching my shoulder urgently with a back paw and hoping Green Snake could be as convincing with Callum as he had been with me.

Assuming, of course, that both Green Snake and Callum had made it out of the garden, and neither of them had been eaten by the dog, and that the bloody snake had made it back to the car before Callum left.

"I've totally got a plan," I said, and Pru sighed.

11

AT LEAST SOMEONE'S GOT A PLAN

No one spoke for a while. I sat there staring at the dirt floor and considering my next move. Callum would come back – there was no question about that – but between the dogs and the necromancers, it wasn't like he could just cruise in and pluck me out. That was assuming he'd made it out of the garden before the woman caught up with him, too. She wouldn't have been able to do much if he was on the street, but if he was still on their property … I set to grooming a shoulder anxiously, my ears twitching with every whisper of noise from outside. The dog was barking again.

When my fur had settled a little, and I hadn't heard any shouting that would indicate the dog was trying to remove Callum's legs, I looked over at Pru. She was hunkered down on her haunches, her tail coiled tightly around her. Her claws looked odd, exposed against her bare skin without any fur to disguise the knuckles.

"It's good to see you," I said.

"I could think of better circumstances," she said, her ears twitching.

"Well, yeah. Are you okay?"

She gave me a flat look. "Just *spiffing*, Gobbelino. I'm in a freezing cold cage, in some stinking shed, waiting for a bunch of clueless humans to do some weird, messed-up ritual with us. I'm *grand.*"

"Right. Sure. I just mean, have they hurt you, have they fed you, that sort of thing."

She sighed. "No one's been hurt yet. Or none of us lot, anyway. They need nine for whatever they're planning, though, so I suppose that'll change now you're here."

"Do you know what they're doing?"

"Turning us into handbags," the ginger tom said. "Does it matter? We know it's not good."

"Well, yeah, it *does* matter, because if we know what they're doing we know what to expect, and we can make a plan."

"I thought you had a plan," he said, wrinkling his snout.

"It's constantly evolving," I replied, and turned back to Pru. "Anyone in here who's actually helpful?"

She snorted. "Don't mind Tristan. He's alright."

I looked at Tristan, who arched his whiskers at me and bared one yellow tooth. "Sure."

"Roll call!" Tristan bawled, making me jump. "Sound off, cats."

"Oh, good," I said to Pru. "He thinks he's an army cat or something?"

"He's been living out back of some sort of veterans' club."

"Fantastic," I said, as a bored voice above us said, "Hey newbie."

"Who's that?" I asked.

"Astrid," the disembodied voice said. "Currently occupying the penthouse shelf along with a lovely yet uncommunicative she-cat of indeterminate parentage."

A growl dropped from the shelves above, something low and rumbling that made my hackles rise. "Gods. Is that actually a cat?"

The growl was even deeper this time.

"Of some description," Pru said. "I saw her brought in."

There was the sound of clattering metal above and Astrid said, "She's trying to head-butt her way out again." She sounded mildly interested.

"*Bottom shelf!*" Tristan bawled.

"Dude," an amused voice said. "We have names. I distinctly remember introducing myself and my esteemed bro."

"Don't call me bro," another voice said, the tones almost identical. "You have *got* to stop watching those American shows. It's grating."

"Like a fine Parmesan."

"That's just your breath on a morning."

"Charlie and Harvey," Pru supplied. "No idea which is which."

"I take offence to that," one of them said.

"You *are* an offence," the other replied, and there was the huff of cat laughter below.

"You're both bloody exhausting," a she-cat said from the same shelf. "Can't you just *stop?*"

"Sorry," both cats said.

"Where's dinner?" a fourth voice asked, the tones querulous. "It must be dinner."

"Almost, Gordie, almost," the she-cat said patiently.

"I want dinner!"

"This sucks, dude," Charlie or Harvey said. "That old boy should *not* be in here."

"First sensible thing you've said," the she-cat replied, then called, "I'm Mitzi."

"Gobbelino," I said, and sat back, looking at my paws. Nine cats, one of which apparently didn't talk and another that sounded like he should've been in the sort of deep fireside basket reserved for the oldest of cats. All of us trapped both by cages (which can't be shifted out of, even ordinary ones. Magic has rules) and the charms carved into the walls. All of us waiting for the necromancers to come and do something necromancer-ish to us, which had absolutely zero hope of being pleasant.

Whatever plan I came up with, it was going to have to be a really, really good one. And really, really fast.

I WASN'T sure how long I'd sat there, ignoring Tristan arguing with Charlie and Harvey regarding who should be in charge of the escape plan. Not that anyone actually had a plan, but Tristan felt he was most qualified to execute the plan once we came up with one, and the more he insisted the funnier the other two cats seemed to find him. Gordie yelled for his dinner now and then, and Mitzi shushed him, and Pru lay with her chin dropped low, almost resting on the bottom of the cage.

"Pru?" I said finally.

She looked at me, her gaze pale and unreadable.

"We'll get out," I said.

Her eyes narrowed slightly, then she said, "I wasn't thinking about that."

"Oh. What were you thinking about?"

"About what that snake's doing," she said, and nodded toward the door.

I pushed my nose against the metal bars and peered down to the floor, where a very small snout was just visible under the door, a blue-tinged tongue flicking cautiously at the magic-tainted air.

"Oh, hey! Green Snake!" I called, and he popped his head into the room, peering up at me. "Have you brought the cavalry?"

Green Snake just looked at me.

"Is that your rescue plan?" Tristan asked. "A *snake?*"

"He's very useful," I said, although admittedly I wasn't quite sure if a prison break was in Green Snake's pool of talents. And, of course, there was the small issue of the fact that it was his fault I was in here. But still, if nothing else, he'd proved himself inclined to bite necromancers, which was in his favour. "Up here, dude."

Green Snake looked at me for a moment longer, as if considering his options, then slithered across the floor. Gordie started yelling about garden worms and if that was dinner, and how he didn't want to eat worms, and Mitzi tried to calm him, and a moment later the snake's head appeared over the edge of the shelf. He might have looked a little anxious, which I figured was the result of the dinner question. He stuck his tongue out at us a few times, then hauled himself up next to Pru's cage. She retreated as far as she could.

"Is that the snake from Callum's pocket?"

"One and the same," I said. Pru had been quite thoroughly concussed when she'd shared a pocket with Green Snake. I was half surprised she remembered.

She relaxed a little, but didn't move any closer. "Does he have a name?"

"Not so far," I said, and Green Snake came to a stop in front of me. He raised the front of his body off the ground so we were at eye level, and tilted his head at me. "Any good with locks?" I asked him.

He looked at the lock, then at me, and eased himself up the bars to examine it. It wasn't just one of those slide and click things, but a proper latch, with a clip slid through it to stop anyone pawing it open. Green Snake flicked his tongue at the clasp, and tried nosing it. Pru, Tristan and I all watched him, and even Charlie and Harvey were silent below.

Green Snake worried at the latch for a while, trying to bite the clip with his fangs or nudging it with his nose, then eventually he just dropped back to the shelf and looked at me.

"I guess that's a no, then?" I said to him, and he tilted his head.

"What's he saying?" Tristan asked.

"I don't know. I don't speak snake, do I?"

"Well, that's bloody helpful." The ginger tom heaved a long-suffering sigh. "I should've known better than to think that any civilians could get us out of this mess."

"Dude, can you do any better?" I snapped. "How

long've you been stuck in here, anyway? I've been here an *hour,* and I'm trying at least."

"*You're* not trying. Your bloody reptile buddy is, and he's useless and all."

I hissed at him, then looked back at Green Snake. "Is Callum here?"

Green Snake looked at the door, and his head drooped.

"Aw, hairballs. He left before you could get back to the car, didn't he?"

A head tilt, which seemed a little ashamed.

I sighed, and Pru said, "So Callum doesn't know where you are, then?"

"Well, he knows I'm *here,* even if not the whole cage situation. He'll come back."

"The cage situation will be the least of our problems," Pru said. "I'm more worried about the fact that they've got their nine cats, and this cage has definitely had previous occupants."

I looked at Green Snake a little despairingly, but he had nothing to offer. Pru was right, though. I could smell other cats in here. Scared cats, and more than that. Cats at the end of everything. I licked my chops, wishing there was a water bowl in here.

"There were a lot more than eight missing cat posters at your cafe," I said.

"And those were only the ones with people looking for them," she said. "Most of this lot aren't up there. Our grabby little friends have been through a fair few cats already." She said it flatly. Cats are nothing if not accepting of reality.

Green Snake wriggled into my cage and tried to curl up next to me.

"Stop that," I snapped, pushing him away with a paw. "It's weird. You're all"—I almost said furless, then remembered Pru sitting in the next cage—"scaly."

He stuck his tongue out in a vaguely reproachful manner, then slipped back out through the bars again and vanished along the shelf.

Pru watched him go, then looked at me. "That was a little ungrateful."

"Well, he hasn't exactly been helpful, has he? And he got me caught."

She shrugged. "At least he's not in a cage like the rest of us."

I couldn't exactly disagree with that, so I just watched Green Snake re-emerge from the shelves and make his steady way across the floor toward the door. He paused when he reached it, lifting his head to look back at me. I nodded at him, and he flattened himself out to vanish under the door. I sighed, then looked at Pru. "How long have you been here, then?"

"I don't know," she said. "A few days, maybe?"

"I've been here at least a week," Tristan said, even though no one had asked him. "I was the first one in."

"Good for you," I said.

He growled. "You know this lot fancy themselves necromancers? Against all the treaties, that is. Death magic's been outlawed for *centuries*. It's meant to be extinct."

"Evidently not so much," one of the brothers said from below.

"We'll have to take them to task," Tristan declared. "It's an unacceptable situation."

I looked at him for a moment, considering that while dealing with cats who accept situations for what they are was easier than dealing with humans, who'll utterly refuse to believe the evidence of their senses if it doesn't fit with their preconceptions, even when said evidence is biting their toes, I still wasn't entirely on board with a military-enthusiast cat who wanted to take necromancers to task. I decided to worry about that later and turned to Pru instead. "Did they grab you at the cafe?"

"No. I was poking around the Headingley house. It was empty, but they were keeping an eye on it."

"What in the realms were you doing there?"

She gave me a narrow look, the nubs of her whiskers twitching. How can a cat get through life without whiskers? I've burned mine off more than once, and it throws your whole sense of the world off. But I suppose you can get used to anything.

"Cats were going missing," she said. "I tried to get hold of Claudia, but I just got a message saying she couldn't do anything. I thought I'd try and find out some more myself."

"Who did you get the message from?" I asked.

"Some Watch cat." She wrinkled her snout. "It didn't seem right. Claudia would want to know about this. She'd want to *do* something about this."

"The *Watch* should want to do something about this. Bloody necros messing around with cats? They should be all over it."

"Yeah, well." She gave me an uneasy look. "They didn't

want to know about Dimly, did they? Or they didn't want anyone *else* to know. I kind of got the feeling Claudia stepped on some tails there."

I shifted around a crawling, sick feeling in my belly. "That was us. Me and Callum. She wasn't even involved."

"She was asking questions afterwards," Pru said. "She wanted to know why Dimly got so far out of hand and no one stopped it. Unicorn horn weapons, for the gods' sakes."

I licked my chops, the air stale and dank. "You remember that sorcerer, Ms Jones? She's been looking for Claudia, too. It's why we went to the cafe and found you were missing. We were going to ask you if you could find Claudia."

We were both quiet for a moment, watching the light grow dimmer as the afternoon leeched into dusk.

"I'm sure she's fine," Pru said finally. "It's *Claudia.*"

"Yeah," I said, then we were quiet again until I said, "Why didn't you come and tell me about the missing cats? You know I would've helped."

"Yes," she said. "I can see that would have helped a great deal."

Tristan snorted behind me and stretched. "It's all in hand. We just have to wait until they let us out for whatever their little ritual is. Then, *bam,* we'll bust out."

I looked at him. "Bust out? Of a warded bunker? Full of necromancers?"

"We can do it," he insisted. "We're organised. I've got tactical knowledge. They don't know what they're up against with me."

"Yeah," I said. "It's not like they know how to trap cats with charmed sacks and metal cages or anything."

He huffed. "Well, with that attitude none of us are getting anywhere."

I pushed my snout against the bars again, trying to see more of the room. "Have you heard of anything like this before? Using cats for rituals?"

Pru shook her head. "No idea. I don't know enough about necromancers or what they get up to, other than that they shouldn't have enough power to get up to *anything*, but this lot obviously do. We need someone with some proper knowledge, someone who really knows the old lore."

Like Claudia. I sighed. "Bloody humans. *Necromancers.* How do they come up with these things? They're all, 'hey, let's try raising the dead! That sounds like a *great* idea. Wait, that's boring and we all got killed off for doing it, so, *I know,* let's try slaughtering a few cats instead and see what happens.'"

"I was in the cellar in Headingley to start," Tristan said. "There'd been some bad stuff go down there. It was *sticky,* like there was so much stale magic in there you couldn't get it off you."

I thought of the freaky toy army and shuddered. "Yeah, that sounds about right. But why leave it when there's all that power there for the taking? That's what I want to know."

"Because they're getting it from somewhere else," Pru said. "It has to be."

"There's nothing here, though," I said.

"This is just a holding cell," Mitzi said from below us.

"Surely you realise that? The charms are all new. They're just keeping us here until they go wherever they need to for the ritual."

"Back to the Headingley house?" Tristan suggested.

"Then why leave in the first place?"

"Ms Jones," I said. "She's been asking questions. I bet it unsettled them, and they decided they couldn't stay. But where—" I stopped, thinking of the magician and the raw, deep-seated power of the house. *"Bloody Lewis."*

"Who?" Pru asked.

"A magician. He just about trapped us this morning. And he's trying to find his son, who might or might not be dead. Not sure on that one yet."

"Necromancers never needed cats to raise the dead, though," Astrid said. She still sounded bored. "Or not that I heard."

"Then they're up to something else. Or something *as well."*

"Old Ones," Gordie said, sounding thoughtful. "Old Ones need nine times nine dinners to open the door. Is there dinner?"

"It's lamb," Mitzi said.

"Oh. I don't like lamb."

"So we've got necromancers working with a magician, and there's enough of us now for whatever ritual they're trying," Tristan said. "And we know other cats have gone missing, so I don't think we can count on them suddenly having a rethink and deciding to set us free."

We were silent for a moment, then Charlie or Harvey said below us, "My cats, we need a plan. Sergeant Pork Pie there is abso-bloody-lutely on the money, if you ask me."

"And as elegant as the snake may have been, a plan he was not," Harvey or Charlie added.

"He could've been," I protested. "Bloody ridiculous clips on these cages."

"*Sergeant Pork Pie,*" Tristan muttered. "That sort of thing could get you disciplined, you know."

"What sort of plan do you think we can make?" Mitzi demanded. "We're all *trapped.*"

"She's right," Astrid said. "By un-extinct necromancers, no less."

"Is there dinner?"

"No, Gordie."

"I'm going to make a plan," Tristan said. "You'll see."

"Sorry, how long have you been in here?" I demanded. "Longest of anyone, you said. And still no plan."

"So I've had time to observe our captors! Gathering intelligence, I was!"

"I want *dinner!*" Gordie wailed.

"There isn't any, Gordie!"

"You'd need to gather intelligence," I muttered.

"I'm a professional," the big tom hissed at me. "I'm going to get us out!"

"Bestow your wisdom on us, oh captain our captain," came from the bottom shelf, along with a snicker.

"I will *have* you!" Tristan roared. "Insubordinate young—"

"*Shut up,*" Pru yelled. "Shut up, the whole scabby lot of you! Where d'you think this is getting us?"

"*Dinner!*" Gordie shrieked.

"*It's lamb!*"

"I don't like lamb!"

"I like lamb," Charlie or Harvey said.

"Old Ones take us all," I muttered, and there was a rattling thud from above, as if someone were throwing themselves against the bars of their cage. "Astrid?"

"Not me," she called back, sounding marginally less bored than before. "I think someone's got a plan after all."

The thud came again, then again, setting up a repetitive, furious rhythm.

"Hey!" I shouted. "Hey, um, cat – go easy!"

The rhythm picked up pace, the rattling getting more ferocious.

"That'll be a no," Astrid said.

"What's she doing?" Pru shouted over the slam of a heavy body against metal.

"Apparently head-butting her way out? I don't—*Whoa!*"

"What?" we all chorused, except for Gordie, who'd given up on dinner and was demanding catnip instead.

"Heads!" Astrid shouted, not that any of us could actually go anywhere. There was one final thud, and as I peered up at the shelf above I saw a cage teetering on the edge, a massive brindled body pressed against the bars. The cage seemed almost motionless, wavering on the edge of balance, and the she-cat gave a growl that I was pretty sure actually scared the damn thing into falling off the edge.

There was a collective intake of breath as the cage and its snarling occupant plummeted to the ground, landing on the old earth with a crash that should've brought half the necromancers in town running. But no one came bursting in the door, or hammering at the lock, and we all just stared at the mass of motionless, matted fur slumped under the metal bars. By accident or intention the cage had landed on one corner and the sides had been bent out of true, warping the edges where the door rested.

No one spoke. Even Gordie didn't ask for his nip. Then the she-cat climbed to her feet, shook her head as if to clear it, and put her nose to the gap in the cage door. She pushed, hard, her massive shoulders surging and her whiskers flattened against her face, and the cage groaned. She growled, stepped back, and threw herself at the door so hard that a collective *ooh* went up from the rest of us on the shelves.

One of the hinges on the cage door decided that this wasn't what it had signed up for and popped open, spilling the she-cat's forequarters onto the floor. She kicked herself free of the wreckage, stood up, and shook herself off, sending a shower of tabby hair scattering around her. She looked up at us with bright green eyes.

"*Dude,*" Charlie or Harvey said. "I'm in love."

She growled.

"I can live with unrequited."

"Shut up, C."

She narrowed her eyes at him, and I said, "Can you do that again?"

"Eight times?" Pru added.

The she-cat sighed and looked at the ceiling.

12

A GLORIOUS BEAST

My new favourite cat slouched across the floor and jumped effortlessly to our shelf. She looked at me and Pru, then leaped to the top of my cage and hoisted herself back up to the top shelf.

"I'm not sure about this," Astrid said. She definitely didn't sound bored now. "Just hang on a minute. Wait. *Wait!*" There was a thud from above, that same hefty impact of cat against cage, and Astrid squawked. The cage scraped across the shelf. The big cat could hit it harder now she wasn't in the cage herself, and it only took a few more thumps, with Astrid complaining the whole time, before cat and cage toppled off the edge and crashed to the floor. Astrid yowled all the way down, and we watched the door pop off a shattered hinge. She lay staring at it, panting.

The she-cat growled and jumped down to our shelf, eyeing me thoughtfully.

"Hi," I said.

She looked at the floor, then at me, her eyes narrowed.

"Not high enough?" I asked.

She shrugged, then peered down at Astrid, who was staggering away from the cage. She had smooth, pale grey fur that was currently sticking out in interesting patterns. The she-cat lifted her nose at me, and hunched one shoulder as if she were pushing the cage.

"You want me to do it at the same time?"

She gave a me a small, sharp nod, and I retreated to the back of the cage. I didn't fancy flying half across the room in some cut-rate metal cage that looked like it had been built to house terriers, but neither did I fancy waiting here for necromancers.

"Let's do it," I said to her.

She braced herself in the gap between the cage and the wall, pushing hard to force it forward. It scraped over the dirty wood of the shelving with a grinding noise that made my ears twitch, and a second push had it hanging half off the edge. She stepped back to the wall, and nodded at me.

"Ready," I said, and we both threw ourselves at the cage at the same time, me lunging the length of the thing to hit the bars where they hung over empty space, her slamming into the back with a thud that made the smarting of impact in my shoulder feel pretty minor.

The cage was already tilting off the shelf with my weight, and when the she-cat hit me the thing spun out into the room, tipping end over end and sending me tumbling with it. I hissed, trying to keep my tail and paws inside where they belonged, bracing myself for the impact. I crashed into the broken cages below hard enough to jar my bones and turn my hiss into a yowl, but the metal clips holding the back of the cage on popped open obligingly.

I scrambled out and looked up at the she-cat, who was regarding me curiously. "I will give you all my custard for a year," I told her. "You *rock.*"

"Back off, dude," Charlie or Harvey said. "I'm already in love with her."

"Do you *want* her to leave us in here?" the other asked, and I blinked at them. They were both sat bolt upright in their cages, two skinny black and white cats with markings that, as far as I could see, mirrored each other precisely. It was disorienting. They tipped their heads together as I stared, the angles identical, and arched their whiskers.

The she-cat growled, and jerked her head at me.

"Right." I jumped up next to her, and together we hefted Pru off the shelf. If anything, she spun faster and hit harder than me, but she didn't even hiss, just grumbled when she couldn't get out immediately. The she-cat jumped down and clawed at the cage until the door shook itself free, then the three of us sent Tristan spinning to the floor. I can't say I felt so bad about him tumbling about the place. He had more padding than Pru, for a start.

"Right," he bellowed once he was free, stomping across the floor with his chest out and his ragged ears up. His tail thrashed wildly behind him, a large bald spot on the tip. "Let's get a handle on this situation. We need a lookout in the window – that'll be you, Astrid. Big cat – what's your name?"

She just looked at him.

"We can't get the rest of these cages open like this," Pru

said, with her paws up on the bottom shelf and her nose pressed to Mitzi's cage. Mitzi was a pretty long-haired black and white cat with remarkably long whiskers. "It's not high enough."

"Just get out, then," Mitzi said. "Get some help."

"Plan," Charlie/Harvey said. "If they need nine cats and they're down to four, that's going to slow things up a bit, if nothing else."

"There's someone out there," Astrid said. She'd jumped onto the old tables lining the wall and had her paws pressed against the window. "I can't tell what they're up to."

"Then move it, kids," Harvey/Charlie said.

"Which one are you?" I asked.

"Charlie," he said. "Not that you'll remember which of us is which. It's insulting. It's not like we're identical." They looked at each other, tails swishing in unison.

"Right," I said, and jumped up next to Astrid.

"Cat! Where are you off to?" Tristan demanded. "We need to formulate a structured approach—"

"Shut up, Tristan," Pru said, without much heat but with a certain authority. It might've been the naked tail, but she sounded like a cat you didn't argue with. Apparently Tristan thought so too, because he just grumbled to himself.

"Where's the *chicken?*" Gordie demanded. "I want chicken!"

"I told you, it's lamb today," Mitzi said.

"I don't *like* lamb."

"I know, love," she said. "So we'll just sit this meal out, okay?"

He grumbled, but puddled into the bottom of his cage, a scrawny old collection of badly kept tabby fur and bones that jutted against his skin. It was probably a good thing we weren't going to be able to bust him out this time around. If we had to run he'd be an absolute liability. On the other paw, the fact that he was in here at all made me want to bite someone in sensitive areas.

Astrid looked at me with pale blue eyes. "Can you see them?"

"Where?" Between having the light behind us and the mucky old glass pressing against the dark it was hard to make out much of the garden, and all I hoped was that we were just as indistinct to anyone looking in.

"They were kind of— *There!*"

I didn't see anyone, but I did spot the red glow of a cigarette swell in the dark then fade again.

"*Callum!*" I bellowed, making Astrid jump away. She glared at me.

"*Ow.*"

"Sorry. *Callum!*" I shouted again, but the cigarette didn't move. I pressed my nose against the glass, trying to see more detail, but all was darkness out there. The streetlights didn't reach the back garden, and the curtains were drawn on the bungalow. I growled, and dropped back to the table.

"And how do you know that's your friend?" Tristan asked, glaring at me. "You could've been shouting at anyone!"

"No one with any sense smokes anymore," I said, and jumped to the floor. "Have we got any way out other than the door?"

"Doesn't look like it," Pru said. All the windows were intact, and there wasn't a drain in the place. Not that I was keen to venture into another one of those, but anything was better than waiting around here.

The big she-cat jumped onto the table and examined the window, the tattered nubs of her ears twitching. She looked at Astrid and jerked her head toward the floor.

"Don't," Astrid said. "You'll hurt yourself."

The she-cat huffed dismissively.

"Never mind that – you'll bring all the damn necros running," Tristan said. "That's all we need."

"Doesn't matter once we're out," I said. "We're faster than they are, and we only have to get over the fence to shift." Well, *they* could do that. I was putting my faith in it being Callum sat in the garden smoking, and him having the car ready for a quick getaway. "It's not like it's going to take long to notice we're missing, even if we sneak out without making a sound."

"Do it," Charlie said, looking at the she-cat. "Go on. That'll be *awesome.*"

"Sure, if she doesn't get lacerated," Astrid retorted.

"Even if that's Callum out there, we won't be able to come back to get you," Pru said. "We'll have to run."

"Do it anyway," Harvey said. "C's right – they can't do whatever they're planning with only four of us. It'll buy some time for you to come back and get us out."

"As the only cat here with military training—" Tristan started.

"*Do it,*" the rest of us shouted at the she-cat, except for Gordie, who was snoring, and Astrid, who jumped lightly to the floor, huffing.

The she-cat backed up to the edge of the table, bunched her muscles under her, and took a deep breath. I could have sworn that, as she inhaled, she actually got *bigger*, as if instead of pouffing her fur up she was actually expanding inside that raggedy coat, and I decided that I'd better follow through on my custard promise. Then she launched herself forward, one bound taking her to just below the window, and the next smashing her into it, her head turned away so her shoulder took the impact.

"Go you glorious beast!" Charlie shouted.

I don't think any of us really thought she could do it. I mean, she was *big*, but while the glass was single-paned, it was tough old stuff that had withstood year after year of autumn storms and winter frosts and spring gales. It wasn't wishy-washy. It was the sort of glass that'd still be standing when the shed fell down around it.

She hit the pane dead centre, and the *crack* as the glass split along half a dozen thin lines sounded like a gunshot. She fell back, collapsing to the table, and Astrid shouted, "You see?" as she leaped up next to the she-cat. The big cat surged to her feet, swiped out at Astrid with one paw to make her back up, then flung herself at the window again with absolute fury, as if in not breaking immediately it had personally insulted her. I think it had, to be honest.

This time the glass burst outward under her weight, and she crashed through to the tune of someone swearing outside and the muted sound of a dog starting to bray enormous, furious barks.

"Scarper!" Charlie and Harvey yelled together, and Pru, Tristan and I surged onto the table and out into the night, carrying Astrid with us.

THE FIRST THING we found was Callum on the ground with the she-cat wrapped around one forearm, cursing and trying to pry her off with his free hand while she gnawed and kicked like she had every intention of making him dinner.

"Get *off,* dammit! I'm not one of them! I'm *not!*"

"It's okay, he's with me," I shouted, loping over to them. The she-cat stopped biting, but she didn't let him go, just eyed me suspiciously.

"Gobs! Are you okay?" He gave up on trying to dislodge the she-cat and reached out to me, resting a hand on my head. "What happened?"

"I got snatched," I said, deciding now wasn't the time to explain that following the lead of a small green snake had been the cause of my being snatched. I didn't need my judgement called into question right now.

"Lovely," Pru said. "But we need to move." She jerked her head toward the house, where the thunderous barking was just about shaking the walls.

"Is this all of you?" Callum asked.

"There's four more inside," I said.

"No time," Tristan said, as lights suddenly flooded the garden. "No good if we all end up back in there."

"Bollocks," Callum said, and scrambled to his feet with the she-cat still clinging to his arm. "Go, *go!*"

We sprinted across the garden as the door to the house flew open and Brutus, the massive Rottweiler-ish dog, exploded out. He was barking, huge, echoing barks that I could feel like a drum beat in my chest.

"*Stop!*" someone shouted, as they always do, even though in the whole history of people shouting *stop,* no one has actually stopped. We ignored it entirely, charging through rundown flowerbeds and hurdling ornamental stones and broken plant pots. The thunder of the dog's paws was so close my tail was twitching as I waited for teeth to close on it, and the necromancers were shouting as they ran from the house. Magic spun and spat in the air as they tried to set up some sort of boundary on the property, and we ran harder. Callum tripped on something and stumbled to one knee, swearing, and the she-cat let go of him, spinning to face Brutus as he raged after us.

"*No!*" I snarled, and slammed my shoulder into her chest with full intentions of keeping both of us running. It was like bowling into a metal bollard, and I bounced off, skittering sideways on the damp grass before I regained my balance. She didn't even look at me, just bared her teeth and *hissed* at the oncoming dog. He bore down on her, all teeth and slobber, and as I recovered and spun back to her she belted him across the nose with one hefty paw.

Brutus yelped and threw himself backward so hard he just about somersaulted. There were people running around the corner of the house now, and Callum shouted, "*Move it!*" as he scrambled to his feet.

"Come on," I said to the she-cat, as Brutus recovered and started barking hysterically, too nervous to come any closer. "*Hurry!*"

She gave me a look that said she didn't hurry for anyone, then made a dart at the dog. He yelped and retreated fast, slamming into a small, overly muscled man and taking him off his feet. The man crashed into a birdbath with a yelp, taking it to the ground with him, and the young woman with the pink hair hurdled him gracelessly.

"Get them!" she shouted at Brutus, waving wildly, and he lunged at me, slobbering hopefully. The she-cat spun around and sprinted for the street with a rather impressive turn of speed, and I legged it after her, my fur lifting as the magic grew and swelled around us, and the dog's breath gusted over my hindquarters.

Wards started to light on the fenceposts like malevolent glow-worms as we raced for the fence line, and Astrid shot through the gate ahead of us to the relative safety of the pavement beyond. Callum was already through, Pru and Tristan at his feet, and they were all shouting for us to run, as if we weren't already at a flat-out sprint. The gate slammed shut almost on our noses, and we hurdled the chain-link shoulder to shoulder. The she-cat's paws hooked the top and she yowled, but we were going too fast and the charms were still forming, too weak to hold her back. I hit the ground still running and she tumbled after me, rolling once and coming up all claws and hackles, glaring around as if threatening anyone to be laughing at her. Callum turned and sprinted down the street, and our little feline force bolted with him. People were emerging from their houses, watching us go with a certain amount of bewilderment.

"What's going on?" one of them shouted at the necromancers.

"Intruders," a slim woman shouted back from inside the fence. "Never mind, we saw them off."

No one suggested calling the police. It wasn't that sort

of neighbourhood. But the presence of human witnesses meant the necromancers couldn't exactly launch deadly toadstool bombs or something at us, at least. Not unless they wanted to be in the cheaper sort of newspapers by the next morning, and as compromised as the Watch might be, *someone* would notice that. Brutus was flinging himself at the fence, yelping with every impact as the wards sparked, then trying again, slobber splashing from his jowls. The neckless man who'd captured me grabbed the gate to pull it open and let the dog after us, then squawked and jumped back, sucking his fingers like a child who's touched a stove. They'd apparently managed to seal themselves in, which gave me at least a little confidence that their skills hadn't improved that much since the zombie chickens.

Callum hauled the door of the Rover open and we piled in past him as a big man in a snazzy neon yellow polo shirt charged down his front path, waving a cricket bat at us. Callum said some sort of prayer to the car gods that evidently worked, because the engine roared into life. The man exploded out of his gate and launched himself at the Rover, swinging the bat furiously. He caught a glancing blow to the back of the car that ended with a crunch as we shot out into the road, cats falling over each other as we tried to brace ourselves on the seat. The car fishtailed for a moment on its threadbare tyres, then Callum slammed up through the gears and left both the angry man and the necromancers in a cloud of exhaust smoke. We tore down the street and through half a dozen intersections without slowing, hung a few rights and a few more lefts, then he pulled over in front of a 24-hour store and stared at us. We stared back.

"Anyone hurt?" he asked finally.

We looked at each other. The big she-cat was crouching in the middle of the front passenger seat, her eyes narrowed as she glared at Callum, while the rest of us tried to find some seat space around her.

"Seem alright," I said.

Callum examined his clawed-up hand and the new hole in the knee of his jeans. "Just me, then."

"Matches the other side now," I said, and he snorted, then shut the engine off.

"Anyone hungry?"

"Yes," we said together, and he sighed.

"Obviously. Back in a moment." He got out and left us sitting in the quiet cocoon of the car. No one spoke, and I wondered if everyone else felt the same vague guilt over our escape as I did. It wasn't like staying would've helped anything, but all I could think of was Gordie calling for his dinner in the cold, unfriendly air of the shed, and no one coming to give it to him.

"Hey," Pru said finally. "It's your buddy."

I looked down as Green Snake lifted his head over the edge of the doorless glovebox and looked at me.

"Well, you found Callum in the end, then," I said, and he tilted his head at me in an agreeable manner. I supposed it was a good thing. Callum would only have wanted to go back and rescue him otherwise, and that wouldn't have helped anyone.

13

AN IMPROMPTU SLEEPOVER

Callum came back to the car clutching a packet of cigarettes, some nondescript tins of sardines, and a small bag of cat biscuits.

"Any custard?" I asked him as he got in.

"No," he said, opening the cat biscuits.

"I promised her custard," I said, nodding at the big she-cat. She narrowed her eyes in a manner that suggested she had thoughts regarding exactly how much my word was worth.

"There might be some at home," he said, giving her an apologetic look. She didn't respond, so he just set the bag of biscuits in the footwell. Tristan immediately jumped down and stuck his head in it, and Astrid checked her front paws as if she thought the car seat might have made them dirty. Which was fair enough, really.

"What now?" she asked. "How're we getting everyone else out?"

"Speaking as a tactical expert," Tristan started, a bit

indistinctly around the biscuits, and Pru hissed at him. "What? I am!"

"Yeah, your help was invaluable," I said.

"And what did you contribute? A useless snake?"

Green Snake lifted his head rather haughtily and glared at the ginger tom.

"He was pretty helpful, actually," Callum said. "He was waiting for me when I got back tonight, and he showed me the shed."

"Which I'm sure you'd never have found on your own," I said. "You know, it being so small and un-obvious. That snake led me into the house and got me nabbed. So, you know. That's how helpful he is."

Green Snake turned his glare on me. I tried not to look at his fangs.

"So that's what happened to you," Callum said. "I thought the dog might've trapped you somewhere." He scritched the top of my head, and I resisted the urge to arch into his hand in front of Pru.

"Why did *you* go into the house?"

"I was just trying to get them to grab the dog, and hopefully think it was barking at me and not realise you were out there. But that woman insisted I come inside while they calmed the dog down, and I figured it might give you time to escape. I didn't recognise any of them from Headingley, so I thought it'd be okay."

"The dog was less an issue than the snake, in the end," I said, and Green Snake hissed.

"I thought your capture was all part of your plan," Tristan said, crumbs in his whiskers. "Wasn't that what you said?"

"Well, it worked, didn't it?"

"For half of us."

I growled, and Pru said, "Back to what Astrid said – what's the actual plan now?"

"Well." Callum opened the new packet of cigarettes and plucked one out. "We can't go straight back – they'll be waiting for us. We'll figure it out, though. I don't suppose you saw any sign of the magician?"

"Nothing," I said. "Just a bunch of pretty cut-rate necromancers. But he's got to be involved. They don't have enough power for what they're doing."

"We don't actually know what they're doing," Astrid pointed out. "So far we have some charms and catching sacks, but not much else."

"Even those take some decent knowledge," I said. "And the wards they were activating on the fences, too. Someone else must've set those up, and my vote's on the magician."

"What's this magician like?" Tristan asked.

"Lewis," Callum started. "He's probably the most prominent magician in Leeds, and his lineage is—"

"Bit round, smells of whisky, microwave dinners, and old-school magic," I said.

"Oh, *him*," Tristan said. "Is he the one you were talking about before as well? Yeah, he was around. Remember, Astrid?"

Callum and I stared at him. "When?" Callum asked.

"Just after we moved from Headingley. A bit less than a week ago, I suppose? He came in and had a look at us – Pru and our large escape artist and those ridiculous brothers weren't in yet – and was talking about how to reinforce the charms and activate the fence and so on."

"So, was it like he was in charge?" I asked.

"Or like a whatchamacallit. Insultant."

"Consultant," Callum said automatically, cupping his hands around the cigarette to light it.

"I dunno. The way he was talking, insultant seems more accurate."

"That mangy cabbage *is* working with them," I said. "I *knew* it. The house was totally a trap."

"Maybe," Callum said, frowning. "But we still don't know why. And there was no one there to actually trap us, which makes the whole thing seem questionable."

"He'll have some nefarious magician reason," I said. "Like he wants to turn us into taxidermied puppets. Or me, at any rate. Maybe he's going to turn you into his new heir."

"Jesus," Callum said, looking alarmed. "I think I'd prefer the taxidermy."

"He probably thought the house would just hold us. He didn't figure we'd find Ms Jones and get out."

"What are you two talking about?" Pru asked.

"The magician was going to hire us," Callum said. "We went to his house—"

"Almost got eaten by dead animals," I added.

"—and found the place a mess. We only got out because Ms Jones happened to be in there, and once we got her out of the walls she got us out of the house."

"The walls?" Pru started, then wrinkled her snout. "Never mind. Who sets a trap and just walks away, though? Are you sure he hadn't just had a scrap with Ms Jones, and you stumbled into the middle of it?"

"Who's this Ms Jones, exactly?" Astrid asked.

"Scary sorcerer type," I said, then added, "Maybe something went wrong. She wasn't meant to be there. She did say she just dropped by for a chat."

"He still could've meant to hire us, and then whatever happened with Ms Jones threw everything off," Callum said, and started the car.

"I doubt it," I said. "I *knew* he was dodgy. And Ms Jones thinks he's dodgy. If a sorcerer says someone's dodgy, you know things are bad."

"I suppose." Callum blew smoke over his top lip as he persuaded the car into reverse to pull out of the parking spot.

Astrid gave a delicate little cough and said, "Can you open a window, at least? Between you and the car, I'm not sure I'll make it without asphyxiating."

Callum looked at her, startled, then wound the window down. "Better?"

"Cold," Pru said, her ears back. "Some of us don't have the insulation."

"Just put the bloody thing out, can't you?" I said to Callum, and the big she-cat growled, although whether at me or him I couldn't tell. He glared at us.

"Don't any of you have homes to go to? You can shift out of here, you know."

"We've got four cats to get back," Pru said. "We're not going anywhere."

Tristan re-surfaced out of the bag of cat biscuits,

crumbs on his whiskers. "Quite. We need to fall back, regroup, and formulate a plan of attack."

Callum looked at us, took a final drag on his cigarette, and stubbed it out in the old cup between the seats. "Well, this is going to be fun," he said, and shoved the car into gear.

WE TRAILED up the stairs of our apartment building, the big she-cat baring her teeth at the gap near the bottom where you could hear the winds of the void still whispering. There were a few scars in the building left over from the reality rips that Ms Jones' book of power had caused, and Green Snake was, oddly, not the worst of them. Callum jiggled the key in the apartment lock until it reluctantly turned, and we trooped into the chill, slightly damp air of our little office/living room/bedroom, with its permanent scent of cigarettes and old books. Callum flicked the desk lamp on, casting an uneven yellow glow across the floors, and wandered into the kitchenette to put the kettle on. He came back with a couple of bowls that he shared the cat biscuits out into.

"I suppose you all want fish, too, do you?" he asked.

"We've had a traumatic day," I said.

"More than a day," Pru said with a shiver. "Don't you have heating in this place?"

Callum sighed and flicked on the little portable radiator, pulling it into the middle of the room. I figured that between that and the sardines he'd just bought, we weren't making this month's rent, let alone what we still owed for last. Trust us to find the one case that ended up being a trap rather than something that actually paid.

The big she-cat jumped onto the windowsill and peered out into the street, then, apparently satisfied, claimed one of the bowls of biscuits and settled over it, crunching loudly. Callum opened some of the sardines, then made a cup of tea and ordered Tristan off his chair so he could sit down. Tristan went reluctantly, jumping to the rickety visitor's chair instead and complaining that it didn't have a cushion.

I looked up at Callum from the desk. "Alright?"

"Alright," he said, rubbing his forehead with his fingertips. "So, what do we know?"

"Well, according to my observations," Tristan started, and Pru talked over him.

"Five necromancers in there regularly. Or, you know – people who think they're necromancers."

"Not much magic on them?" I asked her.

"Not really. They've all got a bit, but it's nothing more than your average cat lady." She wrinkled her already wrinkly snout. "That house in Headingley reeks with power, but I've not seen anyone who has much themselves."

"Except for your magician," Astrid said. "He had some magical muscle on him."

"Not the same, though," Tristan said. "Not quite the blood and bone stink with him."

"Useable, though," she replied. "Power's just power, after all. He can use it for magic charms to sell to shopkeepers to keep their stock fresh, or he can use it to raise the dead. Just because he doesn't smell like he does it regularly doesn't mean he *can't.*"

"You only saw him once?" Callum asked, leaning his elbows on the desk. His fingers were still worrying at his forehead, as if he had a headache starting. It had been at least a few hours since his last cup of tea, so he was probably in withdrawal. Or it was the arguing with cats that was doing it, but I put my money on a lack of caffeine.

"Only once," Tristan said. "And I was in there the longest."

"Not exactly something to be proud of," I pointed out, and he bared his teeth at me. "Just means you were captured for longer, dude."

"I was a prisoner of *war.*"

"It's a pretty small war."

"So far," Callum said, almost to himself, then leaned back in his chair. "They're going to be watching that shed far better now. I don't know how we're going to get in."

"We need a distraction," Tristan said. "You know, like an explosion in the street or something."

We all looked at him. "That might be a touch over the top," Astrid said.

"It would work, though."

"Unfortunately I'm all out of explosives," Callum said. "And after tonight I can't exactly nip back and knock on the door. We need someone else."

"Anyone who goes in there becomes a target," Pru said. "You're not asking my human."

"No," Callum agreed. "It has to be someone who knows what they're getting into."

We considered it. Our pool of acquaintances wasn't

exactly a large or magical one. Until recently I hadn't even wanted much to do with other cats, except for the occasional casual nocturnal encounter. Hey, everyone has itches. With the possible exception of Callum, despite offering him my best pointers.

Regarding other-than-human contacts, though, as we walked a rather fine line between the human and Folk worlds, we didn't exactly seek out magical company that might give us away and get the Watch a little too interested. Recently Folk cases had been finding us far more often than I would've liked, and necessity meant we'd been taking more of them, but we weren't exactly going on picnics with a bunch of fauns, entertaining as that might've been. Which meant our options were pretty limited.

"We don't just need a distraction," I said aloud. "We need backup. If they've got that bloody magician working with them, that lot of greasy necros could probably actually do something."

"More than headless chickens, that's for sure," Callum said.

"Nine cats," I said. "What ritual needs nine cats?"

No one replied for a moment, then Tristan said, "Gordie was talking about Old Ones."

"He was talking about dinner," I said.

"No, he's right," Astrid said. "Something about Old Ones and doors and nine dinners?"

"See, dinner," I replied. "I'm not sure he's the best source of information." But it niggled. The Old Ones had been gone so long that they were almost legend. But like all legends, there was an element of truth to them. Bloodied, unpleasant truth regarding how the oldest necromancers, the ones that had led the march to wipe out Folk and enslave humanity, had been banished from the world. They'd been forced out not just by the alliance of cats that became the Watch, but by the sorcerers and magicians and Folk who had stood with them. And it had been a near thing, that victory. We used the phrase *Old Ones take you* as a curse for a reason.

"That's not possible, right?" Callum asked. "Are Old Ones even real?"

"They were," I said. "Or sort of, anyway. As much as any history is real – it all depends on who's telling it. But what – we think this lot might be trying to raise an *actual* Old One?"

"I've never heard of that even being possible," Pru said, sounding uncertain. "Not even as a story to scare kittens. I mean, that's not just raising the dead. That's raising a *god.* Raising them from another realm."

"They weren't gods," Astrid said, but she didn't sound any more sure of herself.

"Near enough," Pru said.

"It was kind of specific, though," Tristan said. "Gordie saying that about nine dinners or whatever, and the necros wanting nine cats."

We were silent for a moment, then I said, "We need Claudia. She'll know."

"I told you, I can't find her," Pru said.

"Are you sure?" I started, and she glared at me.

"Do you think I'd go poking around a necromancers' house on my own if I had a choice?"

"You did once before," I said.

"Yeah, again when I didn't have a choice. Katja was missing, and I didn't exactly have a lot of faith that you two were going to find her."

"Harsh."

"Seems reasonable to me," Astrid said. "I'm not filled with confidence by you two, either."

"Hey, we got you out," I protested.

"*She* got us out," Astrid said, and we all looked at the big she cat, who'd followed her biscuits with most of a bowl of sardines and gone back to sit on the windowsill. She just returned our gaze flatly.

Callum leaned back in his chair and put his boots on the desk. "We need to get hold of Ms Jones," he said.

"Really?" I asked. "Do we have anything conclusive for her just yet?"

"Well, we have a magician definitely working with necromancers," he pointed out. "That's the sort of thing I'm fairly sure she'd like to know about."

"Is this the sorcerer?" Tristan asked. "That does sound rather risky."

"See?" I said. "And she's probably a bit of an overkill if we're thinking of someone to create a diversion for us, anyway. She could turn the whole street into pumpkins or something, just by accident."

"Quite," Tristan said. "Maybe I could round up a few of my buddies—"

Astrid snorted, loudly enough to silence him. Somehow it still sounded elegant, though. "I thought you hung out with veterans. What're they going to do, throw their dentures at the dog?"

"They're professionals," Tristan protested.

"They're human," Pru said. "Callum's right, especially if we think there might be something to this Old One thing. We need more than a few pensioners waving sticks about the place. Besides, I like Ms Jones."

"You would," I retorted. "I'm sure it was just her bike you liked."

"Claudia trusts her," Pru said. "I know that much."

"That enough for you, Gobs?" Callum asked, flicking through his phone.

I growled. I could still feel the pull of the Inbetween, leviathan beasts moving in the complex planes and voids that ran between the worlds, turning their vast consciousnesses toward me, eternally starving. It was almost as though, in reminding me of how my last life had ended there, she had somehow drawn it closer to me. I didn't like to think of my past lives. They were gone for a reason, and I didn't need to relive them. And besides that, she was a sorcerer before anything else, and I still harboured suspicions that she'd turn me into a goldfish just as absently as she might scratch me behind the ears. It was unsettling.

"It just seems excessive," I said. "We don't really have anything to report yet. We haven't actually seen the magician. What about the reaper? She helped before."

"Reapers don't get involved in this sort of thing," Pru said.

"And now Pru's right," Callum said, and she purred. I narrowed my eyes at them both. "The reaper only helped out on the zombies because they were messing up her souls. She's not going to interfere otherwise."

"We've got *necromancers.* By definition there are going to be issues with souls. Probably lots of them."

"Not at this point," Callum said. "Hopefully not at all, if we move fast enough."

"We're wasting time," Astrid said. "I've never heard of a reaper doing anything outside of lost soul collection, and if we go to whoever this one is to try and persuade them, we'll just be wasting *more* time. You want to leave Gordie in there even longer?"

I sighed. "Of course not. But surely shoddy necromancers are enough to deal with as it is. Do we really need to risk getting turned into hamsters by a bloody sorcerer too? I mean, I'm just talking the possibility of getting caught in the magical crossfire here, not even if she *decides* to turn us into something unpleasant."

"Ms Jones is alright," Callum said, hitting dial and putting the phone on loudspeaker.

"Ms Jones is terrifying," I replied. "And if anyone gets turned into a garden snail don't say I didn't warn you."

Tristan sat up a little straighter. "Is that likely?" he asked. "Because I'm not sure I'm ready to support this idea if there's a risk of snails."

"We're not voting on it," Pru said.

"You call this a democratic society?" he demanded.

"You reckon you're military," Astrid said. "That's pretty much the definition of undemocratic. Deal with it."

The phone clicked, and a recorded voice said, *"You have reached the voicemail of zero-seven-eight—"*

Callum clicked the disconnect button and rubbed his face. "Well. That's that. It's late, anyway. We can try again in the morning."

"Sure, because it's not an emergency or anything," Pru snapped, her tail whipping.

He regarded her thoughtfully. "Do you think they'll do something tonight?"

"They might," she said.

"They need nine cats," I pointed out. "They've got four. They're not likely to grab five more tonight *and* get whatever ritual they're planning organised, are they?"

"We don't actually know they definitely need nine," Pru said. "We're just going on what we've overheard."

"And what Gordie said," Astrid said, her voice low, and we fell silent for a moment. *Old Ones.* The thought sent a shiver along my spine, lifting the hair softly.

"He said nine, too," I said finally.

Pru sighed. "He did. But I really don't like thinking of them stuck in there."

"Me either," I said.

"We'll try Ms Jones first thing." Callum offered Pru a hand, and she sniffed his fingers, then arched her neck so he could scratch her between the ears. "We'll sort this." He looked at me as he spoke, and I could see the frown lines pinching the skin between his eyes.

I licked my chops, sighed, and said, "If anyone wants to check in on their humans, now's the time, kids."

"I'm not going anywhere near Katja at the moment," Pru said as Callum leaned back in his chair again. "I'd rather she worried a bit longer than risk her getting involved."

"Likewise," Astrid said. "Franco'll be fine for another day or so. I hope."

Tristan drew himself up. "I'm an independent cat with

no need of a human. Besides, I'm not leaving you lot alone. You're terribly undisciplined and I refuse to be absent from any planning."

We all looked at the big she-cat and she looked back at us, expressionless.

"We need to call you something," I said. "We can't just keep saying *you*."

She didn't answer, just narrowed her eyes slightly.

"Great," Callum said, and got up to unfold the armchair into his bed. "Sleep where you want."

14

ONE (1) MISSING SORCERER

It wasn't exactly a comfortable night. All of us were jumpy, half-expecting the necromancers to come crashing in the door at any moment. I curled into my bed on top of the filing cabinet, where I could watch the room easily, and Green Snake wriggled his way up to join me. I thought about pushing him out, but he had bitten a necromancer, which went a certain way toward making me feel better about him. Plus it seemed we needed all the help we could get. So I let him curl into one corner of the bed with me, even though the situation was slightly scaly and more than a bit weird.

The big she-cat jumped onto Callum's armchair-bed, eliciting a grunt of protest from him as she walked across his belly, and made herself at home on one side of the narrow stretch of cushions, all but pushing him off. He grumbled but didn't actually move her. I didn't blame him – I was just happy she hadn't wanted *my* bed. Tristan declared loudly that he'd keep watch, and positioned himself in the window for about ten minutes before trying to squeeze in next to Pru and Astrid, who were curled together on Callum's chair, taking up most of it. Pru belted him on the snout and he retreated to the floor, and then all was still, even if I doubted any of us were exactly sleeping.

My whiskers twitched with every shout on the street outside, with the revving of every engine and the smash of breaking glass as someone dropped a bottle. People in our building keep strange hours, and sometimes there were footsteps in the hall outside or the dull thud of something hitting an uncarpeted floor, doors slamming and someone running on the stairs. It's never quiet around here, and now every sound felt like promise of what was to come. That, or an echo of lives lost and deaths best forgotten.

I listened to it all with my chin on my paws, waiting for the long night to crawl close enough to day that we could be up and moving, *doing*. Anything but lying here waiting for … something. The end of the world, maybe. We still didn't know.

EVENTUALLY CALLUM SAT up and shrugged into his hoody, taking the visitor's chair to set it by the window. He sat down and picked his cigarettes up from the table, the yellow light washing through the uncurtained window to give his face hard, tired angles.

I left Green Snake in my bed and dropped softly to the floor, padding over to join him and jumping up to the windowsill. I peered out at the street, but other than two skinny figures sprinting down the alley all was quiet.

"What do you think?" I asked him.

"I think it's a mess any way you look at it."

"Why do you think he'd work with necromancers? Do you think he's actually going to try and raise Ifan?"

"I wouldn't have thought so. Not if he really thinks he's dead. Everyone knows that what comes back after death isn't what was there before."

"Then what's he doing? And what about all this Old One business?"

"I don't know. The necromancers have got to be forcing him to work with them somehow. Surely even Lewis wouldn't want anything to do with Old Ones."

"Can you really force a magician to do anything?"

He drew on the cigarette again before answering. "It depends what they've told him. Maybe they've convinced him that Ifan isn't actually dead. Like Ms Jones said, death can be deceptive. Who knows what he'd do then?"

I'd been watching the street, and now I looked up at him. "If they've said Ifan's just missing, or lost, or whatever – they've found him on their super-duper necro undead scanner or something – maybe he thinks that if they do this ritual, it'll bring him back too."

"Maybe. If it's anything to do with Old Ones, then no one really knows what's possible."

"Well, bad things, I'd say. Very bad things are possible with Old Ones."

"Yeah, well. Grief does strange things to people," Callum said, and stubbed the cigarette out.

I didn't reply, thinking of the dead that had risen from

the cemeteries. They had been tragic and terrible all at once, a brutal parody of life. And maybe whatever the dead-raisers had planned would result in a better class of zombie, but it was still never going to be life.

To wish that on anyone seemed something far more than grief to me. Far *worse.*

WE PILED out the next morning after a rather uninspired breakfast of more cat biscuits and the last of the sardines, Callum muttering that he wasn't a bloody cat rescue as he reluctantly gave the big she-cat the last of the milk. Not that he had much choice in the matter, as she'd jumped onto the tiny kitchen worktop and bitten his hand before he could empty it into his tea.

"I don't *like* black tea," he complained to her, and she shrugged. He glared at me.

"What d'you expect me to do?" I asked.

"We need ground rules," he said, but he drank his black tea while the she-cat lapped the milk from a plate, then he let us out into the hall just as Mrs Smith popped her head out of her door across the hall. She had a strange braided cone of pink-tinted hair going on today.

"Hello, Callum dear," she said, and blinked at us. "I see Gobbelino has some friends over."

I purred at her, and let her scratch me behind the ears.

"It's just temporary," Callum said.

"It's very sweet of you," she told him. "You obviously love cats very much. They're lucky to have you."

He smiled at her and headed for the stairs, mumbling, "That last bit's true, anyway.'

"Sure," Pru said. "I feel *so* lucky right now."

CALLUM HAD TRIED CALLING Ms Jones again, as well as texting, but no one picked up and there was no reply to his messages. Which made things a little more complicated. We didn't know where the sorcerer spent her spare time when she wasn't turning unsuspecting cats into toads, but, luckily or not, we did know where her dentist ex-husband-slash-current-boyfriend worked. Somehow she'd forgiven him for stealing her book of power, which just went to show that sorcerers did still have a trace of humanity left in them. No one else would be silly enough to take back someone who'd not only robbed her but just about broken reality, *and* lost her repository of magic.

I mean, I suppose you could argue that *we* were the ones who had lost her book in the terminal sense, but it had been while saving the world, so I felt that excused us. It certainly should've given us moral high ground on the dentist, yet we were the ones being held to account and not paid for tailing dodgy magicians. Yet another reason not to hang around sorcerers.

We parked across the road from the dentist's office, peering through the morning traffic at the surgery nestled among a nondescript strip of shops and offices. The frosted glass window had blue script swirling across it: *Dentist by Design.* I had no idea whether that meant our Malcolm Walker felt he'd been designed to be a dentist, or had designs on being a dentist, or if he'd just randomly picked a word out of the D section in a dictionary. The last one seemed most likely, given the fact that his own questionable dental hygiene cast doubt on his passion for tooth health.

"Right. Wait here," Callum said. "I'll get another number off him for Ms Jones." He swung himself out of the car and we watched him jog across the road, his coat collar up against the rain. It hadn't stopped all night, a relentless drizzle that sometimes pushed itself into an actual shower before falling wearily back to the same endless spatter.

"I hope this works," Pru said.

"I hope we don't get turned into tadpoles," I said, trying to shift away from the big she-cat. She'd claimed the front seat next to me, and took up an inordinate amount of space.

"I don't think he should have gone in alone," Tristan declared. "He's very scruffy, that man. It gives the wrong impression."

"Your ears are scruffy," Astrid said.

"Those are battle scars," he told her, the ears in question laid back as far as they were able. She shrugged, and we went back to watching the road through the rain-smeared windows.

Callum wasn't gone long. He ran back across the road and onto the pavement, opening the passenger side door. He glanced around to make sure no one was in earshot and said, "Come on. We're going to the cafe down the road."

"What?" I asked. "Why? Is she meeting us there?"

Callum sighed, those frown lines digging into his forehead again. "No. He doesn't know where she is."

"They broke up?"

"No, Gobs. She hasn't been home."

We were silent for a moment, then Pru said, "Missing. Just like Claudia."

"Oh, hairballs," I said, and my stomach did something twisty and unpleasant. "Are we sure?"

"It's looking likely, isn't it?" Pru said. "Ms Jones and Claudia were both looking into the weird stuff happening – the unicorn horn weapons, and the zombies, and the Watch not paying attention to the things they should. If Claudia knew anything about necromancers trapping cats, she'd have been here."

"Maybe she already has been," Tristan said. "We know other cats have been through those cages."

We all looked at him, and I tried to imagine Claudia, with her quick, mis-matched eyes and slouching amusement, snatched up and shoved in a cage, used for some ritual that shouldn't even exist. I mean, no cat is *just a cat,* but Claudia was something else. She was more than just a Watch cat, even. She was the head of some shadowy branch that was meant to keep checks on the Watch itself, and I wouldn't have bet against her in any situation. Then again, she was also just the sort of cat a corrupt Watch would want rid of at the first opportunity.

I licked my chops and said, "Doesn't explain Ms Jones."

"Walker couldn't talk in the office," Callum said. "We'll see if he knows anything else about either of them – he's going to meet us in a few minutes." He looked even paler than usual, his hair darkened by rain and sticking up at anxious angles.

"Do we have time for this?" Astrid asked. "We need to get those other cats out before they get their nine and do … whatever with them."

"Open a door for an Old One," Tristan said. "Or make dinner for an Old One. One of those. Or both."

"I know," Astrid hissed. "You don't have to spell out *everything."*

"Clarity of communications— Sorry," he said as Astrid spat at him. "Right."

"We haven't got anything else to go on," Callum said. "Unless we just go back to the house and ask the necros nicely if they'd mind handing over the cats. And, you know, explain the magician situation and what the hell's going on with Ms Jones and Claudia while they're at it."

"That seems a flawed plan, civvy," Tristan said. "You'd better leave the logistics to more experienced officers."

Pru looked from Callum to me and said, "Let's find out what the dentist knows. It's got to be all connected, doesn't it?"

"That's what I'm afraid of," Callum said, and waved us out.

We jumped out of the car, ears flicking in the rain, and trotted next to Callum as he headed down the soggy pavement. He fished his cigarette packet out, checked it, and swore when he found it empty. He shoved his hands into the pockets of his bedraggled coat instead and hunched his shoulders against the rain, looking a little like some sort of Pied Piper with higher standards with us flanking him.

The cafe had a dog bowl sitting outside it, which the big she-cat helped herself to.

"Gross," I said to her. "Dogs have had their drooly tongues in that."

She looked at me, water dripping from her whiskers, then went back to drinking.

I looked at Pru. "Are we sure she's a cat?"

Both Pru and the she-cat growled at me, and Callum pushed the door open. He checked the room, then mumbled, "Looks alright."

He led the way past a few people perched at small tables, marooned in their own worlds with their laptops in front of them, and sat down at a table in the corner. Green Snake wriggled out of Callum's pocket and curled around his sleeve as I jumped up onto one of the chairs, and Pru joined me. Astrid and Tristan took another, and the she-cat crouched under the table, her eyes on the door and her hackles raised just slightly. I think she was hoping for a dog to come in and offer her some sport. Or morning tea on paws.

A man with a generous amount of well-groomed hair and a short black apron wandered over to us, scratched his stubble, and said, "This is different."

Callum nodded at the door. "It said pet-friendly. Hope this is okay."

"We are pet-friendly, but it's usually dogs. Sometimes a ferret."

"Sometimes I think ferrets would be less trouble," Callum said, and we all glared at him.

The man snorted and said, "Well, they seem well-behaved enough. Just don't let them start any fights. Coffee?"

"Tea, please."

"Sure." The man rubbed the top of Astrid's head and she purred. "I don't suppose they'll eat dog biscuits?"

"Almost definitely not. But they've eaten, anyway."

I *mraow*ed a protest, and Tristan sat up a little straighter.

"Seems they disagree," the man said, and grinned at Callum.

"They always do."

By the time the waiter had brought Callum a pot of tea and had set a couple of small plates of shredded chicken in front of us (giving Callum a sideways grin and saying, "don't tell, or I'll have to do this for everyone,"), we barely had time to scoff what we could before the door was shoved open and the dentist rushed in.

He looked much as he had when we'd first met him – small and a little round, with his glasses spattered with rain. He had an expensive-looking coat on over some sort of pale blue medical top with his name embroidered on the chest, and he hurried over to us, grabbing a chair from another table and pulling it up across from Callum. The big she-cat growled at him when he almost kicked her, and he yelped, peering down at her.

"You've got more," he said, almost accusingly.

"He hasn't *got* anything," Astrid said.

"He's assisting us in our operations," Tristan said.

"Jesus," he said. "I thought that calico one that kept hanging around was bad enough."

"Claudia?" Pru asked. "You've seen her?"

"Not recently," he said, and waved at the waiter, who was tidying something behind the counter. "Latte," he called.

"Thanks," Callum mouthed, giving the man an apologetic look. He just shrugged and started clattering cups around.

"Right," I said to the dentist. "What's happening, then?"

"I was hoping you could tell me," he said. "You're looking for Polly?"

Polly. Somehow I couldn't think of the sorcerer as a *Polly*. It was like a crocodile called Fluffy. "More in the arranging a meeting of colleagues sense than the knowing she was missing one," I said.

"We need her help," Callum said. "Do you have any idea where she's gone?"

"No. I mean, she always has these *business* things"—he said *business* with air quotes, and Astrid bared her teeth —"but she doesn't really discuss them with me. And this time she just hasn't come home."

"Might that be, um, a personal decision?" Pru asked, the ridges above her eyes raised.

"*No,*" the dentist snapped. "She always tells me if she's going to be away overnight. *Always.*"

"She had to ask," I said, then we fell silent as the waiter put a cup of coffee in front of Walker, the top decorated with a frilled leaf of foam.

"Thanks," Callum said, since the dentist evidently wasn't going to, then once the waiter was gone added,

“Do you know anything about what she was looking into?”

“No,” Walker said, emptying three sugar packets into his coffee and stirring it vigorously.

“Any notes?” I suggested. “Journals?”

“She keeps everything online, and I don’t know the passwords.”

“Sensible,” I said, and he scowled at me. “What? You stole her book of power! She lost *decades* of accumulated magic. Or centuries. I don’t know.”

“*You* lost the book,” he snapped. “I just sort of borrowed it.”

“With no intention of returning it.”

“You stole a book of power?” Astrid asked. “You sausage. How are you not turned into an earwig?”

“Don’t insult sausages,” I said, and she snorted.

Walker glared at us. “Are you going to help or not?”

“We were actually looking for help ourselves,” Callum said. “But it might be that both things are connected, so we’ll do what we can.”

“With who?” I asked him. “We can’t do this alone. What about Gerry?”

“He’s got more than enough on in Dimly,” Callum said. “Besides, we don’t want to pull anyone else into this unless we have to.”

"This isn’t going to work,” Pru said. “Those necros might not be too dangerous alone, but the magician is. I mean, anyone who can trap a sorcerer …”

We murmured agreement, and I pushed a scrap of chicken toward Green Snake. He looked at it disdainfully. Or maybe appreciatively. I still couldn’t tell.

"I'll help," the dentist said. "If you think Polly might be involved somehow, I'll help."

"And do what?" I asked. "Wave a toothbrush at them?"

"I know stuff," he replied, straightening his shirt. "Polly's been teaching me."

"Well, I suppose that's better than learning off YouTube like last time."

Callum rubbed his forehead. "This is serious. It could get really dangerous."

"I can do it," the dentist insisted, and pointed at the empty wrappers from his sugar, his face scrunched with concentration. The wrappers shivered, then one of them started to smoulder. There was a flare of flame, and Callum tamped them out quickly, before they could scorch the table. "See?"

"Fantastic, if we want caramelised sugar," Astrid observed.

Tristan coughed and said, "I can still contact my buddies—"

"No," we said together, all except Walker, who just looked confused.

"*What?*" Tristan demanded. "There's no time to waste. We should access all resources and proceed at speed."

"We're not bringing in a load of ex-Army geriatrics," I said. "We've already got a dentist, for the gods' sakes."

"*Hey,*" Walker protested.

"Tristan's partly right, though," Pru said. "We don't have time to think about this too much. They'll be out looking for more cats now, if they haven't actually got them already. Plus they might guess we'll come back for the others, so they're going to do this ritual as quickly as possible. They might not even wait for dark. And that means everyone in those cages is done for. Claudia and your sorcerer too, for all we know. And who knows what's going to happen if they get it right. *There's no time.*"

Callum ran both hands back over his hair, then nodded. "You're right. We're going to have to get back there." He looked at the dentist. "Are you in?"

The dentist took a swig of coffee, then coughed. "Yes," he managed.

"Don't say you can do things if you can't," I said to him. "Can you actually help us?"

"*Yes.* No one ever thinks I can do anything!"

I looked at the others. "It's him or nothing."

Astrid sighed. "Well, when you put it like that … No, I'm still not convinced, but sure."

Callum shook his head. "Hopefully you won't have to do much, anyway, Malcolm. Just help us get in and I'll break the cats out. Shall we go?"

"I've got appointments," Walker said. "I've got a wisdom tooth to take out."

"Reschedule it, then," I snapped. "Don't you want to find your Polly?"

"Of course I do! It's just … my reviews are going to go down if I have to reschedule at short notice. I'm up to 3.4 on Google."

We stared at him, and I wondered who went to a dentist with a 3.4-star rating. He stared back, then after a moment said, "I'll go reschedule them, then."

"Meet us back here," Callum said, and we watched the dentist hurry out the door, trailing an air of panic after him.

Callum wiped his mouth and said, "I think I'm going to need another cuppa."

"You might need more than that," Tristan observed. "I don't feel our unit is really gelling. Should we do some team-building?"

"No," Astrid and Pru said together.

"Just asking," he muttered, and we fell silent as the waiter came back.

"Refill?" he asked Callum.

"Please."

"Looked like a bad conversation."

"Just some disappointing news," Callum said.

"Ah. This one's on me, then," the waiter said, and went to make the tea.

I looked up at Callum. "I like him."

"You like the fact that he gave you chicken."

"I maintain that food is an excellent basis on which to determine likability."

"You should write your own guide to relationships."

"Well, I do have more experience at them than you. Come on, what more d'you want? And he smells nice."

"You mean he smells of food. I have other criteria I base fancying people on." He patted his pockets. "I'm going to need some more cigs."

"The necros aren't enough of a threat to life for you?"

"It's more to deal with these sorts of conversations," he replied, and we both fell silent as the waiter came back with Callum's tea, and a piece of brownie balanced on the saucer.

I couldn't see what Callum *didn't* like about that.

15

BREAKING AND MORE BREAKING

We took the dentist's car to the necromancers' house, partly on the theory that it was more likely to start again when we needed to make a quick getaway (because that wasn't an if), and partly because the necromancers wouldn't recognise it. Even on a street like this, where the cars were either stubby-nosed beasts with tinted windows and oversized engines, or stolid old estates soldiering stoically on well past their sell-by date, our beat-up Rover was still pretty distinctive. Callum said it had character. I said only in the way a Crimewatch sketch does.

Walker grumbled and fussed about getting cat hair on his precious upholstery when he pulled his flashy Audi around in front of the cafe. Callum just opened the passenger door, letting us jump in while he took a last drag on his cigarette. The big she-cat stretched herself out on the backseat and rolled around a few times, then sat up and glared at the dentist while the rest of us snickered and settled down next to her.

"You'd better be right about this," Walker said to Callum. "I'm losing business."

"And finding your sorcerer," Pru pointed out, but he ignored her.

"I'm right about the cats," Callum said. "And we need to get them out before anything else."

"You said we were finding Polly," Walker said accusingly.

Callum rubbed the back of his head. "I'm sure we'll find her. All this is connected." I could hear the *somehow* at the end of the sentence.

"If we don't?" Walker demanded.

"We'll figure something out."

Pru and I looked at each other. *Figuring something out* didn't seem to be the best way to tackle a necromancer clan that was presumably being bolstered by the most powerful magician in Leeds, if not the county. Hell, as far as we knew, the most powerful magician in the *country.* We needed our very own, perfectly terrifying sorcerer to make this work.

"This is off to a good start," I said to no one in particular as the dentist pulled into the traffic.

"Now then," Tristan said, "What's our contingency plan? Escape route?"

"You heard the man," Astrid replied. "We don't have a plan. Nobody has a plan. We're plan-less."

"Well, there's sort of a plan," Callum said. "We go there, Malcolm knocks on the door, and while he distracts them and gets them to keep the dog leashed, we sneak in the back and get the cats out. Once we've done that we can tackle the whole Ms Jones and Claudia situation."

"What d'you mean, I knock on the door?" Walker demanded. "I didn't agree to knocking on doors!"

"What did you think you were going to do?" I asked. "Sit in a tree setting fire to sugar packets?"

"No, but why do you get to go around back and I have to knock on doors?"

"You're the diversion," Callum said. "You just need to keep them busy while we get the cats out."

"How?" Walker demanded. "What if they recognise me?"

"Offer them a teeth cleaning," Pru said, and I snickered.

"*No,* I mean what if they recognise me as a sorcerer in training?"

Astrid choked on something and I said, "*Dude.* You are not a sorcerer in training."

"Polly's been teaching me!"

"*Anyway,*" Callum said, "They won't recognise you. All you need to do is keep them busy. Tell them you're new to the area and are going around meeting the neighbours or something."

"That doesn't sound very believable," the dentist said.

"Say you've lost your dog," Tristan said.

"Too close to losing a cat," Astrid said. "It sounds suspicious."

"Tell them you're one of those religious types," Pru suggested. "Ask if they've embraced the gods of dental decay yet."

I was starting to think she had a very odd sense of humour.

"Just say you're new to the area," Callum said again.

"We won't need long, just make sure you're chatty and say you've seen their dog and would love to meet him or something. Anything to keep everyone in the house and the dog under control."

"These are all terrible suggestions," the dentist said. "I'll think of my own. I did theatre for two years at uni, you know."

We waited expectantly, but he didn't say anything else, and a few minutes later we pulled into the kerb just around the corner from the necromancers' house, in front of a lonely-looking bungalow with one shattered window and another boarded up with old plywood. Its garden was a wilderness of weeds and discarded bottles, and the door was a plaintive record of who loved who carved in weathered knife strokes.

We sat there for a little, cars grumbling past in either direction, none slowing to look at us. The houses were similarly uninterested, the curtains still and the paths empty. No one cared what two men and five cats were doing sitting in an Audi under the cover of the winter rain. Even the dog walkers looked less intent on exercise and more intent on persuading the canines to wee on the nearest thing possible so that they could retreat back indoors.

I wished we had the same option.

"RIGHT," Callum said finally, trying to stop Green Snake creeping off to explore the car. "We're not getting anywhere like this. D'you know what you're going to say, Malcolm?"

He nodded. "I've got my character quite well set in my mind."

"Oh, this should be good," Astrid said.

"You go to the door while we go to the back," Callum said. "Nothing fancy. Just make sure they keep the dog inside or at least on a leash around the front. We'll grab the other cats and get out."

"I'll lead the extraction team," Tristan said. "Who's my second?"

"*No,*" I said. "Callum and I will go for the shed. It needs his thumbs, anyway."

"Glad to be useful," he said, and I ignored him.

"The rest of you, scatter. Even if it's not leashed, that dog can't chase all of us at once. Tristan, you go with the dentist, keep an eye on the dog if he's at that end and warn us if he's loose. Pru and Astrid, you watch the back door. You—" I stopped, looking at the big she-cat. "Seriously, what's your name?"

She just narrowed her eyes at me.

"Well, you just cover everyone. The dog's scared of you, anyway."

She lifted her chin slightly.

"We all good?" I asked, and there was a general murmur of agreement. The dentist was brushing his thin hair to the opposite side, presumably as part of his character.

"My plan was good, too," Tristan muttered.

We piled out of the car and Walker locked it behind us before he headed down the street toward the front garden of the necromancers' house. Tristan shadowed him, leaping into the garden of the rundown bungalow and rustling intently throughout the grasses, popping his head up here and there to check on the dentist's progress with his ears back and his eyes narrowed before diving into cover again. We watched them go, then Callum let us in the gate and we hurried to the back of the property, him trying to look casual and the rest of us not bothering about being seen. That's the advantage of being a cat. No one ever thinks you shouldn't be somewhere.

We were going to have to climb some fences to get into the necromancers' backyard, but none of them looked too high, even given the fact that Callum lacked a cat's natural grace and agility. We paused at the fence, all of us aware that we were about to dive into … something. That we had to get the others out, but we didn't know what was waiting. Maybe the same ineffectual group as before, or maybe the magician, or … who knew. Maybe the ritual had been done already. Maybe there were going to be doors opened onto other realms, and ancient beings come through with carnage in their wake. I lifted my nose to the sky, wrinkling it at the rain. Everything was rendered a sodden grey, the plants bowed with the weight of the water, and I took a snuffling breath.

"This is fun," I said.

"At least it's not dark," Pru pointed out.

"Yeah, we can see what we're getting into," Callum said, and boosted himself over the fence. "Perfect. Come on."

We moved fast, getting through the gardens as quickly as we could, trying not to draw attention to ourselves and hoping everyone was off at work. No one stirred in the first one. As we ran across the second, a woman in a dressing gown threw open the door and yelled at Callum to get off her property.

"Sorry!" he yelled back, and pointed at me. "My cat got out!'

She said something rude about what he could do with his cat, but she didn't chase us as Callum scrambled over the next fence. She just mumbled something about the neighbourhood going to the dogs, which was blatantly inaccurate, and went back inside.

One more fence, and we were crouched at the border to the necromancer's property. Callum huddled down next to a compost bin, trying to make himself inconspicuous if anyone looked out the windows, and Astrid perched on top of the chain-link fence.

"Anything?" I hissed at her.

"Nothing yet," she said.

We waited, the rain whispering on the grass and pinging off the compost bin.

"This is taking too long," Callum said.

"He'll have messed it up," I said. "Why did we use him again?"

"Because we didn't have a choice," Callum said, and the big she-cat grunted then went up and over the fence with startling ease. Astrid shot after her, and Pru and I looked at each other, then followed.

"Right, then," Callum said behind us, but we were already running, scattering across the garden, moving soundless on soft paws with our ears back against the rain. The big cat was heading for the front of the house, probably to see what was happening with our useless dentist, and I angled for the shed crouching in the garden to the back, keeping a wary eye out for the enormous dog.

I skidded to a stop by the shed, tail whipping as I scanned the garden, but there was no movement. No twitch from the curtains of the house, no shout from the front as the dentist was shoved in a dentist-sized sack. Callum ran up behind me, coming to a stumbling stop.

"Aw, bollocks," he said, and I looked up at him. He was staring at the door.

"What?" I demanded, expecting to see some giant unbreakable padlock, or an oversized scorpion holding the door shut with its nippers, or a lock that needed to be fed the souls of kittens before it'd open. I don't know. Necromancers. Anything's possible. Callum just flicked the unsecured hasp, looking at me.

"Aw, *hairballs.*"

He shoved the door open and we stepped into the gloomy interior. We didn't need the lights on to know. I didn't even need to breathe the dank must of unheated earth. They were gone. The cats were gone. All that was left was a dusting of cat hair on the shelves and the faint scent of feline rage.

Callum stepped into the middle of the dirt floor, his hands clenched into fists at his side. "We're too late," he said. "We should've come back last night."

"We couldn't," I said. "They'd have been waiting for us. We'd have just ended up back in cages, and you as well. Or worse."

"We should've done *something.*"

"What? Reported it to the RSPCA? Amnesty International? MI5?"

"Maybe. Anything."

"Dude, it's *just us,*" I said. "We can only do so much. The magician set us up, remember? For all we know, the bloody necromancers are desperate to get hold of you, and it was just luck that none of them recognised you yesterday. Count your chickens and all that."

He looked at me, a muscle in his jaw working. "Blessings, not chickens. And how do you know the trap wasn't for you, anyway? Ms Jones thought it could've been for either of us."

I stared at him. "Chickens are tastier than blessings. And I know it because magicians think cats are as interchangeable as their void monsters. One cat's as good as another to them. You, though, were Ifan's best bud." And whatever else he was besides.

Callum sighed, pushing the palms of his hands against his forehead. "We're playing catch-up, Gobs. If we can't get ahead of this then we're never going to know what's actually happening. We're not going to be able to ask the magician if he's really trying to get Ifan back. And from where."

"He's been messing around with necromancers," I said. "Nothing good is going to come home from that, even if Ifan isn't actually dead. And if the magician's really going to raise an Old One to get his son back, he's trading the whole world for him. Our entire *reality*. We have to stop it. We can ask questions later."

"We don't know for sure that it involves an Old One. We're guessing."

"True. But even if it's nothing to do with Old Ones, we're still talking about letting necromancers get away with killing cats and doing gods know what else, on the off chance that it gets one magician's son back. It doesn't work that way. No one gets to weigh lives like that."

Callum nodded, examining the shed as if it held some final clue for us. "I know. Ifan wouldn't want it, either."

"I bloody hope not. If he did, he wouldn't be worth it."

We were both quiet for a moment, the shed bereft and damp around us, and when Pru spoke from the doorway it was like the ghosts of lost cats creeping up on us. I jumped sideways and bumped into Callum's legs.

"Are you two quite finished emoting about the place?" she asked.

"We're not *emoting,*" I said. "We're merely reassessing the situation based on new evidence."

"Is that what you call it?" She looked from one to the other of us. "No use crying over spilt charms, or whatever. We'll find them. Now come on. The house is empty. Let's see if you can investigate something up."

"Pru's right," I said. "Let's get on. We all have twenty hindlegs, after all."

Callum blinked at me. "What?"

"Well, you know."

"I really don't."

"Pru?" I appealed.

"No idea." She peered into the garden, her snout wrinkled.

"Isn't that a human expression?" I thought about it. "It's weird enough to be."

"It makes no sense," Callum said.

"None of your expressions do. Like, 'you can lead a horse to water but it'll only fish for a day'. What's that all about it?"

Callum looked at Pru. "Let's do that investigating now."

"*What?* Pru, back me up here."

"I don't know," she said. "Katja always says, 'only dead fish howl at wolves'."

"See?" I said to Callum. "Weird."

He snorted, and headed for the door. "*Someone's* weird."

I followed him, Pru shoulder-bumping me lightly as she fell in step with me.

THE DENTIST WAS COMING around the corner of the house as we left the shed, Tristan trotting in front of him.

"Nothing to report," the cat said.

"No answer," Walker said. "I mean, they could be hiding inside, but that seems unlikely."

"No sign of the dog," Astrid said. "They're all out, or all gone."

Callum went to the back door and peered in a window to the side of it. In our line of work we did, on occasion, have to enter places we might not strictly have permission to enter. Usually this entailed me finding a handy window (or – ugh – vent), but apparently Callum was in no mood to wait around. He wrenched a rock out of the garden border and hefted it straight through the window.

"Subtle," Pru observed, but there was no cry of protest

from inside. Callum cleared the glass and swung himself in, then vanished and opened the door for Walker, letting us all into the shabby hall.

"Let's be quick," he said. "Just in case they do come back."

We spread out, scouting the rooms. The place was empty of life, but they hadn't exactly moved out. There were half-drunk mugs of tea on the coffee table, and unwashed dishes in the sink. One of the bedrooms had the covers flung back as if someone had jumped up and run out, and there was a toothbrush lying in the bathroom sink, toothpaste still stuck to the bristles. There was a whiff of dog and low-level magic, but nothing that you'd look twice at. A few cloaking charms, some shift locks. No one was even bottling those rubbish love spells that make your rival come out in spots.

I emerged from under a bed with cobwebs in my whiskers, skirting some hidden magazines, and met Callum's gaze as he leaned in the door.

"Anything?" he asked.

"If the magician's been here, he hasn't been up to much. And I'd put good tuna on no sorcerer even setting foot in the place."

"Right," he said. "So Ms Jones is somewhere else. And Claudia too."

"I'd say so."

"We're going to have to do this alone," he said.

"I know," I said, and sighed. "We're going to have to go back to the magician's house, aren't we?"

Callum ran both hands back over his hair. "It's the

only place that makes sense. Unless there's somewhere else we don't know about."

"In which case we may as well just give up and welcome our new necromancer overlords, because we won't find it in time."

Walker put his head in the door. "Nothing in the living room," he said.

"Great." Callum found his lighter, rolling it in his fingers.

"I'm just wondering if I'm going to make my afternoon appointments," Walker added.

"Dude," I said. "Bigger fish to eat."

"Now that's almost right," Callum said.

"Still makes no sense," I said, and followed him as he headed for the kitchen. "Although I wouldn't say no to some fish."

Tristan had found a bag of cat biscuits in the pantry and pushed it over, and he was crunching his way steadily through them when we walked in while the big she-cat kept watch on the garden from the sink. The tap was dripping on her back, but she didn't seem to notice. Astrid and Pru ambled in after us, and Callum poked at the bits of paper stuck to the fridge without much hope. They looked to be mostly takeaway menus.

"Are we going somewhere else?" Walker asked, checking his watch. "Only I could get back in time—"

"You're not acting in the best interests of the team," Tristan said around a biscuit. "Shape up, man!"

"I'm just saying, you only needed me to knock on the door, and there's no one here. So what now?"

"They must've gone to the magician's house," I said.

"It's like Mitzi said – this place was only ever a holding cell. They've cleared out of Headingley, but if they're working with the magician they can use the power of his house to complete the ritual. Or he can."

"Let's go break into a magician's house, then," Pru said. "This day just gets better and better."

"Really?" Walker asked. "Is that sensible?"

"Definitely not," Astrid said. "But it's that or, you know, stand back and watch the weird ritual that may involve bringing back undead and distinctly unpleasant necromancers who've been banished from this world for centuries."

"They'll be hungry," Tristan said. "I wonder if that's what the dinner thing was about?"

"You don't have to come," Callum said to Walker. "Just drop us back at the car."

Walker scratched his arm. "Do you think that's where Polly is?"

"I have no idea," Callum admitted. "We did just help her get out of there. But it's possible she might've gone back if she figured out what the magician was up to."

The dentist nodded. "Alright, then. I'm coming."

"Joy," Pru said, and I snorted.

Callum started for the door, then hesitated.

"What?" I asked him.

"We're delivering them all the cats they need," he said.

The room was silent for a moment, then Astrid said, "Then we won't get caught. Right?"

"You're only required to give name, rank, and serial number if you are caught," Tristan said. "If anyone's interested."

"I prefer Astrid's option," Pru said.

"It's not like we have a choice," I said. "And no one's taking us by surprise this time."

Callum touched the back of my head just lightly, then headed for the door, the dentist trailing behind and still muttering something about wisdom teeth.

I followed, smelling the harsh tang of loss on Callum's fingers and hoping I was right.

16

WE WORK WITH WHAT WE'VE GOT

We went straight to the magician's house. There was nowhere else to go, and no one else we could turn to for help, although Tristan was still suggesting that we swing by his veteran's club and collect some of his buddies for backup. Callum pointed out, rather diplomatically, that he could hardly explain to a group of retired human veterans that the local cat had suggested they might be able to give us a hand to break into a magician's house, all so that we could rescue some other cats and potentially a sorcerer before anyone started raising the very long dead. Tristan started to disagree, but I added, with possibly a little less diplomacy but perfect accuracy, that a pack of old people with walking sticks were hardly going to tip the balance in our favour. Tristan got a bit sniffy after that, but it wasn't like he'd actually been offering anything helpful.

So now we were parked up across the road from the magician's house, half-sheltered under one of the enormous trees that lined the street. The Audi looked rather as if it belonged around here, but a squirrel had already come down the tree to scream at us, and the few people out in the endless rain still slowed as they passed. They didn't seem as openly suspicious as they had when we'd been here before in our own rather less suitable car, but it just wasn't the kind of neighbourhood where anyone parked on the kerb. That sort of thing was a bit common.

"We're not going to get in without being noticed," the dentist said, as we stared at the high walls and metal gates across the road.

"No," Callum agreed. He had a cigarette in his hands, rolling it between his fingers like he was trying to absorb the nicotine through his skin.

I examined the street, trying to think of ways to get inside other than just walking straight through the gate and saying, "Hi, we're here to bust up your dead thing ring". We couldn't exactly jump into a neighbour's yard, as we had at the necromancer's house. Not only were the walls too high for Callum to get over without a handy shed or tree to help out, I also figured the odds of the gardens around here having things like CCTV and large angry dogs seemed unreasonably high.

"I'll go and have a scout around," I said. "See if they're in there, at least."

"That seems like a bad idea," Callum said. "It's not like they won't be looking for you – for any of us."

"Obviously," I said. "But what else are we going to do? Sit out here and wait for an invitation?"

"It seems risky, though, don't you think?" Walker asked. "I mean, it's broad daylight."

"Would you prefer to wait for dark?" Pru asked, and he looked alarmed.

"Well, no, but—"

"How about you magic us some cloaking spells," I suggested. "*That* would be helpful."

"Um, yes." He pulled out his phone and began to poke at it. "I'm pretty sure I have that on here somewhere."

Astrid growled softly, and Callum folded his arms over his chest, his fingers tapping out a restless rhythm on his arms. "Let's keep an eye on things for a bit. See if anyone goes in or out."

The dentist looked at his watch, and Pru said, "If you say one thing about wisdom teeth I'm going to bite you."

He glared at her. "I wasn't going to say anything about wisdom teeth."

"Well, root canals, then," she said, and he made an aggrieved noise that made me think that was exactly what he'd been thinking about.

"Let me out," I said, pawing Callum's sleeve. "I want to have a nose around."

"You can't go in on your own," he said.

"Look, we have two choices. We wait around here and hope something happens, like the magician opens the gates and rolls out the red carpet for us, or Dentist Dan here remembers how to cast any sort of useful spell, both of which are about as likely as the other—"

"Hey," Walker protested. "That's not fair."

I ignored him. "Or we just get on. My stomach says it's lunchtime already, and that means the necromancers have had half a day to hunt more cats down already. They're not going to be hanging around – they're going to start as soon as they can, which means we lose the cats, maybe lose Ms Jones and Claudia, and we end up facing something *nasty*. Because whatever this whole ritual ends up being, whether it's really going to bring an Old One back or not, we can be damn sure it's not going to result in a new variety of chocolate-covered marshmallows."

"Well said, civvy," Tristan said. "Let's make a plan."

"I think that's what we've been trying to do for the last half hour," Astrid said, sounding bored.

Callum snorted. "And still we're no closer. Gobs, you going in to scout's going to do nothing. Think again."

I growled and peered out of the window. The stroppy squirrel sitting at the base of the tree glared back at me, his tail twitching. No one spoke for a moment, then I said, "Right. We do what we always do. We get resourceful."

"Specifically?" Callum asked.

"You're going to go and buy some peanuts," I said.

"What?"

"Trust me."

THE DENTIST EDGED the car up to the gates and looked at Callum and I, wedged together in the front seat.

"Are you sure about this?" he asked.

"Absolutely," I said.

"It seems a bit ... improvised."

"That's because it *is* improvised, you cabbage. It's not like we've got loads of time and resources to plan this, is it?"

Callum opened the door and said, "Just drive straight up to the house as soon as we get the gates open, and do what you can."

"Run a few necros down," I suggested.

"Gobs."

"What? We can't just leave them wandering around doing necromancer-y things."

"They're still people."

"People who want to murder cats and go poking around in other realms. They need stopping, and it's not like he can throw fireballs at them or anything."

The dentist scowled at me. "I *could* if I had time. I'm just not good under pressure."

"We've noticed," Pru said, following Callum and I out of the car. Astrid and the big she-cat came with her, and I peered into the back seat.

"Where's Captain Codswallop?"

"He said he had something to do," Astrid said. "Shot off when you wouldn't let him help with your master plan."

"Well. At least we're not delivering them nine cats if we do get caught," I said, although right now we needed all the help we could get. As soon as we were through those gates there'd be no shifting even for the cats that could. We were going to have to be fast and smart to get past the dog and the necros, and at least part of my plan rested on the idea that the more of us there were, the less likely it was that we'd all be caught.

Look, improvisation may be my strong point, but you can only work with what you've got.

"Ready?" Callum asked, taking Green Snake out of his pocket and putting him on the passenger seat of the car. Neither he nor Walker looked happy about it.

"If anyone says, 'born ready' I'll bite them," Astrid announced, looking at me pointedly.

"As if," I said, and shook myself off, pouffing my fur up against the rain and what was to come. "Onward, fearless legions!"

"Did you just say *furless?*" Pru demanded, and the big she-cat snorted, whether with amusement or outrage I wasn't sure.

"No." I gave up on trying to motivate anyone and looked up at the top of the wall. "Let's just have at it, then. Everyone try not to get sacrificed."

I RAN for the gap under the gate, scraping my belly and spine as I slipped through and wondering briefly if our glorious beast would make it. The barking had already started by the time I was through, great roaring volleys of it, but it wasn't directed at me. That part of the plan had worked, anyway.

The necromancers had evidently decided they needed reinforcements, because rather than just the one monster, three great dogs were thundering across the garden, slamming through flowerbeds and crashing off the misshapen topiary. They were baying furiously, slobber flying from their jaws, and the whole place looked like someone had let loose a flood of lemmings. Sleek grey forms shot from tree to wall to shrubbery, racing across the dogs' paths and even over their backs when they could, sending the canines into paroxysms of hysterical, frustrated yelping. As I watched, four squirrels hurdled one of the dogs like it was some sort of mobile park bench, bouncing on its back for a moment before scattering. Another dog had two squirrels hanging from its tail and was spinning in a helpless circle, trying to catch hold of them. The third dog had vanished around the back of the house among a flood of furry tails.

Squirrels will do a lot for ten quid worth of peanuts.

"What're we waiting on?" Astrid asked, appearing next to me.

"Just reconnoitring," I said, and ran for the little pillar on the drive that housed the button for the gate. I was quicker about hitting it this time, aware of the dogs barking behind me, and I caught it on the second go. There was a click and a groan as the gates started to move, and the big she-cat burst through the gap as soon as it was wide enough, Callum pushing from the outside until he could slip through after her.

We sprinted for the house, the Audi revving behind us like the dentist was building up to smash the gates down, and as we raced down the drive the front door crashed open. The woman with pink hair ran out, spotted us, and yelled, *"Incoming!"* She started whistling for the dogs, but they were in such a frenzy over the squirrels that they ignored her entirely.

Callum veered off, heading for the side of the house and the window Ms Jones had so helpfully dissolved last time. Pru and I shot after him, dodging jeering squirrels who were doing an excellent line in dog insults as we went.

"Not *arf* bad, are you? You're *all* bad!"

"Bad doggie!"

"Sit! Heel! Fetch! Roll over! Play dead!"

"Bone idle, you lot!"

The big man with no neck crashed out of the house with another woman and a long-haired kid who looked still in his teens following him. Neckless glanced about, spotted Callum, and charged into pursuit, yelling, *"It's him! He's the one!"*

"Hairballs," I muttered, and diverted to intercept the necromancer. Paws thundered after me, and I risked a look over my shoulder, hoping none of the dogs had found us that quickly, but it was the big she-cat, her eyes narrowed as she bolted across the grass, scattering squirrels like tumbleweeds.

The Audi roared behind us, and gravel crunched as it charged through the gate and tore down the drive. The small, muscled man had appeared from inside as well, and he and the long-haired kid ran toward the car, shouting and waving like they were trying to catch a bus. The dentist pulled off the drive and went bouncing through the garden, sending squirrels scattering in every direction.

I shot straight up the neckless necromancer's back, eliciting an outraged yelp, and buried my teeth in his ear. He screamed, then I was abruptly airborne as he tripped over the big she-cat. I flung myself free before he hit the ground, and as he caught himself on his hands the she-cat launched an attack at his face that sent him rolling away, spitting curses.

"And *that's* what you get for putting cats in bags," I shouted at him, and ran to join her attack.

"Gobs!" Pru yelled. "The dentist!"

I spun to see the car with its nose jammed into a small

tree that might have once been carved to look like an elephant, but which was now moulting, misshapen, and partly smashed. The pink-haired necromancer was attempting to drag Walker through the driver's window, shouting that if a single hair on her dogs' toothy heads was hurt she was going to do unpleasant things to his body parts. Walker was clinging desperately to the steering wheel, shrieking that he knew how to Do Things himself and that she'd better stop if she knew what was good for her. The short necromancer with the out-of-proportion muscles was standing next to the car holding a roll of gaffer tape in one hand and one of the dogs in the other, and the squirrels were already beating a rapid retreat. They were never going to be in it for the long haul. Lightweights.

Neckless scrambled to his feet and lunged for the she-cat, who jumped back with a snarl, and from across the garden a woman shouted, "Got one!"

"Astrid!" Pru shouted, as the woman hefted a squirming sack aloft.

"Hairballs," I muttered again. I had hoped the plan would hold together slightly longer. Still, at least Callum should be in by now and freeing the others— The thought was cut off as he came racing back around the house, arms and legs pumping, closely followed by the two remaining dogs. One snagged his coat and he went down with a yelp. I launched myself straight for the dog, and as it lunged to get a mouthful of something more meaty I bounced over Callum's back and slapped it across the snout. It yelped and flinched away as Pru joined me and the big she-cat charged the second dog. Callum rolled away just in time for Neckless to grab him by the front of his hoody and haul him to his feet.

"Aw, bollocks," Callum managed, before Neckless punched him in the belly and he doubled over, wheezing.

"*Hey!*" I yelled. "Uncalled for!"

"*You're* uncalled for," Neckless said. "I bloody hate cats."

"Run," Callum mouthed at me.

"I'm not—" My words ended in a squawk as he lurched half upright and shoved me away before Neckless could grab him again, and a sack slapped down next to me. "You *turnip!*" I yelped, glaring at the woman who'd tried to grab me.

"Here, kitty, kitty," she said, grinning at me, then spun around and slammed the sack down on the big she-cat, who'd been about to leap at her. She hefted the bag aloft, not without some effort. "That's *two!* I am the cat-catching *queen!*"

"Let her *go!*" I yelled, and started forward. She jumped back, and Callum yelped as Neckless booted him in the ribs. I spun around to see him curl in on himself, gasping. I launched myself at Neckless and he tried to dodge me, but I hooked his trousers and clawed my way up his legs, spitting in fury.

"Get off!" he snarled, slapping at me and catching me a couple of good blows around the ears as I scrambled straight up his back and out of reach. "Bloody cats – get it off! *Get it off!*"

A shout went up from the front of the house, "The dogs got the bald cat! Emily, call them off!"

"Drop it! *Drop it* – grab the dogs! *Hurry!*"

The barking descended into snarls and growling, and I craned to see what was happening. The long-haired kid was hovering by the two dogs, who were digging violently at the ground under one of the bushes, doing those horrible dart and bites that didn't mean any good for anyone. The pink-haired woman ran to grab them and tried to pull them back, but no quick sleek form broke cover to run for safer ground. The dogs were too strong for the necromancer, refusing to leave whatever lay under those bushes, and all I could think was, *Pru*. Something in my chest was screaming, wordless and horrified, and I was barely aware of the big man under my claws flailing, trying to reach me where I clung to his back.

"You *parsnips!*" I yowled. "You sodden excuses for blight-rotted *potatoes!*" All I could hear was the thunder of blood in my ears, and all I could see was Neckless' bald, shiny head, and all I wanted was to be big enough to rip it off with one paw. I threw myself at it, determined to at least leave a mark, and a hand grabbed me by the scruff of the neck, painfully tight, tearing me away. I struggled and twisted while hard fingers dug into my bone and soft tissue, and below me I saw Callum trying to grab Neckless' legs as if he'd pull him over. Neckless kicked him again and he curled around the pain, gasping.

And then a rough-edged, slightly slurred, but very loud voice bawled across the garden, "You, woman! *Put that cat down!*"

"*Excuse* me?" the woman in question asked, turning with me still swinging from one hand. My eyes were tearing up from being pulled into a squint by her grip, but I could still see the gate. It was open again, and standing –

well, arrayed – in front of it were four humans, with a big ginger tom stalking in front of them, his head up and his ragged ears twitching.

"Cruelty to animals!" the voice hollered, and a woman stepped forward, leading with a walker that someone had stuck flame stickers on. They were peeling slightly. There was a basket hanging from the crossbar, and a cricket bat stuck out of it, handle up. "How *dare* you?"

Neckless crossed his arms over his huge chest and said, "This is none of your business. Get back to your tea party or whatever."

"Tea party, he says," a new voice snapped, and a motorised scooter rolled forward, one man driving and another hanging off the back. The man driving it had a bald, scarred head and a jacket decorated with medals and badges, not all of which looked entirely legitimate. "You're addressing a colonel," he snarled. "That's tea party, *ma'am.*"

"Not the point, Duds," the woman with the walker said. "But thanks."

"You're trespassing," Pink Hair said. She had finally hauled the dogs away from the bush and put all three of them on leads, dragging them back to where the short muscly man was trussing the dentist's hands with gaffer tape. "Get out before I set the dogs on you."

The man on the back of the scooter jumped off and stepped forward. He had a pot belly under his black turtleneck jumper and only one arm, which was swinging what appeared to be a crowbar. He was at least as big as Neckless. "I wouldn't do that."

"You better not be threatening my dogs!"

"Your friend better put the cat down," the man countered.

They all glared at each other, while my neck ached and my eyes watered, and the dogs growled and strained, and the sacks of Astrid and she-cat flopped about the place in silent fury. The gates eased their way closed, shutting with a clang that made Tristan jump and the fourth veteran, a woman in a spotless apron, spun around to face them, brandishing two very large kitchen knives. A squirrel chittered, and I spotted them lining the walls, sharing their peanuts while they watched with bright-eyed interest, like spectators at a gladiator fight. Still no one moved.

Then there was a quiet yet solid *thud*, accompanied by a muted yelp, and Neckless crumpled to the ground. Callum waved a large, weather-beaten concrete snail at the woman holding me and hissed, *"Put him down."*

"The dogs!" she shouted, backing away from him. "Release the dogs!"

Pink let the dogs go. The colonel grabbed the cricket bat and a ball from her basket, tossed the ball in the air, and hit it toward us with unnerving accuracy. I gave a strangled squawk as it zoomed across the garden, and Callum ducked away. The ball caught the woman holding me on the shoulder and she screamed and staggered, falling to one knee and dropping me. The group at the gates advanced raggedly behind the colonel, who was still hurling cricket balls that sent Pink and Muscles diving for cover behind the Audi. The scooter purred down the drive with Duds screaming insults while the dinner lady–type with the scary knives hopped aboard in place of the one-armed man. She plucked sausages from a shopping bag and hurled them into the garden with lazy accuracy, and the dogs instantly forgot that they were meant to be ferocious guard beasts. They hoovered up the spoils, squabbling over the best bits while Pink screamed at them to heel. The one-armed man chose a moment between cricket balls and charged down the drive, waving his crowbar and issuing dire threats regarding the welfare of cats.

I rolled to my feet and clawed at the nearest sack. Callum grabbed it and upended it, dumping the infuriated she-cat in front of me. She snarled in my face, and I ducked behind Callum, but she was already throwing herself at her captor with a fury that almost made me feel sorry for the woman. Neckless started to get up, one hand clutching his head, and Callum gave him a very un-Callum-like boot to the ribs, sending him back down.

"Alright?" he asked me.

"Alright," I said, looking around. "But Pru …" I couldn't say it. Just her name made it hard to breathe.

"We don't know if they actually got her. Come on." He picked up the second sack and untied it, tipping Astrid out, then ran to intercept our raging cavalry before they decided the dentist was one of the bad guys.

Astrid shook herself off and watched the colonel lob a cricket ball into Muscles' belly just as he dodged around the Audi with his head down, charging toward the one-armed man with his arms out in a tackle. He gave an *oof* and collapsed to his knees.

"Huh," she said.

"My thoughts exactly."

17

ALWAYS THE CELLAR, NEVER THE SUNROOM

We left the she-cat dealing to Neckless and the cat-catcher, and ran after Callum just as a woman in a long, full skirt and a bright pink jumper emerged from the front door of the house, her face tight with fury. She didn't say anything, just surveyed the scene for a moment and shook her head. I paused to watch her. She hadn't been at the necromancer's house. I'd never seen her before, but I suddenly knew why the necromancers had moved, why they hadn't needed the old power in the Headingley house anymore. It hadn't been the magician. Or not *just* the magician, anyway.

The woman clenched her hands into fists at her sides then opened them again, and I spotted blood smearing her palms and caught the whiff of power, rich and strong as deep forest.

"Aw, hairballs," I said, and veered toward her, sprinting hard. She raised her hands and the blood spilled off them in a coil, twisting in the air then plunging into the earth.

The world shuddered, and the one-armed man paused and said, "Was that an earthquake?"

The woman in the door flicked her fingers upward, and the earth *crawled.* Worms twisted out of the ground and beetles scrambled after them as the grass surged up, contorting into living forms. Topiary uprooted itself, branches snapping into fangs and shattered talons. The squirrels vanished as one, and giant spiders made of hibernating bulbs and the roots of forgotten flowers scuttled across the lawn. Bloody necromancers. *Of course* they had spiders.

Callum abandoned the dentist and grabbed the knife-wielding dinner lady, spinning her back toward the gate while she narrowly avoided stabbing him in the arm. "Get out!" he shouted. "Get out! *Run!*"

"Retreat!" Tristan bellowed, jumping back as an oversized centipede made of dead snail shells and small twigs skittered toward him. "Tactical retreat!"

The colonel hustled for the gate button as fast as her walker would allow, but before she could reach it a chasm yawned in front of her. The gate button in its pillar was yanked into the ground, and her walker toppled after it. She let go and teetered on the edge of the void for a moment, then stepped back heavily, almost falling.

I hit the front stairs, hurdled them in one jump, and leaped for the necromancer's hand. I latched onto it, burying my teeth in her wrist just above a thin gold bracelet, tasting power and sweat and some sort of lavender soap. She just looked at me. I growled.

"I've had worse things bite me, little cat," she said, and turned back to the garden. She lifted her free hand higher and the earth fell away below the Audi, swallowing the car as the dentist shrieked in fury. I bit down harder, but she just pointed at the veterans' mobility scooter. Weeds grew up through the wheels, immobilising it. I tried one final bite, feeling the shift of muscles and tendons beneath my teeth, and this time she sighed. She shook her wrist almost absently, and I flew off, slamming into the floor as if she'd taken the colonel's bat to me. I scrambled to my feet and glared at her.

"Save your fury, little cat," she told me, and I watched Callum sink to the waist as the grass gave way to quicksand. "You'll need it later."

This was not part of the plan.

THERE WASN'T MUCH we could do after that. I mean, we put up a good fight, obviously – Callum head-butted Muscles so hard that he was currently still lying on the ground clutching his bleeding nose and making inarticulate noises. Walker worked himself into such a fury about the loss of his car that he ripped his gaffer tape off with his teeth and actually managed to create a couple of charms. One turned Pink's hair a rather unpleasantly mucky green, and the other shredded the sacks beyond repair. I'd have appreciated that more if I'd thought he actually intended to do it, but I'm pretty sure it was just luck.

Tristan's small army resisted wildly. The dinner lady tried to strangle Neckless with a string of sausages, and the colonel proved surprisingly adept with the cricket bat from a seated position, since she'd lost her walker. The long-haired kid just about got knee-capped, and in the end it took a snake made of old garden hose to get it off her. Duds tore his well-decorated jacket and shirt off for some inexplicable reason, pounded on his heavily tattooed but distinctly saggy chest, then clambered off his scooter and ran for the walls at the pace of a limping duck.

"Will you get him before he gets hypothermia?" the woman on the steps said to Neckless.

"He's got no shirt on," Neckless said.

"Genius," I muttered. "Is he going to tell us it's raining, too?"

The woman snorted, and said, "To the best of my knowledge, I don't think him being shirtless is going to hurt you, Ant."

Neckless grumbled, but went and rounded up the old man, who kept slapping his chest and belly and screaming insults. He had a *lot* of tattoos, some of them startlingly graphic, and Neckless didn't seem to know where to look.

"Honestly," the woman said. "Ask him to knock some heads together, and he never hesitates."

"You just can't get the henchmen these days," I said, and she laughed. She had a lovely laugh, warm and open, and not at all like someone who was about to kill us all off in some weird raise-the-dead-type ceremony.

"Emily," she called to Pink, who was trying to squint at the ends of her now-green hair, "Get the dogs secured. I want everyone inside."

"They're going to be *sick,*" Pink said. "All those sausages!"

"Well, leave them outside then," the necromancer said, and looked at the cat-catching woman. She was dabbing at her bleeding face with a sleeve. The big she-cat had apparently tried to remove the woman's face from her skull before a clump of daisies had wrapped around her paws, dragged her to the ground, and smothered her. All I could see were her glaring eyes amid happily nodding yellow and white flowers. "Cerys, round up the cats."

"I'm not going *near* the bloody cats," the woman said, and pointed at her face. "*Look* at this!"

"Everyone's going to behave themselves now, aren't they?" She looked at me as she said it, and I shrugged.

"Best ask them. It's not like I'm in charge. Cats don't work that way."

The woman sighed, looked out across the garden, and clenched her hands again. When she opened them, there was fresh blood on her fingertips where she'd re-opened the wounds on her palms. "*Everyone will behave,*" she said, her voice low. It rolled across the garden like an echo, and everything shivered. The she-cat snarled in her cocoon of flowers, and Astrid lurched off the roof of the old Bentley, where she'd retreated when the garden started getting grabby. She pitched into the gravel of the drive, and it swallowed her, closing behind her as if she'd never even been there.

"*Hey!*" I yelled. "Put her back!"

"That is *not* cricket!" Tristan shouted.

"He's right," the colonel agreed. "That's got to be against the Geneva Convention."

"Will we behave?" the woman asked.

"Yes," Callum called. He was still waist-deep in the

garden, a bruise blooming on his forehead from head-butting Muscles. "Yes, just bring her back."

The woman looked at me for a long time, and I glared at her. "I'm behaving."

"Alright." The gravel burped, and Astrid surfaced, spluttering. "Now then. Everyone can just make their way over here nice and steady, and we'll sort this out."

The garden began to release its prisoners, and I looked up at the woman. "Who *are* you?"

She smiled at me, a smile as delightful as her laugh, as if she were genuinely pleased with me. "Sonia."

"Doesn't answer my question."

"All in good time, little cat."

"I'm actually a perfectly reasonable size for a cat, you know."

"If you say so. You seem a little … scrawny."

"*Rude.* What's the plan here?"

"For everyone to just calm down a little."

"Sure it is. Where's the magician? Are you going to raise his son from the dead? And when are you planning to open the doors between realms and, you know, break the world?"

Her smile faded. "Do you ever stop talking?"

"Not often," Callum said, stopping at the bottom of the steps. His hair was plastered to his head and his jeans were caked with mud, and his coat looked even worse than usual, which I hadn't thought was possible. I checked around. Tristan stood in front of the colonel, looking furious, but the big she-cat looked angrier still as she shook off the last of the daisies. Astrid sat on the drive, still coughing up gravel, and the dentist muttered under his breath as Neckless herded him and the shirtless Duds toward the house. Pink was wrestling the dogs across the garden, and everyone else was assembling on the steps. I could see red flecks on the dogs' muzzles, and something knotted in my chest so hard that I could barely breathe around it.

No Pru.

It wasn't possible. Sure, there had been two dogs after her, but she was quick, and fierce, and they *couldn't* have. I'd have heard her, surely. She'd have called out, something. She couldn't just be *gone*. That didn't just happen. It couldn't.

But she wasn't here.

SONIA LED us into the foyer, where the taxidermied animals were back in their places, staring blankly from the walls and corners of the room. They hadn't gone back quite the way they'd started, though. Not that I remembered from our first visit, anyway. For a start, the birds were still terminally tangled in the mess of wires hanging from the ceiling, so they looked more like some modern art commentary on extinction than they did the centrepiece of a fancy foyer. The skeleton tea party were missing some ribs, and one had a leg where its arm should've been, and a few of the animals seemed to have lost limbs. Whatever magic had put them back together had evidently decided on a waste not, want not approach, so the various cast-offs had sort of glommed together to create new creatures. I spotted a one-legged rabbit with three broken birds' wings sprouting from its neck like a ruff, and an albatross with a fox's tail instead of a wing, and a hare with beaks instead of ears. Ugh. Although the seagull with a human skull instead of its own head was possibly the most disturbing.

I kept an eye on them as we headed inside, just in case any jumped out at us, but I suppose it was job done, the way the necromancer had rounded us up. Nothing stirred as we collected on the cold tiled floor of the foyer, and the big she-cat eased over to me, followed by Astrid. Their warmth was comforting in the magic-stained chill of the place.

"Ant, take our uninvited guests into the kitchen and make them a cuppa," Sonia said to Neckless. "I'll deal with them shortly." He grabbed the dentist and Callum by a shoulder each, and Sonia sighed. "*No.* Those ones we want. The others."

Duds, who was standing with his hands on his hips and his chest puffed out, shouted, "Corporal Dudley Greenwood! Serial number five-five—"

"Quiet, Duds," the colonel said, and he subsided. She was leaning on the one-armed man, and looked up at Neckless. "Milk, strong, no sugar. And you better have biscuits."

"I think we've got some digestives," he said, rubbing the back of his head.

"Pah," the dinner lady snapped. *"Digestives.* Not even chocolate ones? That's a breach of human rights, that is."

Neckless mumbled that he'd see if he could find something better, then headed for the door to the overstuffed living room, the veterans trailing after him. The dinner lady still had one of her knives, and she glared at the necromancer as she went past, raising it pointedly.

Sonia gave her that delightful smile, and, once the little group had gone, turned to the cat-catcher. "Cerys, pop a little something in the tea," she said. The other woman nodded and hurried off.

"*What?*" Tristan hissed. "How *dare* you? I'll tear your face off myself!" He started toward Sonia, and Callum put a boot in front of him. Tristan snarled.

"What's going in the tea?" Callum asked, his voice calm.

"Just a little something so they forget all about talking cats and aggressive gardens," Sonia said. "I'm not a monster. Besides, disposing of four dead pensioners would be more trouble than it's worth."

"I think it's the best we can ask for," Callum said to Tristan, who bared his teeth. "It's not good for them to remember this, anyway."

"They'll remember me," Tristan said. "Well, Duds will. He's been chatting to me forever. Everyone else just thought he was dotty until today."

"Is that the shirtless one?" the long-haired kid asked, startling us all. I'd kind of forgotten he was there. He'd found some frozen peas from somewhere and was holding them on Muscles' face.

"Well. Yes," Tristan admitted. "But he only *acts* a bit dotty. He's not really."

"Wonderful," Sonia said. "So is everyone happy now?"

"Happy as we can be, considering a bunch of necros have just jumped us," I said.

She frowned at me. "You did break in."

"It's not even your house," I retorted.

"No. It's mine," a new voice said, and we turned to see the magician standing at the door to his study, the light from inside turning his greying hair into a glossy halo against his dark skin. "Have you finally got them rounded up? Honestly, Sonia. They can't have been that hard to deal with."

"They had reinforcements," she said. "Irritating lot, really."

The magician examined us. He was wearing a shiny green tracksuit and purple slippers. "I'd agree with that assessment."

"Nice," I said. "And here you were asking us to work with you only a day ago."

"I don't have to like everyone I work with," he said, and frowned. "We're a cat down."

Sonia looked around and swore. "*Dammit.* Where's the other cat?"

"Um," Long-hair said, chewing his lip. "There was sort of a problem."

"*Where is she?*"

"I think your dogs ate her," I said, hating the words as I said them. "Well done there."

Sonia pressed her fingertips to her forehead, took a breath, and pointed at Long-hair. "Take Emily and see if the cat's still useable. *Hurry.*"

He nodded, handed the bag of frozen peas to Muscles, and hurried back out into the rain. The small man leaned back against the wall and pressed the peas onto his face gingerly, moaning.

"Well, this whole situation is fantastic," the magician

said. "*Fantastic.* Everything gets rushed because you let them find the new house, and now we haven't even had time to prepare properly."

"I was thinking it looked about situation normal for necros," I said. "You know, disorganised and ineffectual, just as you should be."

The magician scowled at me. "I'm not a necromancer. And as for you, I think the dogs ate the wrong cat."

"I think the dogs ate the wrong *species,*" I spat. "What did you think we were, dial-a-sacrifice?"

"Gobs," Callum said. "Not really helping."

"What? He tried to trap us!"

Callum opened his mouth to say something, then shrugged. "You know what? You're right. Go for it."

"I should *think* so," I said, but then couldn't think what else to say.

Lewis shrugged. "Worked eventually. I knew you two couldn't keep your noses out."

I growled, and Walker suddenly yelled, "*Ha!*"

We all looked at him, startled, and he splayed his fingers at the magician.

"Ha," he tried again, and made little pinching movements with his hands.

"What do you think you're doing?" Sonia asked.

Walker turned his attention to her and waved a couple of times, then sighed and just made a rude but easily recognisable gesture.

Callum burst out laughing and dug his cigarettes out of his pocket. The packet was half-crushed and muddied. "What?" he asked, looking up to find us watching him. "It was funny."

"It *did* work," the dentist said. "Before."

"It did," Callum agreed, finding his lighter and jamming a slightly bent cigarette into his mouth.

"I must have the gestures wrong." He gave the same definitely unmagical gesture to the magician, and this time we all snickered, even the big she-cat.

"I'd just keep practising," Callum said, cupping his hands to light the cigarette.

"Put that out," Sonia said.

"Make me," he said, and smiled at her.

Lewis shook his head. "This whole thing is a mess, but it'll work anyway. Now you can come along nicely, or I can make you." He turned without waiting for a response and headed into the study. Walker made a few more rude gestures at his back, but Callum just shrugged and followed the magician, shedding mud on the smooth tile. We followed, my whiskers twitching anxiously.

THE STUDY WAS LOOKING RATHER tidier than it had, although there were a lot of gaps in the shelves where the jars and damaged books had been, and a whiff of preserving fluid still hung about the place, fighting with the ground-in scent of old cigars. Lewis led us across the room to where a panel of the bookshelf hung open. I couldn't have sworn it was the same panel Ms Jones had been behind, but I couldn't have sworn it wasn't, either. It felt different, though. There had been nothing behind her – not an empty room, not space – just *nothing,* like the magician kept a handy void in his bookshelves for chucking trespassers into. This time I could see over the threshold to where cold, pale light flooded the space beyond and revealed a landing with the sort of flat white walls and brutally tiled floors that you expect in the better sort of hospital. Stairs led down, followed by a sturdy metal handrail.

The magician disappeared down them without a glance back, and I hesitated for a moment, wobbling on the edge of the study's green carpet.

"Why's it always cellars with you people?" I demanded, and the magician turned to look back at me. "What's wrong with a nice sunroom?"

"*You people?*" he demanded.

"Magicians. Necromancers. Ne'er-do-wells."

"Ne'er-do-wells?" Astrid said. "Have you been watching period dramas?"

"I'm a cat of refined tastes."

"Oddly enough, creatures of the void and demons of the shadowed realms kind of object to being summoned into a sunroom," Lewis said.

"You should rethink your audience," I said.

"I'll take it under consideration." He turned and continued down the stairs.

Old Lewis had really committed to the hospital aesthetic. The stairs were clear of even the smallest amount of dust, and the light reflecting off the tiles was so bright it made me squint. We emerged into a big room lined with glossy white cabinets that weren't marred by so much as a fingerprint. Stainless worktops topped the lower cabinets, and a huge twin sink sat in one corner. There were more shelves stuffed with jars down here too, but, unlike the study, these ones were labelled with neat computer-printed stickers and seemed to contain more chemical solutions and powders than they did seven-eyed piglets and winged frog hearts. The only thing that really screamed *magical cellar* as opposed to *fancy research lab* was the raw dirt floor, packed hard yet disturbingly sticky under my paws.

A bookshelf was jammed with titles like *The Building Blocks of Unlife* and *Elements of the Void*, and a still on one of the benches dripped viscous liquid into a vial. The sound of the liquid hitting the surface was the only noise in the place. It smelled like coffee.

And then someone said, "Well, the gang's all here, then," and a second voice said, "Looks like a party waiting to happen," and I spotted the cages stacked in one corner. The two brothers sat like bookends in their own cages, while Gordie was turned to the wall with his face pressed against the bars of another, Mitzi sitting in front of him with her tail tight over her toes and her ears back.

"If this is a rescue it's a bloody shoddy one," she said.

"Give the cats a break, Mitz," one of the black and white cats said. "That's my glorious beast over there, and I won't hear a word said against her." So that one was Charlie, then.

The big she-cat growled.

"You all *talk* so much," the magician muttered. "Why do you all talk so much?"

"Because we're downright delightful," Harvey said.

Sonia shook her head and opened one of the cabinets. "Shall I start the circle?"

"We may as well," the magician said, and looked at the

rest of us. "Do I have to restrain you, or are you able to accept the situation?"

"Sure," Callum said, and pushed himself up onto one of the worktops, sitting there with his filthy boots tapping a slow rhythm against the cabinet doors. "Why not?"

The magician gave him a suspicious look, but he didn't say anything else. The dentist pressed himself against a wall, looking as if he might throw up at any moment, and Astrid went to touch noses with Mitzi.

I jumped up next to Callum, looked around, then hissed, "What's your plan?"

He scritched the back of my head, and said, "Honestly, Gobs, I don't have one."

"Oh," I said, and looked at Gordie, still wedged into the corner of the cage. "That's two of us, then."

"Yeah." We sat there, watching the magician and the necromancer prepare to break the world.

18

A LITTLE IMPROVISED SUMMONING

We watched Sonia pulling chalk from one of those drawers that are always filled with tea lights and bits of strings and half-dead batteries – apparently even magicians' lairs need one. She set to work in the centre of the floor, drawing a big and surprisingly even circle to start with. I suppose it's no good summoning monsters into ovals. They're bad enough in circles. Who knows what an oval would do? The magician laid a large plain journal leaking Post-its from every corner on one of the worktops and flicked through it.

"So what's the plan here?" Callum asked after a few moments of Sonia sketching and the magician muttering to himself had passed. "You raising Ifan from the dead?"

"He's not dead," the magician said, and I heard Callum's breath catch, but his voice was even when he replied.

"You were pretty sure he was dead the last time we saw you. You know, when you'd just buried him."

"I was misled," the magician said, and scowled at Sonia.

She shrugged slightly. "We were all misled. It was merely the vessel that was left behind. Ifan himself was pulled into another realm."

"Isn't death another realm?" Charlie asked. "You know, technically."

"In every sense, I'd say," his brother said.

"He's not dead," Sonia said, not looking up.

"Well, this should be good," I said. "So, what, you're just going to pluck him back from this mysterious realm all unscathed and happy to be home?"

"Of course he won't be *unscathed*," the magician said. "But he will heal. And we need him back here."

"So you're not raising an Old One, then?" Tristan asked.

"What?" Lewis asked, sounding genuinely puzzled.

"Nine cats," Astrid said. "Isn't that a thing?"

"Don't be ridiculous," Sonia said. "No one can raise an Old One."

"Unheard of," Lewis agreed.

"Not what our sources say," I said, watching the magician.

He looked at Sonia, frowning. "Have you heard of it?"

She waved dismissively. "*Cats*. They'll say anything to distract you." She didn't look up, and I couldn't tell if the tightening of her shoulders was to do with her concentration or with the question of Old Ones. Not that I supposed it mattered. We were about to find out either way very soon.

Callum shook his head. "How'd you find out about Ifan being in another realm, then?"

"We've had communications," Sonia said, stepping back to examine her handiwork critically. She was adding heavy, curling runes to the circle, careful to stay on the outside of it.

"So you're saying Ifan's body died, his soul's been taken into another realm, and you're going to do a bit of a ritual to get him back," I said. "Thought you said you weren't a necromancer, Lewis. This is sounding an awful lot like raising the dead."

"How many times do we have to say it? *He's not dead,*" the magician insisted. "He's in another realm."

Callum scratched his jaw. "Can't exactly be easy, jumping between realms."

"I'm pretty sure the universe dislikes it," I said. "There are rules."

"Do cats listen to those?" he asked me.

"They're a bit more serious than *don't jump on the table,*" Astrid said.

"And more likely to get you turned inside out," Charlie added.

"So, what," I asked the magician, "have you got his body stashed somewhere around here, then?"

Harvey snorted. "Why d'you think he wanted a body with a bit of magic in it? They need a vessel."

Callum and I both looked at Walker, who blinked at us in confusion. "Sucks to be you," I said.

"Not *him,* you sprout," Charlie said. "He's as magic as a flea circus."

"I *am* magic," the dentist protested, then seemed to

think of the possible repercussions. "Well, magic-adjacent, at least."

"You can't mean me," Callum said, and looked at the magician, who was moving Post-its about. "I'm not magic."

"Eh," Harvey said. "You've got a whiff. We know about these things."

"We've got what you might call sensitive noses," Charlie added. "Snouts for skills, sort of thing."

"Well, I'd definitely rather you weren't a vessel," I said to Callum, ignoring the brothers even though I thought their sensitive noses might be right. "That sounds messy."

"I can't be a vessel. *I'm not magic.*"

"You're as wilfully clueless as my son," Lewis said. "He was always running around looking for something *else.* You can't just learn to be who you are, can you? You have to damp it all down with drugs or booze or whatever else it is you shovel down your throats." He sounded honestly disgusted, and maybe a little despairing. "You drown out all the things you could be, drown your potential and your power and your beauty, because why? Because it's scary or strange or, Old Ones forbid, you think you might actually be capable of something." He shook his head. "Well, at least you can be useful now."

There was silence for a moment, and I looked up at Callum. He had a hand pressed to his chest as if he didn't know whether to object or apologise. I couldn't read his expression, couldn't tell if he was hearing something he knew to be true or if he was just confused. Maybe both.

"Dude," Charlie said finally, "that's the most demotivational motivational speech I've ever heard."

"Yeah, your bedside manner could do with a little adjusting," Harvey agreed.

Lewis shook his head. "The sooner this is done, the better. I'm thoroughly looking forward to not dealing with cats anymore."

"We're not loving it either," Astrid observed. "Your son sounds like he's going to be super happy to be welcomed back to the family bosom, though. *Super* happy."

"Good point," I said. "After all, he went to some trouble to make sure everyone thought he was dead. Maybe he's in a realm of heated beds and endless tuna, or whatever magicians are into. I'm sure he'll love being dragged back."

"I like the sound of that realm," Charlie said. "You got an address?"

"What happened to your last necro leader, anyway?" I asked Sonia. "She was less about this whole raising-the-dead thing. Well, other than chickens."

Sonia tucked a curl of blonde hair behind her ear and scowled at me. "Oli was no leader. She was merely a householder for the movement. And she no longer fitted with us. She had some very strange ideas regarding closure and easing the way of death rather than bending it to our will."

"Dead chicken closures do sound pretty strange," Harvey said. "Unless they were roasted."

"Chicken?" Gordie asked, finally looking up from his corner. "Is it dinner?"

"Oh, well done," Mitzi said to Harvey. "I thought he'd forgotten."

"Dinner!" Gordie shouted, loudly for such a scrawny cat. "*Dinner!*"

"It's lamb," Mitzi shouted over him.

"I don't like lamb."

"I know, love."

There was silence then, other than Gordie grumbling to the wall. The magician checked his watch, and I wondered if Oli was still pottering around somewhere, resurrecting cockroaches and chickens, or if Sonia had decided on a more lasting eviction from the necromancers. I hoped for the former, even though the chickens had been seriously creepy.

"What about my Polly?" Walker demanded suddenly. "What did you do to her?"

"Who?" Sonia asked, giving him a puzzled look.

"The sorcerer," Callum said. "The one you had locked in your bookshelves."

"You were the last to see her," the necromancer said, wiping her chalky hands on her skirt. "Old Ones know where she went after you let her out. She was never meant to be here in the first place, although she did come in handy. Would be even handier if we'd had a chance to use her properly. I'm all done here, Lewis."

I wondered how anyone would *use* a sorcerer as the magician picked up his book and started to walk around the circle, peering at the runes.

"I hope you're not double-checking me."

He looked at her over his glasses, like a tracksuit-clad accountant. "Of course I am. We can't have any mistakes."

She sniffed. "I don't make mistakes."

"Other than misplaced sorcerers," I pointed out.

"You misplaced her for us," she snapped, then took a

breath. "I see what you mean about dealing with cats, Lewis. Are you happy with your double-checking?"

The magician made a considered noise, and bent down to rub out a minuscule curl on one of the runes. Sonia looked at the ceiling as if imploring the Old Ones to give her strength.

"Why did you even invite us here?" Callum asked. "I mean, now it seems obvious that it was a trap—"

"I did say there was no way it was a legit case," I pointed out, and he ignored me.

"—but it didn't work very well, did it?"

The magician straightened up and glared at him. "You got the day wrong."

"What?"

"Thursday. You were meant to come on *Thursday,* not Tuesday. That bloody sorcerer turned up asking questions and there was a bit of an altercation. I managed to trap her and bleed some of her power into the house, then went for reinforcements to deal to her properly. While I was out you two came bungling in two days early like the worst sort of holiday guests, set her free before we could drain her properly, *and* broke my window."

I looked at Callum. "I said you needed a diary."

"If I hadn't got the day wrong, we'd have walked into a proper trap," he pointed out.

"End result appears to be much the same," I said, and he grunted.

Sonia put her hands on her hips and glared at us. "I've had enough of all this. Come on, Lewis. Stop faffing and let's get started."

"It has to be right," he insisted. "It has to work this time."

"Batting O for ten, are we?" Charlie asked. The magician gave him a dirty look. "O for six? O for twelve. Let me know when I'm getting warm."

"Don't joke about it," Mitzi said. "That's nine cats every time."

The big she-cat growled agreement, and Callum said, "This is all wrong. Of course it's not working. I mean, I miss Ifan, but this is ... you can't just pull someone out of another *realm*."

"There's no end to what we can do," Sonia said, giving another of those delightful smiles. They were starting to feel less delightful every time.

"Nothing good comes back from another realm," Harvey said. "That's why it's *in* another realm. It doesn't belong in this one."

"*Ifan* doesn't belong in another realm," the magician snapped, and slammed his book closed, looking at Callum. "You say you were his friend. You should know this."

Callum didn't answer, just looked at the remnants of his cigarette with a muscle twitching in his jaw.

"No answer? Typical. Sonia, where are those bloody kids? We need another cat."

"They'll be here." Sonia skirted the circle and grabbed the dentist by the scruff of the neck, doing something I didn't quite see that made him cry out and fall to his knees. "Let's start."

Callum dropped his cigarette and slipped off the worktop. "Let him go."

"Sit down," the magician said, pointing a long, slim knife at him. "We'll get to you."

"Give it here," Sonia said, gesturing impatiently for the knife.

"Leave him," Callum insisted, stepping forward as the dentist squawked in alarm and thrashed in the necromancer's grip. She raised one hand to Callum almost casually, and he was flung back against the cabinets with a yelp. He struggled to claw his way off them but was pinned as easily as if Neckless had been holding him there.

Walker seemed to be similarly trapped, because Sonia let him go and he cowered before her, the tendons in his neck standing out and his face red with effort, but not managing so much as a twitching ear. She lifted one of his arms above his head, pushing his sleeve up to the elbow. The magician handed her the knife, and the big she-cat came barrelling across the floor, all teeth and claws. Lewis booted her casually, sending her spinning into the middle of the circle. She let loose a furious hiss, and the rest of us exploded in a babble of furious shouts. I flew off the worktop and charged the magician, Tristan racing me with his teeth bared and his ragged ears back, and Astrid threw herself at Sonia. None of us reached our targets. We were thrown back as firmly as Callum had been, pinned to the floor by invisible hands.

"Honestly," Sonia said. "We should've just caged the bloody things."

"We'll need them out again in a minute," the magician replied, taking a skinny artist's paintbrush from one of the drawers and checking it for loose bristles.

"I suppose," she said, and casually sliced a long gash down Walker's forearm. He shrieked, and the rest of us contributed some suggestions regarding the necromancer's parentage and relation to various vegetables.

"Now, then," the magician said, and dipped the paintbrush in the blood flowing steadily down the dentist's arm and dribbling onto the hard dirt floor. "Quiet in the cheap seats."

"They're feeling distinctly expensive," Astrid said, and the she-cat snarled and twisted in the centre of the circle, wriggling in her invisible bonds.

THE MAGICIAN WORKED METHODICALLY, not hurrying, carefully dipping the brush in Walker's blood then just as carefully tracing the runes and shapes Sonia had chalked onto the floor. She stood calmly over the dentist, occasionally squeezing his arm to keep the wound open, and clucked her tongue if Lewis went a little over the lines here and there.

At some point, Long-hair came downstairs to announce that they hadn't been able to find Pru in the garden. My stomach curled itself into tight, heavy knots while I wondered if that meant she'd crawled away to safety, or if those bloody awful dogs had actually eaten her. I could still see the red on their muzzles and taste fury like bile at the back of my throat, and I'd have given just about anything to sink my teeth into the nearest necromancer. Not that I was going anywhere right now. The bonds hadn't loosened.

The magician frowned at Long-hair and said, "Just get any old cat, then."

"But fast," Sonia added. "Back here in ten."

The kid ran up the stairs, and Lewis went back to painting. He was three-quarters of the way around now, and I didn't like the way the air was changing in the room. It was thickening, filling with unseen things as he carved a doorway into the walls between the worlds, between the *realms*. I could feel things pushing up against them the way I could sometimes feel the beasts from the Inbetween when they passed close by. Whatever sort of door they were opening, whatever realm they thought they were reaching into, there was nothing good coming from it. I was as sure of that as I was of the fact that the dead should stay dead, no matter how much we miss them. I twisted on the floor, searching for an edge to claw myself out against. There was nothing.

The magician was onto the last few runes, and the room was silent, all of us watching, even Gordie. Lewis traced the flicks and accents, little dots and slices of an ugly, heavy language, the sort you never want to hear spoken aloud. His precision, his complete lack of hesitation, made me wonder how many times they'd already practised this. How many other cats had been trapped down here or in the cellar in Headingley, wondering what was going to come next.

Callum must've been thinking the same thing because he said, "Have you tried this before? Tried to get Ifan back?"

Lewis shook his head, not looking up. "We only made

contact before. We didn't have the right vessel. People like you aren't that easy to come by, you know."

"You've got this wrong," Callum said. "I'm telling you, I'm not magic."

"You're just what we need," Sonia said. "We'll pop Ifan right on in there."

"That sounds cosy," I said.

"Oh, this one's soul's going to pop right out," she said, and smiled. "Someone needs to take Ifan's place."

"Fab," Charlie said. "What about our souls, then? You playing swapsies with them, too?"

"Oh, no. We need some lives to power things. And nobody has as many lives as cats." She lifted the knife and tilted it so the flat white light of the cellar caught the edge, and that was when I saw the multi-hued shimmer that ran across it.

"Unicorn horn," I said, and her smile broadened into a grin. "Godsdamned unicorn horn. You manky runner bean." Because it didn't matter how many lives a cat had left, if someone killed you with unicorn horn, you weren't coming back. It took all of them at once.

"That is *definitely* a contravention of the Geneva Convention," Tristan said. "I object."

"Us and all," Harvey said, and then we fell silent and watched the magician put a final, curling stroke onto the runes.

"Done," he said. "Call the others."

Sonia left Walker bleeding and whimpering at the edge of the circle, walked up the stairs and shouted like she was calling the family in for dinner. They didn't take long to arrive, Cerys with plasters decorating her cheek and

Muscles still clutching his packet of peas. Rather disappointingly, none of them had changed into long black robes or any sort of fancy skull-adorned headdresses. They still looked as if they'd been just about to pop down the shops and had been rudely interrupted.

"Get the cats," Sonia said, and Long-hair grabbed the scruff of my neck and lugged me to the edge of the circle as the force holding me released its grip. Neckless, Cerys, Pink and Muscles were doing the same to the rest of the cats, releasing them from the cages and pinning them down around the circle.

Lewis pointed at Callum and said, "You get into the centre."

"Rather not," Callum said, then yelped as his limbs started moving of their own accord. He struggled against it, swearing and clutching at the cabinet handles, but his arms jerked away and his legs marched him straight into the middle of the circle, moving with a stiff jointed lack of coordination that made my tail puff up. He crumpled to his knees and glared at Sonia.

"There we go," she said. "Don't be difficult. It's only going to make things more painful."

"We've still only got eight cats," Pink said, not quite looking at Sonia. "There weren't any around."

Sonia and Lewis looked at each other for a moment, then he grabbed the back of the dentist's jacket and dragged him to the edge of the circle. "Near enough," he said. "We were never going to get nine cats with nine lives, anyway."

"I'm so glad you're taking this seriously," I said. "Nothing like a little improvised summoning."

"Let's start," Sonia said. "If I listen to him a moment longer we'll be down to seven cats before we start."

"Unnecessary," I said, and stared at the circle. My hackles were raised against Long-hair's hand so hard that my skin was aching.

Nine cats with nine lives, all to bring Ifan back from another realm. I didn't believe it. Didn't believe *her*. There was no way she was helping the magician out of the kindness of her heart. But they were certainly calling out to *something* across the twisted folds of realities. They were going to bring it across the thresholds of countless worlds and into Callum's body, and send Callum himself to whatever outer reaches of unreality displaced souls went to. And maybe it wasn't an Old One, but that didn't make it any better. Because Callum would be gone just as surely as if it was.

I wriggled, and Long-hair squeezed me hard enough to make me wheeze. His hands were sweaty, and I closed my eyes against the sight of Callum kneeling in the circle and the scent of blood and misplaced hope.

Maybe if I willed it hard enough, it wouldn't work.

I didn't seem to have any other options.

19

YOU CAN'T KEEP A GOOD CAT DOWN

So there we were, Callum kneeling in the centre of the circle and the rest of us gathered unwillingly around it, struggling against our captors. Muscles had hold of Astrid and Tristan, who was still bellowing about the Geneva Convention, and the big she-cat was emitting the sort of growls and snarls that belonged in a BBC nature documentary while Neckless trapped her against the ground with an increasingly panicked look on his face. The other cats had been dragged out of their cages, Charlie and Harvey thrashing wildly in Cerys' grip and doing their best to prove that cats can indeed be liquid when required, while Mitzi screamed some seriously inventive curses at Pink, who was holding her at arm's length. Gordie had wandered out on his own, following Mitzi and demanding to know where the chicken was. Sonia had one hand on Walker's shoulder, although he seemed to have given up hope of ever moving again, and just clutched his bleeding arm and stared about with the look of a trapped rabbit.

"Everyone shut up!" the magician bellowed, and there was a moment's silence.

Then, "Is he serious?" Charlie asked.

"He wants us to be silent sacrifices, C. We should listen to the nice man who's about to *slaughter us.*"

"I will *not* die silently, H."

"Too right, C. Too right. Our grievances will be heard."

"Stop bloody *nattering* and *bite their bloody arms off,*" Astrid yowled, and proceeded to attempt exactly that with Muscles, who squawked and squished her against the floor with one huge arm. I wouldn't have wanted to be him. Astrid's pupils were so big I could barely see a rim of blue around them, and everything about her had suddenly become astonishingly sharp.

"Help!" he yelped, while she tore bloody grooves down his arm. "Who's got the gloves?"

"Cats have rights too!" Tristan bellowed. *"We demand fair treatment!"*

"You *monsters!"* Mitzi yelled. "If you so much as tweak Gordie's tail I will tear out your eyeballs and—"

"You said chicken! I want *chicken!"*

"Shut! Up!" Lewis screamed, and stomped one foot onto the packed dirt floor. It should have been some dull little thud, barely audible over the shouting, but it echoed. It shuddered the walls, trembled the very air in the bright cellar, made the lights shiver and my fur leap to attention like I'd stepped outside into an electrical storm. We fell silent. That sense of creatures pushing against the walls of the world was stronger, and I thought I could feel them leaning in, listening for an invitation, scraping against the edges where our realities met and waiting for a crack to

form so they could tear it wide open. "Better," the magician said, and straightened the front of his tracksuit.

"You could've dressed for the occasion," I managed, but I could hear the shake under my words, and my mouth was dry. Astrid looked at me, her pupils still huge despite the lights, then started trying to fight her way free again. We all did, for all the good it did us.

"Now," Lewis said, and Sonia stepped to the opposite side of the circle to him. She was digging her nails into her palms again, and when she raised her hands to her sides they were smeared with blood. Lewis faced her, his own hands open and raised to mirror her. His were bloodless – magicians work their magic differently to necromancers – but I could smell the power coming off him, acrid as stale fear-sweat and old vinegar.

They began to chant, their voices layering over one another, echoing in strange ways, the words running off after each other to bounce against the walls and spill from the cabinets, coating everything in greasy magic, building and swelling and taking on a rhythm of their own. The runes glowed, steam curling from the dentist's blood that outlined them, adding the stink of cooking meat to the stench of power. The ground around Callum shimmered, filling with light as if he were on a floodlit stage, and he squinted against it, finding himself free enough that he could raise a hand to shield his eyes. He staggered to his feet, but when he tried to step toward the edge of the circle he flinched back again, turning his face from the burning runes. The heat of them was singeing my whiskers.

The magic-workers' voices rose, heavy syllables that

should have been clunky and awkward on their tongues, but flowed faster and stronger as the heat and light blossomed across the room. Sonia's pale hair whipped about her face as if trying to take flight, and the magician's face was slick with sweat. Callum staggered, and I saw one of his feet sinking into the floor. He lurched back, pulling it free, but his other foot sank as well, and now he was mired in place, his face pale and taut. I arched and twisted, but Long-hair held me firmly down, his grip panic-tight. I could smell the fear on him. I had the idea that he'd never thought anything would actually happen, that it was just a bit of fun, playing at raising the dead and catching a few cats. No one ever really thinks *what if this works.* It's stories to tell at the pub and games for children.

The floor within the circle was becoming translucent, and I could see something beyond it, something vaguely humanoid but with the proportions all off, the head too big and the body too skeletal, pale and gleaming. It pawed at Callum, the pointed fingertips almost touching his sinking boots, and he fell back, trying to kick himself away. His hands sank into the floor too, and now he was trapped like a fly on sticky paper, twisting and wriggling to pull free as the thing on the other side scrabbled toward him eagerly.

I gave one final buck against Long-hair's hands, but he wasn't budging. And I didn't know what I was going to do if I got free anyway. Run around screaming "the earth is falling"? I mean, it was as accurate as anything, I supposed—

A movement caught my eye. Everyone was watching the thin patch in dimensions growing ever more fragile in front of us, but a small green scrap eased itself out from under one of the cabinets and slithered rapidly across the floor toward me. I stared at Green Snake. He lifted his head for an instant, meeting my eye with that flat stare that could've meant anything, but at that particular moment I rather felt he was expressing a certain level of disdain for how I was handling the situation. Then he shot to my side and buried his fangs in Long-hair's hand.

Long-hair shrieked and let go of me, and I catapulted myself toward the circle.

"*Gobs, no!*" Callum shouted, but I was already crashing to a stop again. The heat was too intense, and I could smell burning cat hair.

The magician clicked his fingers at Sonia, still chanting, and she lifted her lip in a snarl but stopped her recitation long enough to shout, "Get hold of that bloody cat!" The pressure in the room dropped a notch but didn't falter, the spell still rolling across us like a tide.

"Sorry!" Long-hair yelped, and made a grab for me. Green Snake had already turned his attention to Neckless, winding his way up the man's leg in search of delicate regions to put a tooth to. Neckless screeched in alarm, and the big she-cat writhed in his grip, abandoning her efforts of escape in favour of trying to shred his arms. I dodged Long-hair, giving him a good belt across the hand as I jumped away, and flung myself at Neckless' face.

It doesn't matter how dedicated a necromancer flunky you are, or what terrors of the nether realms you're prepared to meet, when you find yourself with a snake halfway up your thighs, a cat in your face and another snarling like a dirt bike in your hands, you're going to rethink your life choices. Neckless let go of the big she-cat and reared to his feet before I could reach him, shaking Green Snake off and staggering into Cerys in the process. She cried out as she stumbled toward the circle, dropping Charlie and Harvey, and in that moment the balance tipped, and the whole room descended into chaos. Cerys fell to her hands and knees just short of the runes, and a flare of heat set her long hair smoking. She screamed and scrambled back in a half-crouch, batting desperately at her smouldering locks, and ran straight into Sonia. Sonia shoved her off, trying to find the rhythm of the chant again, but it was enough that her hold on the dentist faltered. He shot to his feet and bolted for the stairs.

"*Stop!*" Sonia roared, one hand out, and the dentist stopped as if he'd hit a wall, crashing back onto his bum with blood splattering from his nose.

I charged the magician, the big she-cat already a pace ahead of me, and he lashed out at her with one hand, still keeping up his chant. It was feeding back from the walls, as if the house itself were repeating and echoing his summons, throbbing in the air until I could feel it reverberating in my bones. He caught the she-cat a glancing blow, but she barely hit the floor before she was up again, and I tore my way up his legs with my ears back and every claw out. He grabbed hold of me, trying to pull me loose, but now the she-cat was on his other leg, and he staggered back from the circle as he tried to fend us both off. He was still chanting, though, his voice strained but steady, his eyes fixed on the summoning ring.

"Get these bloody animals under control!" Sonia

shouted. Charlie and Harvey were swinging from her skirt, trying to find somewhere to get their teeth into among the swathes of material, and she batted at them furiously, blood staining her hands and the cloth. Green Snake had bitten Muscles and he'd dropped Astrid, although he still had hold of Tristan, who was refusing to be dropped and had his teeth buried in the man's huge forearm. Neckless chased Astrid across the room, but before he could even get close she shot straight between Pink's legs, making her squawk and spin around with a furiously growling Mitzi dangling by the scruff of her neck from one hand. Gordie, who had been cuddled happily into the crook of the woman's free arm, blinked up at her blearily, then turned his head and casually buried his snaggly old teeth in the soft skin of her biceps. She shrieked and dropped both him and Mitzi, and Astrid kept right on going. She leaped at Sonia and wrapped her front paws around one of the necromancer's arms, then applied her teeth and back legs with equal enthusiasm.

"Old Ones take you!" Sonia flung her arm out, sending Astrid spinning away and almost into the circle.

"Help me!" I shouted to Mitzi. "We have to shut the bloody magician up!"

Sonia took up the chant again, ignoring the two cats clawing their way up her skirt, the blood from Astrid's attack spiralling off her forearm and fleeing to join the runes. The room vibrated like glass on the verge of shattering. The dentist scrambled to his feet and made another run for the stairs, and I was dimly aware of the door slamming open above as I clawed desperately at the magician, scrambling up to his waist. He finally grabbed me, ripping me clear and flinging me away like I was nothing more than a nuisance, barely worth the attention. I hit the ground hard, sliding on my side and fetching up against Muscles. I bit him, since I was there, and he howled, still trying to shake off Tristan. Green Snake gave me a satisfied nod, then set off toward the magician with a determined set to his wriggle and the front of his body high off the ground, like he was pointing his own route out with his nose.

Tristan finally let go, gave Muscles a well-judged belt, then roared, "Cats, *attack!*"

"Kind of what we're doing," I said, and threw myself back toward the magician, who was wrestling with the she-cat, still managing some garbled version of chanting, although there was quite a bit of swearing mixed in with it. Not that it seemed to matter – the room, the house, the very *air* had taken up the spell and was casting it back and forth, power running like waves from one side of the cellar to the other, growing stronger with every surge.

"*Get out!*" Callum shouted, startling me. I'd half forgotten he was still trapped in the centre of the circle. Now I spun toward him. He was on all fours, his hair slicked to his face, staring at me, and that distorted, luminous image danced beneath him like a reflection with a life of its own. Life, and hunger. "*Everyone out!* It needs lives, remember? *Don't let it have them!*"

"It's not an it!" the magician shouted. "That's my son!"

"It's not!" Callum almost screamed. "It's not *anything like* Ifan!"

I looked at the glittering figure still trying to force its way through the membrane between the walls, twisting and stuttering in and out of reality, and said, "We're not leaving you."

"No cat left behind!" Tristan shouted. *"Take down the magician!"*

"It's too late," Callum said, his eyes on me. "The charm's got its own momentum. You can't stop it. *Run.*"

I stared back at him. "There has to be a way."

"There's not," Sonia said. She had Charlie and Harvey by the scruffs of their necks, although there was blood on her face as well as her arms. She grinned at me. "It's happening. They're coming."

"Ifan, you mean," the magician said. "*Ifan's* coming."

"I told you," Callum said. "It's not Ifan."

"Of course it is," the magician said. "I *talked* to him—"

"None so blind as those who won't see," Sonia said. "You didn't even want proof, did you? Didn't even care."

The magician stared at her. The she-cat was hanging from one of his arms, gnawing and kicking and emitting the sort of sounds that'd send an alley tom back the way he'd come, and Green Snake had his fangs in his ankle, but he ignored them both. "But—"

"It's not him!" Callum bellowed. *"Get out! Everyone out!"*

The runes pulsed and roared with the rhythm of the summoning spell, tearing blood off the injured and slurping it into the charms, the earth within the circle burning with pale, fierce heat. It was like standing in the sands of the desert as they combusted around us, and it felt as if Callum should've been alight, but all he did was tear his arms loose and struggle to his feet, boots still sinking into the treacherous ground and sweat running down his cheeks.

"Gobs, go," he said, his voice barely audible. "Please."

"Bollocks to *that,*" I snarled, and ran for the circle. I didn't know how I was going to get across it, or what I was going to do if I did, but I gathered myself into a leap, flinging myself at the flames as Callum shouted at me to stop and the heat felt like it'd flay the flesh from me, never mind the fur.

And there was an almighty *phhhwhumpf,* and steam exploded all around me, still hot enough to feel like my eyes were cooking in their sockets, but I wasn't about to be set alight anymore. The room vanished under a cloud of water vapour and I shot through the runes, skidding on the hot, weirdly malleable floor inside. It gave under my paws like jelly, and Green Snake scooted out of the murk after me, twisting and writhing wildly. For a moment I thought he was cooking, and I lunged to pull him clear of the runes, but then I saw he was rubbing himself across them, wearing at the markings. He was trying to break the summoning circle.

"Break the runes!" I shouted. "Hurry!" I scrabbled at the dirt next to Green Snake, and the big she-cat loomed out of the mist with Duds beside her, bare-chested and sodden and wielding a bucket of water. He dumped it over the smouldering runes and turned around in time to hit Muscles on the head with the empty bucket while the she-cat started digging next to me, her ears back. All around us rose shouts and confusion.

"… unfair treatment of prisoners …"

"Gordie! *Gordie!*"

"You'll be hearing from my lawyer about that walker—"

"If you just surrender everyone will be treated fairly—"

"Who let the living bloody dead in here?" Sonia demanded. "And – Old Ones *take* you, damn cats!"

There was a yowl and a thud, and one of the brothers shouted, "That's my bro! I'll have your *eyes* out, you necro toadstool!"

The yelp from the same general direction led me to believe that he was making good on the threat.

"Ifan!" the magician shouted. "*Ifan!*"

"It's not Ifan!" Callum shouted back. "Stop this! Stop this before it gets through!"

The fog was lifting, turning a weird rosy colour, like a sun was coming up somewhere behind it. I glimpsed Neckless, his hands over his head while the scary dinner lady laid about him with what appeared to be the leg bones of one of the skeletons from upstairs – at least, that's where I hoped she'd got them – and Long-hair vanishing up the stairs closely followed by Pink, neither of them looking back. Cerys was trying to go the same way, but the colonel was threatening her with another leg bone and Astrid and Mitzi were making darting attacks at her ankles, and she didn't seem to know which way to turn. Muscles was flat on the ground in a corner with the one-armed man sitting on his back and Duds still hitting him happily with his bucket.

"Gobs, go." Callum was suddenly beside me, scooping me up and shoving me across the fading runes.

"No! We're almost through! It's almost broken!"

The she-cat snarled at Callum as he reached for her, and kept digging. I joined her again.

"Gobs, you have to go! It's coming through." He

pointed behind him at the twisting skin of the circle. There was a tear in it, small but unmistakable, like the first crack in an eggshell, and that warm, glowing light was pouring out. It should have been the promise of new days and spring blossoms, all soft pinks and oranges, but all I could think of was raging infections of the sort that ate your limbs off.

"I'm not leaving you," I hissed, and next to me Green Snake kept wriggling back and forth across the runes, twisting desperately around on himself.

"No one's leaving," Sonia said. "They're almost here."

"They?" the magician demanded. "What do you mean, *they?* What've you done?"

"We," she said, and grinned at him across the murky room. "What have *we* done. Or summoned, rather."

"What are you *talking* about? It's Ifan! We're getting Ifan back!" But he didn't sound so sure of himself, and with that weird light everywhere I didn't see how anyone could be expecting anything good.

"Oh, Ifan, Ifan, bloody *Ifan.* 'Oh, I just want my son back. Oh, I need my heir, we can start again and it'll all be *so much better.*'" She mimicked his voice with her face twisted, then snorted. "When did magicians get so damn *boring?* All that sentiment and desire, Lewis. You should know better. "

Lewis looked at the circle, and Callum and I stared back at him while the she-cat and Green Snake kept working at the runes. "I spoke to him," he said, almost to himself. "I did."

There was a moment's silence, then Sonia gave the sort of world-weary, look-what-I-have-to-deal-with sigh that managers have been giving for centuries, and said, "Just finish the damn ritual, Lewis. Before things get messy."

"Right," the magician said. "Yes. But we're having words after this." And he started to chant.

"You *suppurating yam!*" I bawled at him. "Stop this! *Stop it!*"

"Gobbelino," Callum said, drawing my attention back to him. "You have to go. *Please.*"

I looked up at him, his jaw tight and those anxious lines drawing his forehead together, and said, "Sod that. I feel an overwhelming urge to bite someone, and this seems like a good place for it."

Behind him, the skin of dimensions tore with the sound of the world ending, and something stepped through amid the light of a thousand apocalyptic sunrises.

20

SOME LIGHT POSSESSION

CALLUM TRIED TO GIVE ME A FINAL PUSH AWAY, AND I stumbled back a step or two, but kept my eyes on the figure. We were all looking. You couldn't not. It drew the eye the way a misplaced tile disrupting the perfect pattern of a long smooth wall does, or a rock protruding out of a still pond, or a broken, bloodied bottle in the middle of a sweep of spotless carpet. It didn't belong. It didn't fit. It was *wrong,* and looking at it made you feel that the world was tilting out of kilter, but at the same time you couldn't look away.

The creature didn't climb out of the earth or even shimmer into being. It just stepped through from below the surface of the circle straight onto the top of it, as if dimensions didn't work the same way where it came from. It still had that roughly human shape, but it was hard to be sure of detail. My eyes watered from trying to look at it, and when I glanced around I saw even Sonia was looking at the air above the thing's head rather than directly at it. It dripped with rosy light that pulsed beneath its skin – or *was* its skin, for all I knew. Maybe it was made of the stuff, formed on some base unit entirely different to what formed us. I tried to get a whiff of it, to understand it better, but it was like sniffing the void – flat and alien and terrifying. And *powerful.*

"It can't be," Lewis muttered, breaking a shaky silence. "That's impossible."

"Nothing's impossible," Sonia said, and dropped to her knees. "The Old Ones return. They walk among us."

More silence, then Duds said, "Is she talking about us?" and the colonel shushed him.

"*Bollocks,*" Tristan announced. "You can't go about raising *gods.* I'm not having it. Besides, we're still here. Didn't you need nine cats with nine lives to bring it through?"

The figure turned to look at him – or turned vaguely toward him. I couldn't make out any features.

"Nice one," Astrid said. "Now you've reminded it."

"They were never gods," Sonia said, her voice distant. "They were both more and less than that. Necromancers who truly transcended death."

"What have you *done?*" the magician asked. "What *is* this? You can't just— You didn't tell me this is what we were doing!"

"Didn't you read the small print?" Astrid asked. "*Always* read the small print. Everyone knows that."

"He probably thought he was better than small print," Mitzi said. "I bet he doesn't read instructions, either." The two she-cats shared an agreeable huff, while my fur did its best to separate from my skin.

"Oh, for the gods' sakes," Sonia said. "Why are you *complaining?* Look at what we've done!"

"But I never agreed to this," Lewis insisted. "This is … that *can't* be an Old One! It can't!"

"And yet it is. And they will bring your precious son back, if you serve them." Sonia's voice was reverent.

"No. No, this is all wrong. We need to reverse—" He was cut off as she raised a hand to him almost absently. He grunted and fell to his hands and knees.

"Now we come into our own," she whispered. "Now we rise."

"You're not bloody bread dough," Charlie said. "What's one orange alien going to do?"

I looked at Callum. "Get out of there."

"I can't." He nodded at his knees, and I saw that they were still trapped in the dirt, as if the floor inside the circle had become some very stiff, crumbly sort of mud pool. There was blood on his jeans, and I couldn't imagine how he'd even made it across the short distance to reach me. He shuffled a bit to prove his point, and the earth cracked and reformed around him, as if he were a tree trying to uproot itself.

"Fine. I'm coming back in." I started forward, and the big she-cat grabbed me by the scruff of the neck like I was a kitten, holding me in place.

"Hey," I managed, half-strangling. "Unacceptable. Everyone needs to keep off the neck."

"Keep him there," Callum said to the she-cat, and she growled agreeably.

"Callum. *Callum!"*

He ignored me and twisted in the cracking earth,

dragging himself around until he could face the Old One. I couldn't tell if it was looking at him or not, but suddenly it wasn't *over there,* it was *right here,* leaning over Callum without seeming to have moved.

"Lewis!" I shouted, as well as I could with the bloody she-cat still leaning on me. "Stop it! That thing has to go back! It *has* to! It's nothing to do with Ifan! You *know* this! Put it down!"

"I can't … I don't know …" He half raised a hand, and Sonia clicked her fingers with a hiss. He screamed and pitched sideways onto the floor.

"You think I didn't take a drop of your blood for a little insurance?" she asked. "No one's going anywhere. The Glorious One will take its vessel, and then it will take all the lives it needs to sustain the transition."

"Glorious my fluffy tail," Harvey said. He was limping as he approached the edge of the circle. "Cats put you death-dealing lot down once. We can do it again."

Sonia barely glanced at him. "I doubt you're up to the task, mittens."

"Mittens, she says." Charlie ambled over to his brother. "Like it's an insult to be compared to a highly useful article of clothing."

"I think it kind of is, C."

"Only if we decide it is."

They nodded at each other, and I strained to pull myself out from under the she-cat, but it was like trying to break free of a large, determined beanbag. So I just shouted, "Stop blathering and *do something!*"

"Just get out," Callum said. His voice was flat and furious. "I'll hold it as long as I can."

"You *can't!* It's going to rip your damn soul out!" I could hear the yowl on the edge of my words, but it hardly mattered.

"Get out!"

The Old One – the thing, the ancient almost-god, the damn necromancers' sweet dream – reached for Callum as if it was going to haul him to his feet by the front of his hoody, and its hand slid smoothly into his chest. He screamed, his back arching, then lashed out. I expected his hand just to pass through the thing, or bounce off it, but it connected with a strange hollow *thock* that echoed somewhere beyond hearing. The Old One lurched back, and the orange light intensified to bright yellow, making me squint. Callum clawed at the ground, pulling his legs a few centimetres clear, then the thing was on him again, hands diving into him.

"Where is my son?" Lewis bellowed, struggling to his feet. He flung a hand out at Sonia, and power surged across the room. She fell back with a startled yelp. "Give me my son!"

"I don't know where he is," she shouted back. "Get *down,* you miserable spell-caster! I have your blood! I *command* you!"

"You can *choke* on your damn commands! You think you can hold *me?*" Lewis roared. "This is *my house,* necromancer! You stand on *my land!*"

Sonia snarled and raised her torn, bleeding hands, and Lewis did something fancy, and abruptly there was an explosion of power crackling across the ceiling of the cellar, two forces meeting and combining and shattering against each other, curling around the overhead lights, making them spark and glow brighter, flooding the whole place with stadium-level lighting.

"Ooh," Tristan's army said appreciatively, and Neckless bolted for the stairs, knocking Duds over on the way. Cerys took her chance and legged it after him, leaving Muscles screaming for help behind them, and the colonel and the dinner lady shouting dire threats as they helped Duds to his feet.

The Old One paid no attention to the theatrics going on outside the circle. It clawed at Callum with both hands as if it intended to open him up like a roast chicken, and Callum gave another of those agonised screams. I put every scrap of strength I had into my legs and *bucked.* The she-cat slid off me with a startled grunt, and I scuttled forward, tearing the skin of my neck out of her teeth. I plunged over the runes, leaped to Callum's shoulder, and flung myself at the Old One without thinking.

Some things you just don't stop to consider. It's best not to.

It was like diving into the centre of an intelligent ice storm. I didn't bounce off, or even collide softly with it the way Callum's fist had. I sank into the thing, warm light spearing through me even though I squeezed my eyes shut against it. I clamped my jaw down on a yowl as impossible cold bit through my bones, gnawing with the sort of terrible, furious hunger that can never be eased. It was the hunger of dying stars, of collapsing worlds, of eternity for an end, of the seas for the land and the stars for darkness. It could tear you apart, that hunger, and I wasn't going to hang around to give it the chance to do so.

I exploded out of the thing, and it didn't even turn to

look at me. Or maybe it was looking at me the whole time. Just because it had a vaguely head-shaped bit didn't mean that's where its eyes were. I gathered my legs under me for another assault, but before I could leap Pru sailed past me, her flanks scored with bloody gouges, and flung herself at the Old One in a fury of ripping claws.

"*Pru!*" I shouted, and followed her.

The horrified inertia broke, and the other cats poured into the circle, while above us magic crackled and spat and the room surged with power as Sonia and Lewis battled across the circle. We surrounded the Old One, trying to drive it back from Callum, but it was like attacking a luminous jellyfish. Any scrap our teeth tore away just drifted back to the whole. The stuff it was made of gave way under our paws and reformed after we passed, and it paid as much attention to us as humans do to feathers in the wind. We hissed and spat and raged and tore, and it didn't even bother to push us away.

And yet somehow Callum's blows landed. He was still mired in the unforgiving earth, but he'd managed to pull himself free to the mid-calf. He shoved the thing back, his fists sinking into it but somehow finding something to push against, forcing it away over and over again. He was sweating and panting, his skinny shoulders high, and I shouted, "His feet! Dig him out!"

We abandoned the Old One and flung ourselves at Callum's legs instead, clearing the sticky, membranous dirt away from him. He kicked and struggled, trying to pull himself free at the same time as still swinging clumsy blows at the brilliant creature in front of him, and suddenly one leg was clear, his boot lost to some other realm. He threw everything behind one furious punch, driving the Old One back and to whatever passed as its knees, then he braced himself on the ground and pulled his other foot free.

"Go!" he shouted at us, scooping up Gordie, who was still pawing happily at the ground, nowhere near his feet. "Out of the circle! Out!"

We bolted. There was a flash of heat behind us, and I glanced back, expecting the Old One to be reaching out its greedy hands for Callum, but it was still struggling to its feet, incandescent as an emergency flare. It wasn't quite *here* as a creature yet, still nothing more than a single-minded drive to take a vessel.

Callum jumped the runes, stumbling to one knee on the far side, and we surged after him, spinning to see the Old One walk to the edge of the circle. It tipped its head down to the markings and started to drift forward.

"We broke it," Astrid said. "We broke the circle. It can come through."

"Old Ones take us," Tristan muttered.

"I think this one might," I said, taking a step in front of Callum.

Then Green Snake slithered neatly across the gap and lay there, his chin firmly on the ground. There was a startlingly loud *snap*, and the runes started to glow. So did Green Snake, but he just flattened himself a little more tightly against the earth. I thought I could see his ribs through the soft pattern of his scales.

The Old One stopped, still with its head tipped toward the ground, then tried moving forward again. It hit Green Snake and came to a shuddering halt. Green Snake hissed.

"No!" Callum said, starting forward.

"Don't! It can't get out," I said.

"But Green Snake …"

"We really have to give him a name," I said, staring at him. He tilted his head slightly, without lifting his chin. The Old One tried getting across the runes just behind the snake, but the circle snapped and twisted, pushing the thing back. The orangey colour of the Old One intensified, and I could feel the icy hunger of it shivering across the room toward us even over the heat of the runes.

"I like that snake," Pru said.

"Me, too," I agreed, examining her.

"He's good with dogs," she added.

So that was how she'd got away. I looked at Callum. "Okay, it's trapped in there. How do we send it back where it came from?"

"You're asking me?"

"You were the only one who could do anything to it."

"I don't know," he said, and Sonia gave a sudden shriek, falling to her knees as the magician's power surged across the room.

"Give me my son," he roared, taking a step forward.

"I don't know where he is!" she shouted back, clawing at her own hands to start the blood flowing again.

"You *used* me." His voice dropped to a hiss, and he made a quick gesture at the necromancer. She snarled with pain, dropping back onto her elbows and glaring up at him.

"You couldn't *wait* to help. Anything for your little lost son." She spat the words. "Maybe the Old One will bring him back for you, if they feel generous. But you need to kneel before them. Kneel before your god!"

"I do not kneel," Lewis said, his voice flat and furious. "I will *never* kneel." His eyes were fixed on the necromancer as he stepped toward her, and I watched with a numb sort of horror as his purple-slippered foot came down on the runes.

"*No!*" Callum shouted, and dumped Gordie unceremoniously on the floor, charging around the circle. Sonia gave a shout of triumph, balled her bloodied hands into fists, and *pulled*.

Invisible hands swept around the magician, and he fell into the circle.

CALLUM SPRINTED around the circle with his tattered coat swirling about him, skidding to a stop as close to the magician as he could get. "Get out!" he shouted, leaning dangerously far over the runes, one hand outstretched. "Hurry!"

The magician floundered toward him, swimming in the sticky earth, reaching for his hand with wide, terrified eyes. The Old One flashed across the space, one moment toeing the runes around Green Snake, the next leaning over Lewis.

"*Come on!*" Callum waved desperately.

"I'm trying!" Lewis clawed at the earth, cringing away from the creature. "Help me!"

"Callum!" I shouted, sprinting around the circle after him. "Get back! Leave the bloody turnip!"

"Please," Lewis begged, stretching toward Callum.

"I'm here." Callum teetered on the edge of the runes, straining to reach the magician's hand. Their fingers brushed over each other, caught on the tips, then Lewis screamed as the Old One shoved its luminous hands into his back.

"Lewis!" Callum started over the circle and I flung myself at his legs, trying to drive him back.

"Don't! It's too late!"

And it was. The Old One pulled the magician's body apart effortlessly, opening some hole in the back of him that wasn't in the flesh, but in something deeper and more vital. Lewis screamed again, clawing at the Old One, but his hands passed through it just as our paws had done, and the creature pulled the gap wider then stepped into it, the way a human might step into a costume. It wriggled a little, making space for itself, and Lewis' screams reached a pitch that tore at the heart.

Callum stepped over me and into the circle.

"No!" I bolted after him, clawing at his tattered jeans. "No, Callum—"

"Get out," he said, and grabbed the Old One around its neck. His hands sank into it, but somewhere they found purchase and stopped. *"Out.* This is not your place."

He pulled, and the Old One clung onto Lewis, trying to claw its way deeper into him. Lewis had stopped screaming – I couldn't tell if he was dead or *gone* or just passed out – and his body flopped unpleasantly, the creature sticking half out of his back like some sort of grafted tree.

"Callum," I hissed, every hair on my back standing to attention. "He's gone, leave it."

"Out," Callum snarled again, and *heaved*. The Old One let go and slid out of Lewis effortlessly, faster than seemed possible, like elastic recoiling. It landed on Callum, wrapping itself around him and sinking into him, moving with that same effortless speed. Callum cried out, trying to push it away, but whatever purchase he'd had on it was gone. It was moving too quickly, eating into him, *absorbing* into him like liquid into a sponge, and Sonia was chanting some delighted, raging prayer from outside the circle, and cats were shouting, and one of the veterans was saying something about unacceptable forms of punishment, and there was nothing, *nothing* I could do as some ancient, unknown *thing* swallowed my partner whole.

I clawed at Callum's jeans helplessly, feeling the fabric of the Old One part under my claws, and he managed to say, "Gobs, run," then his eyes rolled back and he collapsed to the ground.

Everything became still. Even Sonia fell silent. No one spoke, and the only sound was the persistent hiss and spit of the runes. I nudged Callum's arm with my nose, smelling that vast, hungry cold, searching for the cigarettes and sorrow scent of him underneath, lingering like a shadow on the edge of day.

"Callum?" I whispered.

For a moment there was nothing, then he sat up. There was no preamble, he just rose to sitting as if lifted by an invisible hand, his eyes still closed. I stared up at him, waiting. I already knew he wasn't there. Not in any way it counted.

Then he opened his eyes, and unpleasantly candy floss–hued light washed from them.

"*Kneel, organic things,*" he said, and rose to his feet with the same spooky effortlessness. "*Kneel before your god.*"

21

EVERY TRUE GOD SHOULD BE AN INFLUENCER

"Glorious one," Sonia cried, and threw herself to the floor. "We've waited so long!"

"Open the circle."

"At once, at once—" She crouched to place her hands on the runes, and the shocked stillness shattered. The colonel shouted for her to stand down, and seven cats shot across the cellar and descended on the necromancer. I was still staring at the thing that had been Callum, and Gordie was purring happily as he rubbed his face against Muscles' cheek where he lay trapped under both the one-armed man and Duds. Muscles wasn't even struggling anymore, just staring at the Old One with a look on his face that said very clearly that this was not what he'd been expecting. Sonia shrieked as the cats attacked her, rolling away from the circle as she tried to dislodge them, but that's a lot of feline fury to extricate yourself from, and she wasn't doing it any time soon.

"Callum," I said, pawing at his jeans. "Callum, are you

in there?" That cold void scent filled my nose, mixing with the burned blood stink of the runes.

"Ugh. Do not touch me, organic thing." The creature in Callum's body tried to kick me away, but it hadn't got the hang of human physics yet, and stumbled as I sidestepped easily.

"Callum," I tried again, and it turned away from me. I looked up at it, Callum's head lolling on its shoulders, his fingers twitching, and for a moment I just wanted the porous earth to open below me, so I wouldn't have to see this parody of him in front of me. But I couldn't look away. Wouldn't. If that was all I could do, I'd do it. I wouldn't look away. I wouldn't turn my back and let him be swallowed alone. I'd bear witness, even if my chest felt like one of the dogs had hold of it and I could barely find breath in the sticky confines of the cellar.

"Let me out, organic things," the creature said to the room in general, but the only person who seemed likely to do that was currently still tussling with cats.

"Rav, break the circle!" she shouted at Muscles.

"Stand down, that man," the colonel said, shaking a leg bone threateningly.

"Yeah, I'm good," Muscles said, and worked one hand free to scratch Gordie's chin. He purred.

"I grow impatient," the Old One declared.

"Callum," I said. "If you're still in there, pick your nose or something."

The colonel and the dinner lady had crossed the cellar to Sonia, but they couldn't actually do much, given the cats swarming over her. At least she was otherwise occupied for the moment.

"Callum," I said again.

The creature didn't look at me, but one hand jerked up, pawed at its face, and dropped again. Its expression twisted, then it said, *"Let me out or there shall be consequences."* But it didn't sound as sure as before, the words less booming pronouncement and more plaintive request.

The colonel lunged at Sonia between a gap in the cats, brandishing her leg bone, and the necromancer flung an arm out. The colonel staggered back a few paces, using the bone as a crutch, and Sonia's face contorted with effort. She was panting, blood smeared across her hands and arms, and her exhaustion was almost palpable.

"Come on, Callum," I said. "Don't hang around being polite about things. Just kick the bloody monster out!"

The Old One contorted, body staggering around to face me, and it pointed at me, that ugly, glossy light curling around its fingertips. *"I weary of you, organic thing."* Power surged within the circle, but the creature's arm jerked off to the side as it released its spell, and there was a puff of dirt and a whiff of ozone next to me. That terrible weight was still on my chest and belly, but I could breathe.

"Stop messing about," I said. *"Get it out."*

"Enough," the thing said, and reached for me with both hands, its movement smoother but still uncoordinated. I almost thought I could hear Callum screaming behind the strange flatness of his own face for me to get out of the way as control of his body slipped further and further from him.

I backed up, looking at the Callum-thing's twitching

fingers and said, for no reason that I could think of, "Want a cig?"

The thing paused. *"What is this, organic thing? Is it a sacrifice?"*

"An offering," I said. "Very traditional."

"Show me."

"Ah – right. One moment." Well, what the hell. While the thing was thinking about cigarettes, it wasn't thinking about tearing the world apart, or evicting Callum from his own body, so why not? "Try your coat pocket."

"My pockets?" The thing looked down at itself. *"What are these?"*

"Seriously? Did you not have pockets back in the day?"

It gave me a disapproving look. *"I am very old and very wise. I do not remember these pockets, so I imagine they were unimportant."*

"Pockets are very important," the colonel said from where she was still waiting to take a shot at the necromancer, who had rolled further from the circle. "That's why there are never decent ones in women's clothing. There's no telling what we could do with decent pockets."

The Old One looked at her curiously as she waved to the scary dinner lady, who lowered her leg bone and stepped tentatively toward the circle, digging in the pocket of her apron.

"I do not understand this."

"Me either," the colonel said. "I think it's a conspiracy, personally."

The dinner lady stopped at the edge of the circle, lighting a cigarette with a bright pink lighter. Her fingers were shaking.

"There we go," I said, before the pocket debate could derail things too much. "Have a nice cigarette."

"Don't listen to him, Glorious One!" Sonia shrieked. Duds and the one-armed man had abandoned Muscles (admittedly, he didn't seem to need much guarding anymore – he was sitting up with Gordie cradled protectively in his lap, still staring at the Callum-thing in horrified astonishment). The two veterans had managed to get hold of the necromancer and were pinning her to the floor while the cats circled around her in a growling guard. "He's a cat! He's the enemy!"

"Are you?" the creature asked me.

"Well, I am a cat. The rest's open to interpretation. Have a cigarette."

The creature's fingers twitched toward it, then drew back. *"This is a trap. Cats were our enemies. This I remember."*

"It's just a cigarette." I couldn't have said why it seemed so important that the thing have it, but it did. It was in the twitch of the creature's fingers, some Callum memory trapped in the craving for nicotine. "No trap."

The thing bent at the waist and examined the cigarette the dinner lady was still holding out cautiously. *"How does one have it, organic thing?"*

"Don't touch it!" Sonia screamed, and Tristan shoved a paw in her mouth, which sent the scream up several octaves. The creature didn't look around, and I watched the smoke from the cigarette drift toward it. It sniffed.

"Is it on fire?"

"It's meant to be."

"And one sniffs the— Oh, *get out* you freaky *monster!"* Callum roared suddenly, straightening up and grabbing at

his chest as if he were about to do a male stripper routine. His hoody tore at the neck, but something else tore too, and feathers of orange light washed around him. He snatched the cigarette off the dinner lady as she jumped back, and jammed it in his mouth. *"No organic thing I do not—* Out! *Out!"*

There was a surge, a sudden flood of burnt yellow and orange, then Callum was staggering back, the cigarette still in his mouth, wrestling with the fluid, glowing form of the Old One. It twisted and spilled through his hands, tendrils wrapping around his head and neck, trying to claw its way back in while he struggled to keep hold of it.

"Callum!" I yelled, and flung myself at the Old One like it'd do any good. I flew through the bone-crushing cold effortlessly, and the thing stopped trying to get back into Callum, twisting wildly in his grip instead as it tried to flee. He flailed at it, balling it into some gunky mass in his hands as it strained away from him.

"Let go!" I shouted. "Let go and get out of the circle!"

"No," he started, and the thing abruptly slithered away from him, falling through his fingers like an egg yolk and diving into the magician's body. The body snapped and jerked, then surged to its feet, power snapping in its hands.

"Oh, hairballs," I said, as Lewis spun around and fixed us with rosy eyes.

"Bollocks," Callum agreed, and took a step toward the creature.

"This is better," it said. *"The power is closer here."* It raised one hand and all of us – Tristan's veterans, and the cats outside the circle, and Sonia, and Callum and me – spun

across the room like dandelion fluff. I slammed into a wall and fell straight down into a sink, which seemed reasonable, until the dinner lady landed on the worktop and slid on top of me, almost squishing me, and we both yowled. I shoved my head through the gap between her bony hip and the sink and stared out at the Old One. Green Snake was still clinging desperately to the runes, but as I watched the magician-thing flicked his fingers and the snake spun into the air and across the room, twisting helplessly.

"Better," it said again, and I craned my neck to look at Callum, who was slumped on the floor below me. He took the cigarette out of his mouth, looked at it, then put it back again and inhaled deeply.

"I knew there was no point quitting," he said. "No effect whatsoever on life expectancy. I think it bought me five minutes, even."

"I bet a cup of tea would've worked just as well," I said, and he looked up at me and grinned, a tired yet perfectly Callum grin, and I really regretted the fact that we were about to be devoured by an ancient almost-god. It seemed unfair.

The thing in the magician's body looked around at us all, slumped against walls or sprawled on worktops, and said, *"Organic things, offer yourselves for my delectation."*

"Nope," Charlie said. "Pass."

"This is what we get for listening to Duds," the colonel said. "I thought we were rescuing a few cats from a dog-fighting ring."

"Well, that's what he said," Duds replied, pointing at Tristan.

"To be fair, I hadn't anticipated the whole soul-eating situation," Tristan said. "And I thought the necromancer angle might take too long to explain."

"Silence. You will not talk."

"Good luck with that," Callum said, pushing his hair back off his face and looking at his feet. "They never shut up for me." He wriggled his toes. "I liked those boots." He was down to one sock with a hole in the toe, his other foot bare and bloodied.

Sonia stumbled forward a step and dropped to her knees. "Glorious One, I have brought you all these lives to feed on—"

"Hold up," the one-armed man said. "That's a bit much."

"Shut up and accept your fate," she snapped.

"I will have this one first," the creature said, and pointed at Callum. *"He irritates me."*

"You're not the only one," I said, hooking my paws over the edge of the sink. "But no. Unacceptable."

"Shall I eat you first then, organic thing?"

"I'll give you hideous indigestion," I said. "Just FYI."

"I imagine he's right," Callum added. "It's just his nature."

"I'd be insulted if I didn't feel that giving indigestion to gods is quite a positive trait."

"I do not remember organic things talking so much. You should cower before me. Quietly."

"Times they are a-changing, rosy dude," Charlie said. "Or have a-changed. Whatever."

"Cower," the thing in the magician's body insisted, and

no one moved. It huffed and folded its arms. *"This is unacceptable. I shall exterminate you all."*

"Not seeing the difference between that and the devouring, to be honest," Pru said. "No real incentive there."

"The one offers the glory of serving me."

"Same end result," Astrid said.

"Is there an option three?" Harvey asked.

"Stop it!" Sonia hissed. "You will serve your god! *Kneel!*"

"Why don't you do it, then?" Mitzi asked. "Go on, you first."

The magician-thing turned to the necromancer expectantly. *"Offer yourself to me, organic thing."*

"Well, no, I'm your servant. Your priestess. I called you here – I opened the door for you!"

"Then it shall be an honour for you to be devoured first." The creature leaned forward slightly, then frowned with its new face. *"The movement does not work. This body is defective."*

"You have to use your feet," Muscles said helpfully, and the big she-cat hissed at him. "What? He's going to work it out anyway."

"Ah. I remember." It stepped forward, a little carefully, raising its feet too high, like a foal working out how its new muscles work. It crossed to the edge of the circle where Green Snake had been, examined it, then stepped out. There was no flash of power, no tearing of dimensions, not even a sudden dimming of the lights. The return to our fragile world of an Old One, one of the original necromancers, the

closest to a god a sorcerer has ever become, the purest form of power the world has ever seen, was entirely unremarkable. It nodded to itself, apparently satisfied.

Sonia scrambled to her feet and retreated, pressing her back to the bookshelves. "Glorious One, I offer you all these cats first. They have many lives for you to take." She waved the knife at the creature. "I even have a knife that will release them all at once!"

"Good Lord," Duds said. "I'm not liking the sound of that."

"Me either," Astrid said. She was crouching on the worktop above him. "Although I've only got one left, anyway."

"I desire a willing offering first." The Old One shook its limbs out. *"I am unsure of this body yet."* It stepped forward again, still moving in a way that was not quite right, as if it wasn't certain where or in which direction its limbs should bend. Sonia tried to scoot away, but the colonel poked her in the side with a femur.

"I don't *think* so," she said.

"You need a priestess!" Sonia yelped. "You need someone to serve you and help you in this new world!"

"All will worship me."

"Only if you're killing it on Instagram," Charlie said.

"True. You need to be an influencer," his brother said. "That's where the true religion is these days."

"What do these words mean?"

The two black and white cats looked at each other. "Stuff," Charlie said vaguely.

"Metrics?" Harvey offered.

"I will have your souls next. Priestess, come here." It beck-

oned imperiously, and Sonia was flung toward the creature, hitting the floor on her knees so hard that all the humans let out an *ooh* of sympathy.

"*No!* No, please, I have fought for your return, I have searched for the rituals, I have waited and hoped and opened the doors, I have found you the vessel, I—"

"*You serve me well.*" The magician-thing patted her awkwardly on the head, flattening her hair.

"Yes, yes, I do. And I will continue to do so, Glorious One. Just let me serve you."

It considered it, its hand still resting on her head, and I think we'd have just sat there and waited for it to make up its mind if it hadn't been for Green Snake. He came inching across the floor, covered in dirt and burned rune blood, looked at us all with his flat disapproving gaze, then buried his teeth in the magician-thing's ankle.

The Old One shrieked, power exploding from its hands, and Sonia threw herself to the ground, rolling away from it. The rosy essence of the Old One wavered, hauling itself half out of the magician's body as it tried to escape the snake, and Callum bounced to his feet and charged. He hit the magician in some sort of rugby tackle, carrying him back into the circle, shouting for someone to close it, and poor bloody Green Snake started slithering desperately back to his station. I hauled myself out of the sink and bolted after him, grabbing him up in my jaws as gently as I could and carrying him the rest of the way. Callum was still wrestling with the Old One, which was half in and half out of the magician's body, and the colonel hobbled after him on her leg bone crutch, shouting to her troops.

I dropped Green Snake next to the runes and stared at the circle. It was torn up in more places than the snake could mend, and I flopped myself down in one of the gaps, shouting for help as the snake settled himself nose to nose with me. We stared at each other as cats raced across the packed earth and Callum struggled with the magician, and for one moment I thought we'd do it, thought we were going to send the bloody thing back where it came from, then the earth *surged.*

I went flying, catching sight of the snake twisting in the air with me, and hit hard, claws out as I slowed my slide. I came up facing back into the centre of the room to see Sonia lift her bleeding hands from the ground, her face set in grim, exhausted angles. She staggered as she got up, almost falling, then helped the magician-thing to its feet. Callum lay in the circle with them, struggling to push himself up to his elbows, and the rest of us were sprawling across the room, the one-armed man nursing a bleeding nose and Duds clutching one leg as he rocked in agony.

"Enough!" Sonia shouted. "Enough of this! Glorious One, take what you need."

The thing in the magician's body cricked its neck, resettled itself, and said, *"This one first."* It leaned over Callum and laid its hands on his chest, and the orange light drifting in an aura around it grew stronger. *"Yes. This one has what I need."*

Callum cried out, trying to shove the thing away from him, but whatever strength he'd had before was gone. The creature didn't even flinch.

"Callum!" I bolted for the circle, but an invisible hand

grabbed me, sweeping me off the ground and clutching me so tightly around the middle that I could feel my ribs groaning. I yowled and twisted, fighting against something unseen while Sonia glared at me and Callum screamed, and the sunset light flooded the cellar, growing stronger and stronger as the Old One fed.

I caught sight of other cats hefted aloft, the humans writhing against bonds none of us could see, and even Green Snake was trapped. Sonia's face was white with effort, her bleeding hands shaking as she held them out like she was stopping traffic, but she wasn't faltering. I yowled for Callum, but I couldn't even hear myself over the roar of power and the pound of my own pulse, and the room was coming in and out of focus with every surge of blood.

We weren't going to make it.

We weren't going to *stop* it.

The Old One was feeding. It had risen.

22

HOLIDAY, INTERRUPTED

I WASN'T SURE HOW MUCH LONGER I'D STAY CONSCIOUS, OR even how much longer I *wanted* to stay conscious. Callum might have an annoying affection for ethics that seriously got in the way of us living our best life, but I had no desire to see him turned inside out by some ancient, pastel-coloured almost-god from a different realm. I also wasn't sure I was keen on being awake for my own turn at going inside out, and I certainly didn't want to discover what losing my remaining five lives all at once was going to feel like. One at a time had been unpleasant enough so far.

So I wasn't trying too hard to resist the swells of dimness coming over me as power surged within the cellar and the necromancer's grip constricted my breathing to almost nothing. But the sound of something *ripping,* a sharp hard noise that shook the cellar, did catch my attention. The grip on me faltered, and I sucked in a hacking breath that hurt my ribs, colour returning to the world. I squinted at the circle, the magician-thing still crouched over Callum, Sonia with her hands outstretched, but both of them seemed to have paused. She looked around, puzzled.

"What is this noise, priestess?"

"I'm not sure," she said.

"It is not time for my brethren to come through yet. We need more sustenance."

Oh, good. It had *brethren.*

"The door was only opened for you, Glorious One."

The creature straightened up, and Callum slumped, gasping.

"There is something coming." It took a step toward Sonia. *"What have you done, priestess? Do you betray me?"*

She backed away. The grip on me loosened a little further, but I couldn't find the energy to try and fight my way out.

"I haven't done anything!" she protested.

"Then I must feed quickly. I need to gain my strength." It looked back at Callum, who raised one hand weakly. I thought he was trying to fend the creature off, then he just made a rude gesture that the dentist probably would've recognised. A cat huffed with pained laughter – probably one of the brothers – then the air began to thicken with sticky magic again, and whatever little moment of grace we'd had passed. I went back to willing myself to pass out before I had to watch anyone get eaten.

And this time the noise *shattered* the room. It sounded as if the very fabric of the world was being rent apart, shredded to rags by something vast and furious as it hunted for what it needed. The magician-thing staggered away from Callum, and the unnaturally warm-edged light of the cellar was swallowed by a blast of smooth, sweet darkness shot through with the scent of salt winds and strange flowers, as if a tropical night had fallen suddenly, swallowing the creature's poisonous sunset.

The dark exploded across the cellar, and the invisible hand gripping me vanished. I crashed to the floor, half-expecting to plunge into soft sands or warm seas, and heard the others falling with yowls of surprise. Heat washed over me – a gentle, sun-warmed glow, not the infected flush of the other realm – then was gone, and the lights inset in the ceiling came back on, stuttering their cold illumination over the room and leaving it pale and human-looking and a little bereft.

I managed to get my front paws under me and lifted my head, blinking to clear my vision. Callum still sprawled on the ground. Sonia and the magician-thing were standing over him, but they were looking at someone else entirely.

They were looking at a barefoot man who'd just appeared in the circle, wearing sodden chequered shorts and an equally drenched Hawaiian shirt that clashed with the shorts hideously, but somehow looked as if it *intended* to clash, and was therefore entirely acceptable. His dark skin was dusted with sand, and his close-cropped hair was dripping wet, and he looked at the magician-thing and said, "What the hell have you *done?*"

No one spoke for a moment, then Callum rolled toward the man and said, "Ifan?"

"Huh," I said, at the same time as Pru said, "*Interesting.*"

Callum and Ifan stared at each other, ignoring us along with the startled necromancer and the Old One, then Ifan said, "That's not Dad, is it?"

Callum shook his head heavily.

"What is this new organic thing?" the Old One demanded. *"I do not like it."*

"Old Ones *take* you – what's going on?" Ifan asked.

"Pretty much that," Callum managed, going back to looking at the ceiling.

"Is that the one that's meant to be dead?" Tristan asked. "He's looking alright."

Sonia shoved her hands forward, her face drawn in tight lines. I could see her shaking from here. Not even a necromancer can keep using the power she was without rest, no matter how much they're willing to bleed – or to make others bleed.

Ifan made a quick, irritated gesture, and there was a sound like mud swallowing a stone. Sonia stumbled, and one of the lights smashed as the magic rebounded. I tried to get to my feet, but my legs seemed unwilling. Green Snake crept up next to me and rested his head on one of my front paws, so I stayed where I was. He deserved a break.

"Who did this?" Ifan asked Sonia. "Did *you* do this?"

She glared at him. "We worked together."

"I shall devour him," the magician-thing declared, and started forward.

"Not in my house," Ifan snapped, and it hesitated.

"This isn't *your* house," Sonia said. "This is *his* house. *His* power." She pointed at the creature. "Bow before the Glorious One, child!"

"That's nothing but a body," Ifan said. "A shell. Which means this is my house now. My power." He raised his chin as he spoke, and you could almost miss the tremor in his voice. *"I claim it."*

"You can't!" Sonia shouted. "It's *his!*"

"I claim it," Ifan repeated, and every light in the place surged brighter.

"Kneel, organic thing," the creature hissed, and the rosy glow roared around it, washing across the floor like blood-tinted soap scum and sweeping up the walls, wrapping around Ifan's ankles and twining up his arms.

"Not a chance," he said, and the overhead lights burned so bright I had to squeeze my eyes shut against them. Bulbs popped in a cacophony of shattering glass, and when I opened my eyes again everything was wreathed in pink light.

"Kneel."

"See, if you were still Dad, you'd know how well ordering me around works," Ifan said, and he took one step forward, grabbing the magician-thing by the back of its neck. "Get *out* of him!"

The creature seized the front of Ifan's gaudy shirt, pulling him so close they could have kissed. *"If you say this is your house, I will take you instead."*

Luminous Old One muck swirled out of the magician's body, diving at Ifan, and he tried to twist away, but the creature had too tight a hold on him. The rosy mist sank into him, burrowing into his skin, and his body arched in agony. His face twisted with the effort of trying to hold the thing off, but it was pouring into him, flooding his body with that awful infectious light, and he cried out, stretching one hand out pleadingly.

"Callum," he managed.

Callum heaved himself up far enough to roll toward Ifan, hair in his face as he reached one shaking arm out. Sonia took half a step forward, as if to stop him, and I staggered to my feet, kicking Green Snake off and stumbling toward the circle. The ground was treacherous beneath my feet, pliable and full of that sense of presences pushing against the edges of the world. Things were *thin.* Callum rose to his knees, still straining toward Ifan. Their fingers met, brushed, then twisted together, and I felt a *snap* of connection somewhere on the edge of my senses. The world trembled. Sonia staggered back, and Callum dragged Ifan closer, reached his other arm into the murky sunset-hued mist, and *pulled.*

Two screams went up, and the room plunged into darkness, lit only by an intense yellow glow that washed over Callum and Ifan's faces. Their hands were still locked together, and between them the Old One twisted and writhed, condensed into a ball of fury that swelled and throbbed like a star about to go supernova.

"The circle's still holding the door – Ifan, *open it!*" Callum shouted, and there was a terrible, bone-shattering squeal that shook the entire room as worlds and realms – *realities* – tore open. For one moment all was incandescent orange again, the earth surging beneath my paws. Currents sucked and washed at the room, like the pull of a rip tide, and Callum and Ifan were both shouting something I couldn't hear, and *things* screamed in rage and hunger, but I couldn't tell if that was here or wherever that terrible sunset light was coming from. It grew brighter, brighter still, until we were all lost in a horrifying postcard-pretty haze, then there was a thud that shook the world, and it was gone.

The room was so dark I was only sure we hadn't been plunged into the void because I could feel the dirt beneath my feet. Or I thought I could. Nothing seemed too certain right now.

Then there was a click, and orange light flared, a small flame shining over Ifan's face. "Callum?" he said.

"Here," a tired voice came from somewhere around my head height, and I picked my way toward it.

"Dad?" Ifan tried, without much hope in his voice, and there was no answer.

Something rustled, and I smelled tobacco as a second flame flared inside Callum's cupped hands. He sat up as I reached him and put a hand on my back. I could feel him shaking, and still smell the stink of spent magic and alien worlds on his fingers.

Ifan swore suddenly, and dropped the lighter. "Bollocks," he said, and stumbled his way out of the circle. "There must be candles down here."

"You'd think," Pru said in the darkness. "Bloody magicians and their summonings. There are always candles."

AND THERE WERE CANDLES, of a sort, in the magician's everything-drawer. They were those fake battery-operated ones, which I supposed were useful if one were worried about rogue creatures from the void knocking real ones over and starting a fire, although they did lack a certain aesthetic appeal. Ifan switched half a dozen of them on, lighting the place in a weird gloomy orange glow that was much more pleasant than the Old One's light, and handed more out to Tristan's veterans, who clutched them like aged carol singers.

Callum hadn't moved, and was still sitting in the broken circle with his forearms resting on his knees, smoking quietly while I sat next to him and listened to the echoes of lost things fading. We were alone within the runes. The magician - or what was left of him - had vanished, and I didn't know where Sonia was. It had been too dark to be sure what had happened in those last, world-breaking moments. Maybe they'd both fallen through the door to whatever sunny, nightmarish realm the Old One had come from, or maybe the sheer power of what they'd been playing with had consumed them like firewood. I didn't much care either way.

Ifan wandered over and stared down at us. "What the hell was all that?" he asked.

"I could say the same thing," Callum said. "Where've you been, the eternal beach party?"

Ifan looked at his shirt and brushed it off a little self-consciously. "Mustique," he said.

"When magicians die, they go to Mustique?" I asked.

"Well, Ibiza initially. But it's winter now."

Callum rubbed a hand over his face. "You git."

"I could say something stronger, if you like," I offered.

Ifan scratched one arm. "Look, the necromancers were getting weird, and Dad was getting all pushy about me joining the family business. It was all very magician-

Godfather-y, and you know I'm not into that stuff. I needed a break."

"So you faked your own death." Callum sounded less surprised than resigned.

"Gods, what d'you do when you need a day off?" I asked him. "Break a leg?"

He grinned, a broad, slightly knowing grin that curled at the corners. "Sure. Not mine, though."

"So how did you know to come back?" Callum asked.

"Oh. Yeah. Dad called me."

"What, he just happened to have your phone number?" I asked.

"No. Not that sort of call." Ifan rubbed his face, and Callum offered him his cigarette packet. It looked very much as if it'd been crushed in gardens and involved in magical tussles, and Ifan shook his head. "I tried to ignore it – he's tried to find me before, and I didn't want anything to do with it, but this time he was really pulling. Summoning me, really. I had to work to keep hold of where I was. But I was dealing with this sorcerer at the time. She just showed up, gave me a bollocking, and told me I had to get home. I said no way, and we had a bit of a … well, *altercation,* shall we say. Next thing she's shoved me in the water, and then while I was distracted Dad snagged me and I went under. I didn't really have a choice in the matter." He patted his pockets and sighed. "I think I left my wallet on the bar."

I looked at Callum. "I want a break from cellars and magicians and the end of the world. Can we go to Mustique?"

"Sure. I'll just pop it on the credit card, shall I?"

We both snickered, and Ifan looked at us in the way people do when they don't quite get the joke, and probably got their first gold card at ten or something. He held out a hand to Callum. "Come on."

Callum looked at the other man's hand as if unsure if it might bite, then took it and let Ifan haul him to his feet. The magician's son was shorter and more solid than Callum, his shoulders broader, and they stared at each other for a moment before Ifan pulled Callum into one of those awkward human hugs where no one seems to know what to do with their arms. I listened for the whisper of magic, for that strange *snap* of connection I'd felt when Ifan had reached for Callum before, but there was nothing except the confused ache of missed years and broken promises. I looked at my paws.

Callum pulled away first, patting his coat down as if checking he hadn't lost anything, and Ifan looked around the cellar. Muscles was still cuddling Gordie, the old cat lying in the man's enormous arms with all four legs pointed to the ceiling, purring rustily. The veterans and the rest of the cats looked back at us curiously.

"Right," Ifan said. "Well. Anyone for a drink?"

"Oh, aye," Duds said immediately. "You got any whisky?"

"Probably," Ifan said. "Try the cupboard above the fridge in the kitchen."

"Sold." Duds hobbled for the stairs at a good pace despite his injured leg, Tristan padding next to him. Muscles tucked Gordie into the crook of his elbow and used his other arm to all but lift the colonel off her feet. The scary dinner lady wiped her knives off on her apron and they followed Duds, the colonel pausing to glare at Ifan.

"I don't trust you," she said to him.

"Join the club," I said, and Callum snorted.

"So unfair. You don't even know me," Ifan said, pressing a hand to his heart.

Mitzi followed Gordie, leaving the rest of us standing in the dimness of the cellar.

"So that's it?" Pru asked. "What about your dad?"

Ifan shook his head, and for the first time the faint curl at the corners of his lips was gone. "The house wouldn't have let me claim it if he was still here. And I could feel it as soon as I arrived – the house was adrift. Wherever the body went – if that *thing* took it or not – it was just the vessel. All that mattered of him was gone before I got here."

We were silent. Callum put a hand on Ifan's shoulder, shifting like he'd say something, then just let it drop away again. I was suddenly glad for the candles. I didn't want to see Ifan's face any more clearly than I could. Loss is loss, no matter when or how it comes. Maybe Ifan had already been lost to his father, maybe they'd always been lost to each other. The pain was still there.

"What about the necromancer?" Astrid asked finally, her voice low. "Do we think she's gone too?"

Callum and Ifan looked at each other. Callum shrugged. "Don't know. It was all a bit messy there."

We were quiet again, then Charlie said, "Messy, maybe, but you two *rocked* it."

"Couldn't've done better ourselves," Harvey agreed.

"Well, we'd have had more style," Charlie said. "A little more flair, you know?"

"Pizzazz," Harvey suggested.

"Zing."

"Groove."

"Elegance."

"Je ne sais quoi."

"Shut up," Pru said, and the big she-cat growled in agreement.

"Right," Ifan said. "Anyone hungry?"

"Thought you'd never ask," Charlie said. "I'm fair Hank Marvin, I am."

"Shut up, C," Harvey said.

"What?"

"I'm just getting in before they do."

Ifan clapped Callum on the back lightly and headed for the stairs, the cats trailing after him. Callum and I looked at each other.

"Alright?" I asked.

"Alright," he said, running both hands back over his hair and looking at his boot-less feet. "I suppose."

I thought of all the things I could ask or say, about the way he'd held off the Old One, the way he'd ripped it clear of Ifan's body when the magician's son couldn't do it himself, the way Ifan had known to reach for him, begging not just for help but for *power.*

But instead I just said, "D'you think there's chicken? I could go for some chicken."

"Who ever heard of a magician without chicken?" Callum asked, and crouched down as Green Snake flopped his way toward us. He stopped and looked from

Callum to me, his head smeared with grime, and tilted it wearily.

"Dude," I said, "You're my favourite snake ever."

"I think we should call you Rerek," Callum said.

"Derek? Why would you do that to him?"

"*Rerek.* Egyptian serpent god of chaos," he said, scooping the snake up and trying to wipe some of the gunk off him. The snake drew back from his fingers as if horrified.

"You can't do that either," I said. "He's like the *opposite* of chaos."

Green Snake tipped his head to me in agreement.

"We can't just keep calling him Green Snake."

"Call him Derek, then. Better than calling him after some god. Gods are way too much trouble as it is. There's no call to be using their names on blameless snakes."

"You have a point there," Callum said, and offered me his arm. I scrambled stiffly up it to his shoulder, feeling every tumble and fall as I did so, and we climbed the stairs together, leaving the scarred, lonely cellar behind us.

I wished that it would be so easy to leave necromancers and missing magicians behind too, but I didn't think so.

We never seemed to get away that easy.

23

NOT EVEN WORLD-SAVIOURS CAN GET CHIPS AROUND HERE

We found the kitchen through the foyer (two of the skeletons were now legless, which at least reassured me that our aged special ops team hadn't been robbing graves for their weapons) and across the overstuffed sitting room that looked as if it had been breeding floral ottomans and spindly side tables. The door at the far side of the room, the one we'd tried to get through to escape the taxidermy army, stood open onto a vista of glossy black cabinets and white tiles that was bright enough to make my eyes twitch, and filled with a babble of feline and human voices.

We ambled into a kitchen that was almost as clinically clean and smooth as the cellar had been before we'd got our paws on it. Callum leaned on a vast kitchen island between the one-armed man and the dinner lady, touching his bruised forehead cautiously, and I jumped to the worktop and squinted across the expanse of slick, white marble to the far wall. A shiny black kettle was boiling on even more white marble worktop, next to an enormous black range that looked like it probably still had the shop stickers on it. It was as glossy as the black wall cabinets, and the walls themselves were tiled with long, shiny white rectangles. The whole effect was sort of like being immersed in a giant, wipe-clean zebra skin. I wasn't sure if that was the look they'd been going for or not. You never can tell with humans.

A bottle of whisky was being passed enthusiastically around the island and slopped into the sort of tumblers that had probably been handed down for five generations, and Callum waved it away as Muscles offered it to him.

"I'll take a tea," he said to Ifan, as the other man leaned on the opposite side of the island and grinned at him.

"Tea? What happened to our Callum?"

Callum shrugged slightly, fishing his cigarettes out of his tattered coat, and I said, "Oddly, alcohol and magicians tearing holes in dimensions don't mix so well."

Ifan gave me an amused look and added another mug to the ones already lined up next to the kettle. It looked like Callum wasn't the only one in need of caffeine.

"I'd just like to know where that woman went," the colonel announced. "The one that tried to poison us."

"Put stuff in the tea, they did," the dinner lady said, sounding indignant. "As if I couldn't sniff that out instantly!"

"Good call, Lulu," the colonel said. "We might've drunk it if not for you."

"And they were definitely going to do something distasteful to you cats," the one-armed man said. "Shouldn't be allowed."

"Excellent work, troops," Tristan said. "We appreciate

the assistance enormously. Extra rations all round, I'd say."

Duds poured himself another measure of whisky, and waved at Callum, cadging a cigarette off him. "Told you they talked. *Told you.*"

"Duds, we might've taken you more seriously if you'd remember to keep your shirt on," the colonel said. "It doesn't befit an army professional, that sort of behaviour."

Duds thumped his saggy, tattooed chest. "With this body? Why would I deprive people of it?" He winked at Lulu the dinner lady rather lewdly, then flexed his old muscles and made a naked couple on his chest bounce suggestively. She snatched the whisky off him, shaking her head.

"I've got standards, Duds. *Standards.*"

Pru limped across the island to sit next to me, and Callum scratched her head gently. "Those look nasty," he said, nodding at her side.

"Should see the dogs," she said. "Your Green Snake has excellent aim when it comes to snouts." She lifted her nose to Ifan as he slid a tea in front of Callum. "This sorcerer – did she have a cat with her? Calico one?"

"Didn't see one," Ifan said. "It was all pretty quick, though. She didn't mess around, that one."

"Sounds like our Ms Jones," I said.

"How does a sorcerer get to Mustique so quickly?" Callum asked.

"Probably best not to think about it," I said, then added to Ifan, "Do you have any chicken? Callum reckons magicians always have chicken."

"I was not aware of this universal law. But I'll see."

Callum wrapped his free hand around his tea, scratching his forehead with the thumb of the hand holding his cigarette. "What happened to Walker?"

"Best not think about that, either," I said. "Especially don't think about what happens when Ms Jones gets back and finds out we've lost her dentist. Sort of an insulting injury, that one, after the book of power thing."

Callum groaned and swigged his tea like it was whisky.

TURNS OUT, magicians do have chicken. And not just any old chicken, but chicken from the sort of shops that sell them in fancy waxed cardboard and paper bags, rather than a foil tray and a plastic bag. I bet that chicken had an upper-class accent and all. Tristan threw himself at it before Ifan could even get it out of the bag, and the big she-cat nipped his ear hard enough to make him squawk.

Everything settled down after that, the humans drinking whisky and tea and eating a fruit cake that Ifan had found in one of the cupboards, us eating chicken and Green Snake soaking in a sink full of warm water, trying to get the grime off his scales. I offered him some of my chicken, but he preferred Ifan's whisky. Fair enough. I don't know what snakes eat.

Finally Duds nodded off with his chin on his chest, and Muscles only just caught him before he fell off his stool.

"We best get off," the colonel said, climbing down off her own stool.

"Do you need a lift?" Ifan asked.

"No, we brought the club van," she said, and Lulu jingled a set of keys at him.

"About all this," the magician's son – or just the magician, now, I supposed – said, and the colonel cut him off with a brusque sweep of her hand.

"What, you think we're going to be running about the place shooting our mouths off about talking cats and warring magicians and ancient gods coming through doorways from pretty orange dimensions?" She snorted. "We're all one set of misplaced dentures off being banged up in care homes as it is. No one's talking."

I arched my whiskers at Tristan, and he lifted his chin. "Duds 'n' me have been chatting for years. He doesn't tell anyone about it."

"He tells *everyone* about it," the one-armed man said. "But he was talking to cats when he was twenty, too, so it's not like anything's changed."

"Fair enough," Callum said, and got up, offering the colonel an arm to lean on. "Come on. We'll go and see if we can get the scooter out."

"Nice one, young man," Duds said, shaking off Muscles and taking a slightly unsteady step toward the door. "Someone else might have to drive, though."

We headed through the overstuffed living room to the foyer, and opened the front door onto a damp early evening, smelling of overturned earth and crushed grass and spent magic. Ifan flicked the outside lights on, and the churned-up, overgrown garden was flooded with dull colour, revealing the dentist sitting damply on top of the broken-down Bentley with his arms wrapped around his knees. An enormous dog looked away from its guard duty and growled at us. The big she-cat growled back, and the dog flopped onto its back, exposing its belly.

"Well," I said. "At least we haven't lost him."

"The man of the hour," Charlie said. "Couldn't have done it without you."

"I was making sure no one came in," the dentist said. "You know, sneaked up and took us off guard or something."

"How's that going?" I asked.

He scowled at me, and Muscles went to grab the dog's collar. It wagged its tail and ducked behind his legs, keeping them between it and the she-cat. She purred.

Walker slid off the car and looked at Ifan. "Who're you?"

"Might ask you the same thing," he said mildly, and we headed for the gates. I checked for the other dogs, but it appeared Pink had grabbed them on the way out. The dentist complained about his missing car, pointing at the bare, scarred earth of the garden, and the colonel promised to drop him home, which didn't seem to cheer him up much. Callum, Ifan, and Muscles managed to pull the mobility scooter out of a flowerbed while Walker pointed and waved and strode around the place and eventually gave it a little push when it was almost out, then Ifan opened the gates with a click of his fingers, since the button and its pillar were still underground somewhere. There was a generously scuffed silver van lined with windows sitting outside, the back still open and the lift for the mobility scooter down, and the veterans loaded up. Muscles, the dentist and the dog went with them, as did Tristan. Gordie was back in Muscles' arms, unbothered by the dog, and Mitzi jumped in after them.

"Joining up?" Tristan asked her.

"Sod off," she said, and Callum pulled the door shut.

We watched them go, then Astrid said, "Best get on. Franco'll be beside himself. He's probably already arranged my funeral." She touched noses to Pru, then stepped sideways into nothing, leaving behind only the soft scent of her smooth grey fur.

"Aw," Harvey said.

"I'm not bothered," Charlie said. "My glorious beast is still here." He tried to rub his shoulder against the she-cat, and she stepped sideways, leaving him staggering.

"My name," she said, her tones precise and clear, "Is Tam. Call me a beast again and I will eviscerate you."

We all stared at her. "You speak," I said.

"Genius," she replied.

"But you've not said anything before. At *all.*"

She narrowed her eyes at me. "You talk too much. *All* of you," she added, as the other cats snickered.

"Her name's Tam," Charlie said, flopping to the damp ground and rolling onto his back. "*Tam.*"

She huffed and walked away, sitting down on the other side of Callum. Pru leaned against her, soaking up her warmth.

"Where's your car?" Ifan asked Callum.

"At the dentist's office," he said with a sigh.

"I'll give you a lift." He turned back to the house, and I wondered if magician's cars didn't run like regular ones. That Bentley was going *nowhere*.

We watched him go, then Harvey turned green eyes on

us and said, "We're out of here, then. Before my brother gets his nose torn off."

"It's true love," Charlie said, gazing longingly at Tam, who narrowed her eyes at him.

"Thanks," Callum said. "You know, for everything."

"Likewise," Harvey said, still staring at us.

"Have I got chicken in my teeth?" I asked, and the brothers exchanged glances.

"Mind how you go, Gobbelino," Harvey said, his voice low.

"Always do." But I was uneasy under his gaze.

"The Watch are *touchy* these days," Charlie's voice was as quiet as his brother's. He glanced at Tam, but she was ignoring us, cleaning the muck off one back leg while Pru crouched next to her with her eyes closed, shivering gently. "And you don't seem to learn from previous lives too well."

"What's that supposed to mean?" I demanded.

"Just step careful," Harvey looked up at Callum. "Both of you. We'll be in touch."

"What for?" Callum asked. If he'd been a cat his hackles would've been as high as mine. I could hear it in his voice.

"Let's just say Pru wasn't the only one who got caught while looking for an old friend," Charlie said.

"You know Claudia?" I asked, and they just looked at each other again.

"We need to go," Harvey said. "Come on, C." He stepped away into the night before we could even protest, and Charlie gave us a last nod.

"Catch you later, kids. Good doing business with you."

Then he was gone, leaving Callum and me staring at each other, the rain gathering softly on my whiskers and dripping to the sodden ground.

Turns out magicians' cars run just the same as any other, but the magician's garage housed a sleek, low-slung black car that stank of oiled leather and money. Ifan rumbled up to the gate in it and we got in, Callum sinking deep into the bucket seat.

"*Nice,*" I said.

"Yeah. I'm glad Dad kept her," Ifan said, running his hands over the wheel. "I missed this car." He'd pulled a coat on over his still-damp shorts and shirt, and found some shoes. He pulled into the broad street, the gates swinging closed behind us, and we rumbled down the road in a cocoon of low music and warmth.

We didn't speak much on the way to the dentist's office. Ifan pulled up behind our car, and we all stared at it, dripping rust and oil in the night.

"Is that going to start?" Ifan asked.

"Why does everyone always ask that?" Callum said, opening the door.

"Cal." Ifan caught his arm, and they stared at each other for a moment. Ifan looked into the backseat at Tam, Pru and me, then back at Callum. "Thank you," he said, and there were so many things swirling about unsaid that the weight of them made my chest hurt. That's humans for you. And they can't even smell the memories and regret and hope and hurt washing off each other, so they just swap words like trading cards that can never fill the gap that yawns between them. Maybe it's easier, but it didn't feel like it to me. It felt like the loss of things that had never even been had.

"Sure," Callum said, and got out. We trooped out of the car after him and stood in the rain as the two men looked at each other. "See you, then," Callum said finally.

"Definitely," Ifan said, and the grin came back. Callum shut the door with a heavy *thunk*, and the magician pulled away into the night.

Callum watched him go, his fingers worrying at his thumbnail, and eventually I said, "I know the car might leak, but it's drier than this."

He looked at me, as if startled to find us there, and said, "Right. Come on."

We jogged to the car and piled in, finding it cold and musty and stale after the warmth of the magician's car. But it also smelled less of magic and more of exhaust fumes and something rubbery burning away to nothing, which was, oddly, an improvement.

"Shall we drop you off, Pru?" Callum asked, once he'd managed to get the engine going. For one horrible moment it had seemed like it'd refuse altogether, as if in a huff about our vehicular infidelity, but finally it caught and belched into life.

"Yeah," she said. "I don't fancy shifting right now." She sounded tired, and the blood on her flanks still looked too fresh and sticky.

"What about you?" he asked Tam, and she just shrugged. She'd apparently used up her quota of words.

"You can get the reward, too," Pru added.

"What reward?" I demanded.

"Katja will've offered one," she said, trying to make herself more comfortable. "May as well take it."

"We can't do that," Callum said.

"Rent, remember?" I said. "Food, possibly. Maybe get you some new boots."

Callum looked down at his feet and wriggled his toes. "Doesn't seem right."

"She'll practically force you to take it," Pru said.

Callum made a doubtful sound, and I thought that if Katja didn't force him to, I would.

KATJA DID FORCE HIM TO, and it wasn't a small reward, either. She clawed the money out of the shop safe, Pru cradled in one arm and her phone jammed against her ear as she called the emergency vet, and shoved the cash at Callum without even counting it. He tried to give it back, and she hit him around the ear so hard that he yelped and scared the vet, who started shouting down the phone, asking if Katja needed emergency services. She just pushed the money into Callum's coat pocket and shooed us out of the cafe, her car keys in her teeth. We stumbled out, and she lowered the phone for a moment.

"Thank you," she said. "Come to dinner next week."

It wasn't a request. "Um," Callum said.

"I'll see you Wednesday at seven," she said, and hurried across the road, beeping a deep blue VW Beetle open as she went.

We watched her go, then I looked up at Callum and

said, "I knew I liked her."

"This isn't right," he said, looking at the money.

"Look, *someone's* paid us. We might not get turfed out on the street now."

"I suppose," he said doubtfully. "And I can always bring it back on Wednesday."

"And you've got a date."

"That is *not* a date."

"It's so very much a date. You're like her hero."

"Gods," Tam said, almost to herself, and turned and marched away down the damp street.

"Hey," I shouted after her. "Where're you going?"

"To find someone who doesn't talk so much," she called back, and jumped onto a bin then a wall, then vanished into someone's backyard. A dog yelped in alarm.

"Well done," Callum said.

"She was talking to you, too."

We looked at each other, then he said, "D'you fancy fish 'n' chips, or are you full of chicken?"

"I'm never too full for fish," I said.

"Good." He crouched down. "Lift?"

"In this rain? Definitely." I scrambled onto his arm, and he tucked me inside his tatty coat. Green Snake lifted his head from the inside pocket and flicked his tongue out at me thoughtfully. I returned the favour, and he looked startled.

Callum headed down the street to where the fish 'n' chip shop spilled its welcoming neon over the waterlogged pavement, spinning a siren song of vinegar and hot oil, and I leaned against him, thinking of the brothers and their guarded warning. Wondering what that meant for the days to come, and hating the sneaking sense of memories scratching at the back of mind, like the sorcerer had thinned the wall between me and them. And I thought, too, of the raging Old One and the torn world, and Ifan reaching out. Thinking of that *snap* of connection and the raw pulse of power. But Callum didn't feel any different. I didn't feel any different. *Nothing* felt any different.

And maybe, in this moment, nothing was. Because this moment was, as ever, just me and the cigarette-scented, thoughtful warmth of him, holding back the cold damp world for each other while we stood together at its centre. And it wasn't pretty, and it wasn't comfortable, and sometimes it didn't seem like we could hold back much more than a damp poodle – probably a small one, at that – but it was real. It mattered.

And it was all we needed.

It's all anyone needs, I suppose. Someone to help moor us against the chaos.

Or at least to help us ride it out.

We stepped into the bright light of the shop, and my whiskers twitched with the scent of battered fish.

"Out!" the man behind the counter bellowed, before the door could even close behind us. "You can't come in here in that state! This is a respectable establishment! No bloody junkies!"

"I'm not—" Callum started, and Green Snake and I popped our heads out to see what was happening.

A young man with a neck tattoo screamed and fell off his stool, and a little girl said, "Look, Mum! He has a *snake!*"

"*Out!*" the man behind the counter yelled, waving a greasy chip scoop at us.

"Right," Callum said with a sigh, and stepped back out into the rain. "Well done, you two," he said, heading back toward the car.

"It was your coat was the problem," I said. "Or possibly the missing boots, but I'm going with the coat."

"He might've come round if you'd kept your heads down."

"Anyone that won't serve a reasonable variety of species doesn't deserve our custom."

"Now, that's true enough," Callum said, and scratched my head.

I snuggled back into the warmth of his coat, and outside the night roared on, full of persistent rain and unfriendly chip shop owners and confusion and misapprehension and beauty and loss, and we walked into it wrapped in our own strange and wild and unrespectable magic.

Which was all anyone could ask for, really.

Well, that and to not have a Green Snake trying to cuddle you, but I was willing to let it go just this once.

For now, anyway.

ON THE NAMING OF SNAKES

Lovely people, I realise that the question of Green Snake's name was left largely unresolved in this story (because Gobs has a point regarding both the invoking of gods' names and the fact that Green Snake is rather less chaotic than the rest of their lives). However, this does not mean it shall remain unresolved.

Especially not when I have lovely readers who give me wonderful ideas regarding the naming of small snakes. And, in fact, some names so splendid that they spark their very own stories.

So pop the link below into your browser to read an entirely free, no-sign-up-required story regarding the naming of snakes! Or of one snake in particular, anyway…

www.kmwatt.com/greensnake

Read on, lovely people! And special thanks to Carolyn and Geoff for the really very wonderful name. Green Snake just wishes everyone would listen when he asks them to use it…

FREE STORIES!

Cats always have that air, don't they?

The one that suggests they know something we don't. Possibly a lot of somethings we don't.

And maybe . . . just maybe they do.

Discover eight tales of cats with good intentions but bad execution, cats that may or may not be cats, and cats that could really be a lot more helpful than they actually are (but you try telling them that).

They inhabit some worlds that may seem familiar, or near enough to be only a step away. Others not so much. Or hopefully not, anyway.

But they all share one key characteristic.

They've all got issues with cats.

Disclaimer: your cat may or may not be living a secret second life. But don't say I didn't warn you. And if they wink, *always* wink back.

Download your free book now!

www.subscribepage.com/catstories

AUTHOR'S NOTES

Lovely people, thank you so much for picking up this book. I know there are huge demands on all of our time these days, and I appreciate it hugely that you've chosen to spend some of yours reading about mercenary feline PIs and their human sidekicks.

I have one request, and one gift for you (because that seems fair).

Reviews are a bit like magic to authors, but magic of the good kind. Less raising-ancient-orange-almost-gods, more get-more-readers-and-so-write-more-books variety. More reviews mean more people see our books in online stores, meaning more people buy them, so giving us the ability to write more stories and send them back out to you, lovely people. Less vicious circle, more happy story circle.

So it would mean the world to me if you left a review at your favourite retailer, on Goodreads, or at any other website of your choice. It doesn't have to be long – "liked it" or "would rather clean up cat's hairballs" will do just fine. Of course, if you'd like to leave a longer review, that would also be wonderful!

And finally, if you jump to the link below, you'll be able to grab yourself some free stories! You'll need to sign up to the newsletter, but that'll get you first dibs on advance reader copies of new books as well as being able to enter giveaways and receive unsolicited cat photos. Ahem.

The Cat Did It: 8 Tales of Troublesome Felines
(www.subscribepage.com/catstories)

And if you'd rather just jump into more novels, head to my website (www.kmwatt.com) for details on *all* the books, plus to read blogs and short stories, and view potentially incoherent book review videos, because the talking is harder than the writing.

Thank you once again for being so entirely wonderful.

Read on, lovely people!

Kim

ACKNOWLEDGMENTS

First and always, thank *you,* lovely reader. Thank you for your faith in scruffy PIs of both the human and feline variety, and for trusting in me to get them out of drains, summoning circles, and squirrel ambushes. Thank you for reading, thank you for believing, and thank you for the lovely chats on social media and via email. They mean everything. *You* mean everything.

Thank you to my wonderful editor Lynda Dietz, of Easy Reader Editing, who does so much more than just correct my dodgy hybrid NZ/UK/US English. We find beautiful friends in the most unexpected yet loveliest places. All good grammar praise goes to Lynda. All mistakes are mine. Find her at www.easyreaderediting.com for fantastic blogs on editing, grammar, and other writer-y stuff.

Thank you to my amazing beta readers, who are friends, cheerleaders, and occasional *Kim, stop*-ers. I need all of these, and my stories would not be the same without you. You are all entirely amazing.

Thank you to Monika from Ampersand Cover Design, who didn't even flinch at my request to "make it look magic-y". That's true professionalism, there. Find her at www.ampersandbookcovers.com

And thank you to my friends who are family, and family who are friends. The ones that have been bright lights not just in the complex times of a pandemic, but always. Online, offline - no matter. Life would be a lot darker without you, and I love you. Although I don't expect you to be willing to bring me back from the dead. That would be weird.

ABOUT THE AUTHOR

Apparently this bit should be done in third person, but the Little Furry Muse refused to do it for me. She says lending her muse-ship to my writing is more than enough.

So hi, I'm Kim. I write funny fantasy set in a world not so dissimilar to ours (and in fact sharing many locations). I write about mystery-solving dragons with a strong affection for barbecues and scones, and reapers running petting cafes featuring baby ghouls. I write about myth and reality clashing in small and spectacular ways, and about the healing magic of tea and a really good lemon drizzle cake.

I write about snarky feline PIs, and about the Horsemen of the Apocalypse upgrading to Vespas, and about the very real force that are women of a certain age.

Most of all, I write about friendship, and loyalty, and the importance of looking out for one another. Because these, above all things, are magic.

And you can find me rambling on about all this (and more) over on my website (www.kmwatt.com), or join me on Facebook, Instagram and Twitter for bad puns and many, many cat memes. Many.

Come join me!

ALSO BY KIM M. WATT

The Gobbelino London, PI series:

A Scourge of Pleasantries (Book 1)

A Contagion of Zombies (Book 2)

A Complication of Unicorns (Book 3)

A Melee of Mages (Book 4)

The Beaufort Scales Series (cozy mysteries with dragons):

Baking Bad (Book 1)

Yule Be Sorry (Book 2)

A Manor of Life & Death (Book 3)

Game of Scones (Book 4)

The Beaufort Scales Collection (Books 1 - 4, e-book only)

A Toot Hansell Christmas Cracker - a festive short story & recipe collection

Book 5 coming Summer 2021!

Head to kmwatt.com/my-books for details!

Made in the USA
Middletown, DE
29 May 2021